She went ahead and unbuttoned her shirt. Then she moved around while looking in the mirror to make sure it wasn't too revealing. It was close, but you couldn't really see anything unless she bent down. She would remember that. The doorbell rang. She took a deep breath. *Here I go. God, please let Boggs like what she sees.*

As always, Toni looked out the peephole before opening the door. It was a little distorted, but she could tell Boggs was wearing black jeans, a white T-shirt and a soft black leather jacket. She looked incredible to Toni and she found herself biting her lower lip in anticipation. She opened the door and looked into Boggs's green eyes.

Boggs started to take a step inside and froze. Her mouth opened, but no words came out. She just stood there staring at Toni.

"Are you coming in?" Toni asked, thrilled at Boggs's reaction. She'd noticed.

Boggs blinked several times and then stepped inside. "Holy shit, Toni."

Toni kept her eyes locked on Boggs's and took a small step toward her. "Do you like it?" she whispered.

Boggs nodded several times. Then for the first time Toni saw Boggs's gaze trail down to her chest. A smile formed on her lips. Toni saw Boggs swallow hard. Toni took Boggs's hands in hers and pulled her closer. Not close enough to touch, but just close enough for Boggs to get a great view down her shirt.

Visit

Bella Books

at

BellaBooks.com

or call our toll-free number

1-800-729-4992

BORDERLINE

The Toni Barston Series

TERRI BRENEMAN

Bella
BOOKS

2007

Bella Books, Inc.
P.O. Box 10543
Tallahassee, FL 32302

First Edition

Editor: Christi Cassidy
Cover designer: Stephanie Solomon-Lopez

ISBN-10: 1-931513-99-6
ISBN-13: 978-1-931513-99-7

Acknowledgments

This book would not have been possible without the love and support of many people. A very special thanks to Christi Cassidy, my editor, who continues to teach me. A huge thank you to Robin Schultz, R.N., who continues to give me medical insight along with her friendship. I would also like to thank Ernie Birch, my weapons expert, and Lucy Liggett for her knowledge of state law. But most of all, I thank my partner, Cat, for continuing to believe in me and support me on every level. She makes the sky bluer and the grass greener in my world, and for that I am forever grateful.

About the Author

Terri Breneman was born and raised in a suburb of Kansas City. She received a Bachelor of Arts degree in psychology and sociology from Pittsburg State University in Pittsburg, Kansas. While living in Germany she earned a master's degree in counseling. As a psychotherapist specializing in borderline personality disorders, she worked with high-risk adolescents, juvenile sex offenders and their victims. She also worked with multiple personality disorders. She decided to change careers and attended St. Louis University School of Law. After graduation she opened her own practice. One year of that was quite enough and she was fortunate to find her current job as a research and writing attorney, working in federal criminal law.

Terri lives with her partner, Cat, in St. Louis, where they share their home with three cats—Dexter, Sam and Felix. The cat featured in this series, Mr. Rupert, was a longtime companion. Rupert Eugene died in 2003 at the age of 17. He is still loved and missed terribly.

Borderline: 1) not fully classifiable as one thing or its opposite; 2) not quite up to what is usual, standard or expected; 3) personality disorder with a pattern of unstable and intense interpersonal relationships varying between over idealization and devaluation, impulsiveness, and a lack of control of anger.

Collegiate Dictionary, 11th Ed., Springfield, Massachusetts: Merriam-Webster, 2003.

Diagnostic and Statistical Manual of Mental Disorders, 4th Ed., Text Revision. Washington, D.C. American Psychiatric Association, 2000.

Chapter 1

The woman sat at her kitchen island, sipping coffee and planning her day. There was still so much left to do and just not enough hours in the day. Still, it would be worth the wait. She wanted everything to be perfect for the love of her life. She closed her eyes and imagined the two of them snuggled together on the couch watching their favorite movie. Or drinking coffee together in the kitchen while muffins baked in the oven. Or better yet, making love for hours on new silk sheets.

She was so filled with excitement she could barely sit still. The time was almost right. As soon as she finished rehabbing the loft they could finally live together as a couple. She giggled at the thought of all the fun they would have and all the secrets they would share. Mmm. The woman of her dreams was smart, beautiful and kind. She was also extremely shy. In fact, she had never even voiced her love and admiration to the woman, but she didn't need to. The woman knew. She had known from the first time they met and they actually shook hands. Her hand was so soft. She could tell by the look in her eyes that it was love at first sight. And that was good enough, at least for now. They didn't need words. At least not yet.

She looked at her watch. *Time to go to work*. She closed her eyes one more time and imagined kissing her lover good-bye before going to work. Mmm. Kissing her woman. Her Toni. She could hardly wait.

Toni Barston pulled out the bottom drawer of her old gray metal desk, leaned back in her chair and propped up her feet. She closed her eyes for just a minute. She was having difficulty concentrating this afternoon, so she attempted to center herself and regain her focus. It didn't work.

She worked at the Metropolitan Prosecutor's Office in Fairfield, Missouri. Fairfield was a growing city with a population of over one million. The city had its fair share of restaurants, minor league sports teams, museums and, of course, crime. On her desk in her small office was a photograph of her cat, Mr. Rupert. He had been with her longer than any human and seeing his face made her feel warm inside. She looked at the wall and smiled when she saw her law degree hanging there. She hadn't decided to go to law school until she was thirty years old and she was still getting used to the idea of being an attorney. Her old job as a psychotherapist, however, seemed much less complicated at this moment.

She looked back down at her desk. The number of cases stacked there was close to unmanageable and she was feeling a little overwhelmed. She had only been on the job eight months and was just beginning to get the hang of misdemeanor cases. Now she had her first felony trial coming up and she was a little nervous. It wouldn't have been too bad if that was all she had to worry about, but, of course, this was the real world. She still had to contend with a variety of other cases in various stages, as well as life in general.

She took a deep breath, yawned and stretched. This resulted in untucking her silk blouse from her slacks. Since she had kicked her shoes off an hour ago, she felt a bit disheveled, which made her smile in a completely different kind of way. Another reason she had difficulty concentrating was Victoria Boggsworth. Everyone called her Boggs and she was the best investigator in the prosecutor's office. She was about five feet six and her light brown hair was short and stylish. She had beautiful green eyes, her voice deep and a little gravelly. At thirty-nine years old she was still turning heads. Boggs was also the star shortstop of the department's softball team. And Toni was in lust.

Toni and Boggs had gotten close during a very strange investigation last fall. A serial killer had escaped from custody and Toni's boss had assigned Boggs as a bodyguard. The two attempted to remain professional during this ordeal but failed miserably. They began dating shortly thereafter but the time they'd been able to spend together was not nearly enough for Toni. It was a difficult situation for her. Although she was by no means closeted, she was well aware of the homophobia within the good ol' boys' network of the legal world. She was also aware of the downside of dating someone you work with. Things could get messy and uncomfortable if the relationship went sour. But none of that mattered whenever she saw Boggs. She just couldn't get enough of that woman.

Toni shook her head and again tried to push the image of Boggs from her mind. She looked out her window to the parking lot. Nothing unusual. She'd been having a strange feeling the past couple weeks that someone was watching her. She never saw anyone but the feeling wouldn't go away. Maybe she was just being paranoid, she told herself. *But it isn't paranoia if it's true.* Toni sighed and picked up the Johnson file from her desk.

David Johnson was charged with home burglary and although it looked like a pretty good case, Toni didn't feel right about it. Maybe she just had too many other things on her mind.

She read over the police report again. One of the back windows of the house had been broken and the crime lab had found a piece of cloth on a broken shard of glass. There was also a blood drop on the windowsill, but the sample was too small to test for DNA. The burglar had ransacked the bedroom and study and had broken a lamp and a vase. Judging from the crime photos, the scene looked more like the work of an amateur rather than a professional burglar. The items taken included a Smith & Wesson .38 revolver, part of a coin collection, PlayStation 2, a DVD player and forty dollars in cash. The police report noted that a neighbor had seen a green Volkswagen Beetle in the driveway the night of the burglary and had remembered the personalized license plate. It said "GREEN." The homeowners were away for the weekend and did not report the break-in until Sunday night.

Toni reread one of the supplemental police reports. The suspect drove the car seen by the neighbors and when police went to his apartment to question him, they noticed a cut on his hand. He consented to a search of his upscale apartment and police found all of the items missing from the home. The twenty-one-year-old kid was arrested immediately but made no statement. His attorney bonded him out in record time.

Although Toni had only been an assistant prosecuting attorney for a short time, something didn't seem right about a run-of-the-mill burglar being bonded out so quickly. The process usually took a little longer. That had been a couple months ago and she still didn't have a good feeling about the case.

A week after David Johnson's arrest, the preliminary hearing had been held in front of Associate Judge Linda Allen. Johnson's attorney, Butch Henley, had filed a motion to suppress evidence based on involuntary consent to search his apartment. Judge

Allen had quickly denied his motion and the hearing had continued. Toni brought in one of the homeowners to show that Johnson did not have permission to enter the home. She also questioned him regarding the value of the property taken to establish that it was well over five hundred dollars. This made the burglary a felony.

Toni had put one of the police officers on the stand. Officer Kelly Hardson was new on the job, but she did fine. She quickly went through the process of identifying the owner of the Volkswagen, the questioning of David Johnson and his consent to search the apartment. Butch Henley asked only a few vague questions. At the end of the hearing Judge Allen found probable cause had been established and set the trial date. The trial would be in front of Circuit Judge Timothy Smith. Toni remembered that Butch Henley had smiled and winked at her after the hearing. It had made her uncomfortable.

The trial was now only three days away. Toni had written her opening statement and taken notes from her witnesses. She felt her case would go well, but she wasn't sure what to expect from Butch Henley. In the last few months she had learned that he was a high-powered defense attorney and that David Johnson was the son of a corporate bigwig in Fairfield. Her office had been willing to let Johnson plead to a lesser charge, but his attorney insisted on going to trial. Toni wasn't sure whether he was just that cocky about his chances of getting an acquittal or if David's father was trying to teach his son a lesson. Either way, Toni thought, the trial should only last a day.

Toni closed the file and glanced at her watch. Almost three o'clock and that meant Boggs would be arriving any minute for their "meeting." She pulled out her little mirror from her desk drawer and checked her hair. She retucked her blouse and slipped on her shoes. Good enough. She popped a mint in her mouth.

Two minutes later Boggs appeared at her door. She was carrying a stack of files and she winked at Toni before sitting in the only available chair in her small office. "Hey, Toni." She smiled. "I want to get through these cases pretty quick. I've got a hot date tonight."

Toni blushed. They were going out to dinner tonight. "I'll see what I can do. I'd hate to interfere with your love life."

It took over an hour to go through the pending files and decide what action needed to be taken on each case. Toni was usually all business during the workday, but it was sometimes difficult to remain professional with Boggs in the room. She closed the last file and looked into those sexy green eyes. Boggs winked at her again.

"Stop that," Toni said. "We have a deal, remember? Work is work."

"What did I do?" Boggs leaned back in her chair and grinned. Her dark blue blazer fell open and Toni could see she was wearing her gun in a shoulder harness today. Even though Boggs was wearing a white blouse, pressed khakis and loafers, Toni was imagining her with much less. She could almost feel Boggs's powerful arms holding her. Undressing her. Making love to her. Toni blinked away the image and saw that Boggs was still grinning.

"You're making this very difficult," Toni stammered. "Stop looking like, well, like that!"

Boggs straightened up in the chair. "Okay, okay. I know. No fooling around at work. Why don't you go to the bathroom and pull yourself together while I look over the Johnson file. I know you're a little nervous about the trial."

Toni smiled and nodded. "Be back in a sec. Thanks." She handed Boggs the file on her way out.

Toni glanced in the mirror and shook her head. Her face was flushed. She checked the stalls and thankfully she was alone. *God. That woman can get me hot with just a look. I'm a mess.* Thank goodness the day was almost over.

Toni was patting her neck and face with a wet paper towel when she heard the bathroom door open and close. She was barely able to turn before Boggs's arms were around her, pulling her close.

"Are you crazy?" Toni gasped. "What if someone walks in?"

Boggs pulled her back toward the door. "If someone tries to come in, the door will bump into me."

She pulled Toni close and kissed her. Toni could feel her knees go weak.

"If someone comes in, just head for one of the stalls and I'll go out," Boggs whispered in her ear.

Toni could only nod. The feeling of Boggs's breath in her ear had almost sent her through the ceiling. Her entire body hungered for Boggs as she wrapped her arms around her. She felt Boggs's hands slide down her back and her body shift as her leg pushed between Toni's. The kiss began slow but grew more passionate quickly. Toni forgot about her work-only rule and pulled Boggs closer. Her breathing quickened and her heart was pounding. She wanted more of Boggs. Much more. Boggs's hand had just slipped inside Toni's blouse when the sound of the doorknob turning acted like a small explosion between the two, sending Boggs backward toward the door. Toni quickly spun around and was closing a stall door just as one of the secretaries, Cindy Brown, opened the bathroom door. It opened only partway, bumping into Boggs.

"Oh, sorry," Cindy said as she realized she had bumped Boggs.

"That's okay," Boggs said as she left the bathroom. "No harm."

Boggs was sitting in Toni's office when Toni appeared five minutes later, her face still warm. She sat at her desk. "What the hell were you thinking? We almost got caught."

"You drive me crazy," Boggs murmured. "And we didn't get caught. Hey, what took you so long to come back?"

7

Toni rolled her eyes. "Cindy wouldn't shut up. I walked out of the stall as soon as you left and washed my hands. She was fixing her hair in front of the mirror and she just started talking. I didn't want to be rude, but I swear she's in the bathroom *constantly*. At least seventy-five percent of the time I go in, she shows up and she always wants to talk. I don't know about you, but I don't like to chat in a public restroom."

"What *do* you like to do?"

"Jeez, Boggs," Toni said, blushing. "Get the hell out of here. I need to go over a couple things before I go home. I've got a date tonight too and I need time to get ready."

Boggs grinned. "Do you want to go back to The Cat's Meow?" It was a new gay bar in town. They had gone to the grand opening a few weeks ago. The food was typical bar food, but it was good and not very expensive.

Toni nodded.

Boggs stood and leaned over Toni's desk. She was only inches away. "I'll pick you up at seven," she whispered. She left without saying anything else.

Toni pulled out her mirror. Her face was still flushed and her body still tingled as she thought about that kiss. *Damn that woman.* She checked her schedule and the docket for tomorrow. Everything was in order. She looked out her window and again felt as though someone was watching her. She shrugged off the feeling and began packing up her briefcase. She wasn't going to get anything more done tonight. Might as well go home. She passed the bathroom and smiled. *For as long as I live I'll never be able to go into that bathroom and not remember that moment.* As she walked through the offices at Metro she noticed that all the secretaries were gone. *I must not be the only one getting out of here a bit early.*

8

Chapter 2

The woman sat in her 2004 black Suzuki Grand Vitara, a small SUV, and lit another cigarette as she looked at her watch. It was four forty-five and Toni should be leaving the building soon. She was parked at a meter only a half block from the Metro building. She knew that Toni would leave the garage parking lot and turn south on 12th Street. She took another drag. *There's nothing like a cigarette to help clear your mind.*

She was on her second cigarette when she saw Toni's car pull out of the garage and turn right. She started her car and eased out into the traffic, keeping one or two cars between her and Toni. She knew Toni was a careful driver and rarely drove fast. This made following her even easier. She was only one car back when Toni stopped at the light on Hudson. She could see Toni glance in the rearview mirror and then run her fingers through her hair. She wished it were her fingers in Toni's hair. Hmm. It wouldn't be long, now. Then they could be together.

The light turned green and Toni eased across the intersection. At the same time a little blue pickup truck was speeding down Hudson toward the intersection. The driver obviously was trying to make the light, but it had already turned red. He was heading straight into Toni. Her heart pounded. *No! Not my Toni. God, please, no.*

Toni reacted quickly. She floored it, probably knowing that slamming on the brakes would leave her in the path of the truck. She made it through the intersection and pulled over to the right. The truck barely missed the back end of her car, but it clipped the Impala behind her. The truck spun around twice and slid into a light pole.

The woman took a drag off her cigarette and slowly drove around the Impala and through the intersection. She passed by Toni without looking at her and then pulled over to the side of the road. Several other cars were doing the same thing. She watched in her rearview mirror as Toni spoke on her cell phone. She was probably calling the police. Toni then got out of her car and talked to the old man driving the Impala. Both seemed to be fine. The old man was smiling and pointing to the front end of his car. It looked like a minor scratch in the old, heavy steel bumper. The driver of the truck, a young guy wearing faded jeans and a torn sweatshirt, was inspecting his damage and cussing up a storm.

Sirens could already be heard. The woman longed to run to Toni and cradle her in her arms, but this was neither the time nor the place. It would cause too much of a scene. She had to wait until the moment was right. She had waited this long. She could wait just a little longer. There were just a few things left to do. Watching Toni in her mirror, she felt her heart beat faster.

She stayed in her car as the police cars arrived. She was parked just a few feet in front of Toni's car and had her window rolled down. She was able to hear most of the conversation. One of the officers was standing behind Toni's car taking down her statement when the truck driver approached them.

"That crazy bitch almost hit me," he screamed. "Goddamn woman drivers."

Another officer pulled him away as Toni explained to the first officer what happened. "My light turned green and I started across the intersection," she said.

The woman smiled to herself. Toni always seemed so calm in situations like this. Clearly she was a little shaken, but not angry or aggressive. *That's my woman.* She was amazed at Toni's control. She herself had a difficult time sitting in her vehicle when she'd seen the truck driver come over to Toni. But she knew she really shouldn't interfere. At least not yet.

Toni continued to explain the situation to the officer. The old man from the Impala came over and told the same story. Apparently several other motorists who had stopped all said the same thing. The truck driver clearly ran a red light. He continued to scream at Toni from across the intersection and it appeared he only quieted down when the police threatened to arrest him. *How dare anyone talk to my woman like that? Son of a bitch.*

Other drivers who had stopped were beginning to leave so the woman started her SUV and drove off. She didn't want to be noticed, but she hated leaving Toni. She turned on one of the first side streets so she could turn around in someone's driveway. She had to wait almost a full minute for traffic to clear. By the time she got back to 12th Street, she couldn't see Toni's car. *Damn it. She's gone.* She lit another cigarette and waited, not sure of what she wanted to do. Two minutes later the blue truck drove past her. She took another drag and pulled into traffic behind him. Maybe this was her lucky night after all.

Chapter 3

By the time Toni arrived at her townhouse she had calmed down from her near accident. She opened her door and was greeted by Mr. Rupert. Twenty pounds of fur pushed against her leg and he meowed loudly.

"Hiya, buddy. You won't believe what happened on the way home."

Toni scratched his head just before he bolted toward the kitchen in anticipation of dinner. She scooped up the mail from the floor by the mail slot and put it and her briefcase on the dining room table. She headed to the kitchen, leaving her shoes by the table, and filled Mr. Rupert's bowl with half a can of wet food. He had finished eating it before she had put the remainder in the refrigerator. He was washing his face when she turned around.

"You know, Mr. Rupert," she said, looking at his huge face,

"maybe I should cut back a bit on the food. You seem to be filling out a little."

Mr. Rupert seemed offended by her suggestion. He stopped washing and stared at her. Then he cocked his head and meowed. He was too cute for his own good.

"You're right," she answered. "You look fabulous. Let's read the mail."

Toni skimmed the day's mail and tossed most of it in the trash. She gave Mr. Rupert a credit card offer that was addressed to him and he happily began chewing on it. This was the second one he'd received. She wondered where these companies got their information. The only mail she kept was the Land's End catalog and a psych journal. *I wonder why I got this. My subscription ended over a year ago.* She put it back on the table, grabbed her shoes and headed upstairs.

Toni's townhouse wasn't too big, but it was just right for her and Mr. Rupert. The bottom floor had a large living room/dining room area with a galley-type kitchen. It was a corner unit so she only had neighbors on one side. The place was furnished in what Toni's friends called "garage sale/dorm room" décor. In the living room a large, old dark green sectional couch curved around one corner. The opposite wall held a floor-to-ceiling bookcase made of cinder blocks and boards. It held her television and stereo along with a few photos and books. The dining room table was in a corner by a window. Its main purpose was to hold Toni's briefcase and mail. She almost always ate while sitting on the couch.

Upstairs was Toni's bedroom and bath, separated by a huge walk-in closet. Toni's queen-size waterbed took up half of her room. She had a small desk in the corner with her laptop computer and several books scattered about. There was also an overstuffed chair and ottoman in the far corner. This was one of her favorite places to read.

Toni carefully took off her blazer and hung it in her closet.

Then she stripped off her remaining clothes and tossed them in two piles. One was for the dry cleaner and the other for the hamper. She hated taking clothes to the dry cleaner and had promised herself to only buy washable clothing from now on. That wasn't easy and washable suits were out of the question. Still, the cost was getting out of control. *Oh, well. That's the price you pay for buying suits. Too bad I can't wear jeans and a T-shirt every day.*

In the bathroom she caught a glimpse of herself in the mirror. She thought she still looked decent at thirty-four, but she could use a bit of toning. She really needed to find some time to work out. She leaned closer to the mirror to inspect her hair. It was almost shoulder-length and she had been contemplating a shorter style. *Maybe this weekend I'll take the plunge.* She looked again and noticed one white hair nestled within her brown waves and promptly yanked it out. Mr. Rupert was sitting on the counter looking at her in the mirror.

"See this?" she said to him, holding the single hair in front of his face. "With all the stress I've been through in the last few years, my hair should be all white. Thank God for good genes."

Mr. Rupert looked at the hair closely then rubbed against her arm.

"Thank you, buddy," she said, knowing he didn't care what she looked like. "I love you, too." She rubbed his head and decided not to dwell on her looks. She jumped in the shower.

By the time Boggs arrived at seven, Toni had showered, dressed, looked through her catalog, skimmed most of the psych journal and drunk a glass of wine. When the doorbell rang, she looked out the peephole and opened the front door.

Boggs stepped inside and wrapped her arms around Toni's waist. "I missed you," she said, nuzzling her neck. "I've been ready for an hour."

"You should have come over earlier," Toni replied. "After I showered I just sat here and read."

Boggs grinned. "Maybe I should have been here for the shower. We could've gotten a head start."

Toni laughed. "Don't tempt me. But I'm afraid I'm too hungry to be very focused. I skipped lunch. How about a quick dinner then coming back here for, um, dessert?"

Boggs agreed and she drove them to The Cat's Meow. The bartender smiled and nodded at Toni as they headed past the bar. The bartender was about 5'8", lean, and looked to be in her late twenties. She had short, wavy light brown hair that looked like it had never seen a comb. She was wearing black jeans and a tight black leather vest with no shirt. Her breasts were barely covered. There was a barbed-wire tattoo around her right bicep.

Toni and Boggs spotted an open table near the pool tables and they grabbed it. A woman with a variety of piercings took their order and brought their drinks. Toni's glass of wine was much fuller than Boggs's glass. Boggs pointed out the obvious disparity but the waitress only shrugged and left.

"I think the bartender likes you," Boggs said.

Toni shook her head. "That's Bert. I chatted with her for a while when we came to the grand opening. She's nice. Don't you remember? She used to work at Gertrude's Garage."

"Bert, huh? She looks pretty rough." Boggs leaned back to see the bartender in the next room.

"Oh, she's a real sweetheart underneath," Toni said. "Not like some people I've run into. Listen to this." She drank her wine and told Boggs about her adventure on the way home. "The guy was such an asshole. I mean, his light turned red before he even made it to the intersection." She shook her head. "Then he had the nerve of accusing me of trying to hit him!"

"Did the cops arrest him?" Boggs asked.

"I don't think so. I saw one writing him a ticket. There wasn't any damage to the old guy's car, just a huge dent in the side of the truck." Toni sighed. "I guess I'm just thankful something worse didn't happen, you know?"

Boggs reached across the table and took Toni's hand in hers. Toni could feel the warmth of her hand but it was the warmth in her eyes that filled her entire body. They ordered burgers and chatted throughout dinner.

It was only after the last french fry disappeared that Toni mentioned the near accident again. "I just can't believe that guy."

"Well, I'm glad you're okay," Boggs said. Her gaze lingered for another minute. "Let's get out of here," she said, glancing at the check.

Toni felt the shift in Boggs from genuine caring and concern to genuine lust. Both emotions felt good. She tossed a twenty-dollar bill on the table next to Boggs's and grabbed her jacket. They were back inside her townhouse in less than fifteen minutes.

"Want something to drink?" Toni asked.

"Water would be good."

Toni opened the fridge and pulled out two bottles of water. One plain and one lemon-flavored for her. She tossed the bottle to Boggs, who was leaning against the wall in the kitchen. Toni struggled to twist off the cap. "Damn it. What do they do? Glue these damn things shut?"

Boggs took the bottle from her. In one easy movement she removed the cap and handed the bottle back to Toni.

"Thanks," she said a little sheepishly. "I guess I'm a little on edge tonight."

She leaned against Boggs and snuggled against her neck. The feel of Boggs's arms around her made her sigh and relax just a bit. Even though Boggs probably would have preferred to head up to the bedroom, she guided Toni over to the couch.

"Let's just sit for a bit, okay? You've had a long day."

Toni nodded and curled up next to her on the couch. Mr. Rupert joined them and Toni absently began petting the huge cat. He kept pushing his head against Toni's leg and purred so loudly that both Toni and Boggs looked at him and laughed.

"Well, he's happy and content," Boggs said.

"That's my boy. He likes it when I'm home with him."

The three of them sat quietly for a few minutes until Boggs said, "Are you okay? You seem a little preoccupied or something."

Toni sighed. "I'm sorry. I guess I am. It's stupid, really."

"What?"

"Well, I know this sounds really paranoid, but I feel like someone has been watching me," she explained. "I'm sure it's just some leftover feelings from all that crap that happened last fall, but it feels real."

Boggs's entire body stiffened and she automatically scanned the room. Her gaze settled on Toni's blinds, which were open, and she got up to close them.

"Maybe it is just old stuff," Boggs said, sitting back down. "You are under a lot of stress at work, especially with this trial coming up and all. But is there something specific you can tell me? Like, when do you feel someone watching you?"

Toni thought for a few moments. She turned to face Boggs. "It's hard to explain. Like today in my office, when I looked out the window. It's not as though I saw someone or something unusual—it was just a feeling."

Boggs was sitting about two feet away and she reached her arm out and caressed Toni's shoulder. "Any other time?" she asked.

Toni smiled. She felt safe with Boggs. "I'm probably just a little paranoid, but I did feel it when we went to the grand opening of The Cat's Meow a few weeks ago. It was really strong then, but I just ignored it. There were so many people there and everything."

"Maybe someone there has the hots for you," Boggs said, smiling. "I mean, you are pretty good-looking."

"Stop it. I'm being serious."

"Me, too." Boggs raised an eyebrow. "Seriously, there could

have been someone staring at you there. You were on the news last fall. Maybe some woman is lusting after you but doesn't have the guts to actually come up and talk to you. That could explain why you're feeling this way."

"I guess so," Toni agreed. "But what about outside the office building?"

"That's a little different," Boggs said. "Maybe we should be extra careful."

Toni pulled up her knees and wrapped her arms around them. She was choosing her words carefully. She didn't want Boggs to think she was nuts. "I don't know how you feel about this, but I trust my gut feelings. They usually end up being right. There are some things I just *know*. I don't know why, but I do."

Boggs was nodding. "I understand," she replied. "I guess I'd call it instinct or something, but I don't doubt you at all." She pulled Toni closer and put her arm around her.

Toni felt safe and peaceful. Telling Boggs was the right thing to do. *Maybe I'm not crazy.*

Boggs looked at her watch. "Shit. It's almost nine. I hate to do this, but I've got to go over to Dave's house and let his dog out. He had to go out of town for a few days and I volunteered for night duty. I can't believe I almost forgot." Dave Berry and Boggs had been in the air force together for many years as officers in the military police and remained friends ever since. Dave had gone into the private sector while Boggs opted for the prosecutor's office. "I can come back afterward. Maybe an hour and a half?"

Smiling, Toni hesitated. "Normally I'd be all over that," she explained. "But I'm really wiped out tonight. Is that okay?"

"Sure, babe," Boggs said, obviously disappointed. She kissed Toni lightly on the lips and got up to leave. "I'll see you in the morning."

Toni walked her to the door and hugged her tightly. "Thanks for understanding," she whispered in her ear. "I'll be more myself tomorrow. I just want to get a few things settled and then crawl into bed and sleep. I'll talk to you in the morning, okay?"

Boggs hugged her back and kissed her again before leaving.

Toni felt bad about not wanting Boggs to come back over. She just needed a little time to shake the feeling of being watched and to blow off the near miss with the jerk in the truck. She felt like she was rotten company and didn't want Boggs to see her that way. This was the best thing, she told herself. She wanted Boggs to see her at her best, not nervous and cranky. She made herself a cup of hot tea and snuggled on the couch with Mr. Rupert. Tomorrow would be much better.

Chapter 4

The next morning, Toni sat at her desk going over what was on her schedule for the day. She was working on a motion when Cindy knocked on her door. Toni waved her inside.

She handed Toni a stack of papers and said, "I thought you'd want these right away, so I brought them over to you instead of just putting them in your mailbox. So, how's your day going?"

"Good, thanks," Toni replied. She noticed the papers were from Butch Henley, the defense attorney in the Johnson case. "I appreciate your bringing these in to me."

Cindy was beaming. Toni realized that if she didn't cut this off now, Cindy would linger in her doorway forever.

"In fact, I better get on this right away." Toni turned her attention to the papers and attempted to look completely engrossed. It seemed to work.

"Okay, see you later," Cindy said as she turned and left.

Jeez. I hate it when she does that. Toni now actually looked at the papers.

What the hell? It was a motion to suppress evidence based on an involuntary consent to search Johnson's apartment. It was basically the same motion that Judge Linda Allen had denied months earlier. This time it would be in front of Circuit Judge Timothy Smith. Toni was still reading the motion in disbelief when Chloe, the receptionist, buzzed her.

"Ms. Barston, Judge Smith's secretary on the line for you."

"This is Toni Barston," she said as she picked up the call.

"Good afternoon, Toni. This is Maggie. Judge Smith has scheduled a suppression hearing on the Johnson case at ten o'clock tomorrow morning."

Toni blinked in disbelief. She took a deep breath. "Um, thank you, Maggie. I'll be there." She hung up the phone and just sat there. What the hell was Butch Henley doing? Why would Judge Smith grant a hearing when Judge Allen had already denied this motion? *What is it that I'm not seeing?*

Toni gathered up everything she had on the case and buzzed Dorothy Whitmore, her boss's secretary and gatekeeper. Dorothy had been around for more years than anyone really knew and she protected her boss, the prosecuting attorney, like a mother lion. She also knew the ins and outs of everything in the entire Metro building.

"Hi, Dorothy. It's Toni Barston. Is Anne available?"

"She's pretty busy, Toni. Can Elizabeth help you?" Elizabeth Sampson was Anne Mulhoney's first assistant and right-hand woman.

Toni hesitated a moment, then decided that Dorothy would know who she should talk to. "Well, I just got handed a motion to suppress in the Johnson case," she explained. When there was no response from Dorothy she continued, "It was filed by Butch Henley. He filed one with Judge Allen a few months ago and she denied it, but he filed another one with Judge Smith."

Toni barely got the last word out when she heard a click. For a moment she thought Dorothy had hung up on her. Less than thirty seconds later Dorothy was back on.

"Come down in about fifteen minutes, Toni," Dorothy said, her voice warm yet professional as always.

Toni made sure she had everything related to the case to take to Anne. She felt a little stupid going to the prosecuting attorney with this, but she felt like she must have missed something big. She didn't want to do something idiotic in front of the judge. Maybe this was just routine for a defense attorney. After all, this was her first felony trial. She sighed. Maybe she wasn't ready for felony trials. Would Anne pull her off the case and put her back on misdemeanors? Ugh. How embarrassing. By the time she arrived at Anne Mulhoney's office she was sure she would receive a lecture from her boss. Her face must have shown her emotions as she went into Dorothy's office.

"It's okay, Toni," Dorothy said as soon as she saw her. "Go on in."

Anne was sitting behind her huge desk when Toni pushed open the heavy oak door. She was dressed impeccably as usual in a navy suit with an ivory silk scoop neck blouse underneath. There was a scar on her neck from her brush with death last fall, but she did nothing to hide it. Anne exuded a quiet sense of confidence and power no matter what she wore or said.

She motioned for Toni to sit. "Let's see the motion."

Toni handed her the papers and sat in one of the leather club chairs facing Anne's desk. Anne was shaking her head slowly as she read the motion.

"And Judge Allen denied this?" she asked.

Toni nodded.

"Did Butch ask the police officers any questions?"

"I only put one officer on the stand," Toni explained. "Officer Kelly Hardson. She was the one who wrote the report. He asked a couple really vague questions."

Anne was tapping her pen on the desk. "This stinks," she said. "Butch has connections all over Fairfield. I've always believed he had something going on with Judge Smith, but I've never been able to get anything solid enough to do anything about it." She handed the motion back to Toni. "All I can tell you is to do everything by the book, not that you wouldn't. But put on every bit of evidence that you have, okay?"

"I was planning on putting on the officer who wrote the report, Kelly Hardson, but I guess now I should also put on the other officer for this hearing. I don't really have anyone else."

"That's fine," Anne replied. "Spend as much time as you have today looking at the suppression cases he cited in his motion. He's trying to say that David Johnson was either so drunk or so stoned that he couldn't have legally consented to the search. If he convinces Judge Smith, our case goes out the window. Talk to the officers again and see if they had any indication that Johnson was under the influence."

"Thank you so much, Anne. I was beginning to feel like I was missing something, or was just ignorant."

Anne smiled broadly. "Don't worry, Toni. You're doing a great job. The only thing you're ignorant of is the politics here in Fairfield. You have to be around a while to understand who plays by the rules and who likes to twist them into knots." She motioned toward the door. "Go on, now. You'll be fine."

Toni left Anne's office feeling both a lot better and a lot more nervous. She hurried back to her office, stopping at Cindy's desk. "Could you please get ahold of Officer Kelly Hardson and Officer Jack Benson. I need to speak with them today. It's urgent."

Cindy was grinning from ear to ear. "Absolutely. I'm on it."

Toni went into her office and immediately got on her computer. She pulled up the cases that Butch had cited in his motion and printed them out. She was logged on to Westlaw, a Web site that had every case ever decided in the United States, and was doing her own research when Cindy buzzed her.

"Officer Hardson is on line one for you. I haven't been able to reach Officer Benson yet, but I will."

"Thanks, Cindy." Toni punched line one. "Hi, Officer Hardson. I'm going to need you to testify tomorrow at ten o'clock for a suppression hearing on the Johnson case." She quickly gave the officer a rundown of how the hearing would go. "Could you come by my office this afternoon so we can chat?"

"Sure, counselor," Officer Hardson replied. "Be glad to. How about three o'clock?"

"That's fine. See you then," Toni said. "Oh, you don't by any chance know where Officer Benson is, do you? He's still your partner, right?"

"Yeah, Benson's my partner," Officer Hardson answered. "But he's on vacation this week. The lieutenant gave him some time off. I've been working with Sergeant Davis while he's gone. Is there a problem?"

Toni swore to herself. "No problem," she said. "I'll see you at three."

She was ready to tear her hair out. Why hadn't she made sure Officer Benson was available? She should have called him. The trial was supposed to begin in just two days. She was screwed. Damn it.

She buzzed Dorothy again, who put her right through to Anne. After she told Anne about Officer Benson's vacation, she heard Anne sigh.

"Butch isn't stupid," she explained. "He knew that in normal circumstances you'd only put one officer on the stand, the one who wrote the report. But I'm guessing that Officer Benson's vacation was not planned by him in advance. It just seems a bit too coincidental that he's on vacation and unavailable."

"Do you think I could get a continuance?" Toni asked.

"I doubt Judge Smith will go for that. You're running a bit too close to the time limit and I sincerely doubt David Johnson will waive his speedy trial rights. Go ahead and ask for the continuance, but be prepared to proceed with the hearing tomorrow. Just do the research and do the best you can."

Toni hung up the phone not feeling much better about the situation. She was still researching case law when Officer Hardson appeared that afternoon right at three. She was wearing khakis and a white polo shirt. She looked like she could be in high school.

"Have a seat," Toni said as she pointed to the only chair in her office. "Thanks for coming by. Can I get you some coffee or a soda?"

Officer Hardson shook her head. She looked nervous and nearly dropped the notebook she was carrying. "Did I do something wrong?" she asked.

"No, not at all. The defense has filed a motion to suppress, that's all." Toni tried to sound as though this was normal procedure. She didn't want the young officer to get more nervous than she was already. "Can you tell me again about the arrest and search? Start from the beginning."

"Okay." Officer Hardson took a deep breath. "Jack and I got the call from Detective West. He said to go over to David Johnson's place and see if he was home. I guess he figured no one would be there because he told us to call him back and let him know the lay of the land or whatever."

"He didn't ask you to interview the suspect?"

Officer Hardson thought for only a moment. "No. Like I said, it didn't seem like he was expecting anyone to be home."

"Okay," Toni said, taking notes. "What happened next?"

"Well, I rang the bell."

"Where was Officer Benson?"

"He was looking at the Volkswagen Bug in front of the building. He came up the walk when he heard the front door of the apartment open."

Toni nodded for her to continue.

"The guy opened the door and I asked if he was David Johnson. He said yes. Then I asked if that was his vehicle out front, the green Bug. He said yes. That was when I noticed there was a cut on his hand. Then I told him why we were there and I asked if we could come inside. He said okay."

"What did he look like?" Toni asked. "Was he dressed?"

Officer Hardson took another moment to reflect. Toni was pleased. This would look good on the stand.

"He was wearing blue shorts and a white T-shirt. No shoes or socks."

"Did he look tired or wired or anything?"

"No, not really. I mean, not that I noticed. When he said we could come in, I just started looking around the room. I saw the PlayStation Two on the floor next to the television and a stack of boxes that I recognized as coins on the coffee table."

"What happened next?"

"I looked at Jack and he just grinned. He put the cuffs on him and read him his rights. Everything from the burglary was in plain view, right there in the living room. Once we walked inside and turned the corner, there it was."

Toni nodded again. "Can you remember anything else about him? The way he talked or walked or anything? I'm trying to establish that he wasn't drunk or high."

"Oh, no." Officer Hardson shook her head. "I don't think he was under the influence of anything, but I only spoke to him for a minute." She seemed almost apologetic.

"That's fine," Toni said. "You're doing great. Do you have any questions for me regarding the hearing tomorrow?"

"No, I don't think so. I'll be there early, just in case," she said, smiling. Clearly this young officer was anxious to do a good job. Toni reassured her again and sent her on her way.

Toni looked through the police reports again. If Butch was going to try to show that Johnson was under the influence of drugs or alcohol, he'd need to have something concrete. She placed a call to the police station and talked to the desk sergeant. After a full explanation of the situation, Toni was transferred to the booking officer.

"If there's anything you can remember about Mr. Johnson, that would be very helpful," Toni said after detailing the reason for her call yet again.

The officer said he was looking in the log book. After a couple minutes of silence he responded. "Pretty much routine, counselor. We booked him and stuck him in a cell. The only other note in here is that he was sleeping in the cell when the noon check was done. Nothing else."

"Is that normal for a guy to sleep after he's booked?" Toni asked.

"Everything is normal around here." The officer chuckled. "Some guys scream and yell, others just sit there and some sleep. Nothing unusual here."

Toni thanked him for his time and hung up. This was not good. Butch could easily argue that David was "sleeping it off" or some such nonsense. She needed Benson. She buzzed Cindy again. "Any luck finding Officer Benson?"

Cindy sighed. "Some of the guys think he's up at the lake with his wife doing some fishing. He's not answering his cell phone. And you just got another filing from Mr. Henley. I'll bring it in."

She appeared a moment later and Toni took the papers from her. It was a list of witnesses that Butch was going to put on the stand in the morning along with short blurbs about their expected testimony. Johnson's father would say that his son had had a problem with alcohol for quite some time. Two others were friends of Johnson who would testify that they were with David before his arrest that morning and that they had all been drinking heavily. A third was classified as a "friend of the family" who would say he called David just a half-hour before his arrest and he was nearly incomprehensible. Great, she thought. Three people were going to say that he was drunk out of his mind. She had a desk sergeant who would say he slept in the cell and a rookie cop who wasn't really sure. Her only hope was that she could find Officer Benson and the judge would believe her cops.

She buzzed Boggs at her desk. She needed to find Benson in time for the hearing in the morning. She explained everything to Boggs.

"I'll make some phone calls and see what I can find out," Boggs said. "Someone has to know how to get ahold of the guy."

After hanging up from Boggs, Toni felt a little better. At least she was doing all she could do for now. She was still berating herself, though, for not making sure Benson was available for trial. In order to calm herself she went back to her research on suppressing evidence. It was almost five o'clock when Boggs finally called back.

"So far nothing," she said. "The only info I've gotten is that he's at 'the lake,' but no one seems to know which lake that is. He's not answering his cell phone; it goes straight to voice mail. The emergency number he left is his brother's. He, conveniently, isn't home. One of the lieutenants over there gave Benson the time off, and he was no help. In fact, he was pretty rude about the whole thing. He acted like I was personally attacking the guy for taking some much-needed vacation time. Blah, blah, blah. Everyone else I've talked to so far didn't even know he was gone."

"What about asking Vicky to nose around?" Toni suggested. Vicky Carter was a detective on the Fairfield police force and also a friend of Boggs and Toni. She had helped them with the serial murder case last fall.

"I left her a message," Boggs replied. "I'll let you know when I hear from her. Are you getting ready to head home?"

"I think so. There's not much else I can do here. I've got a bunch of cases to read tonight so I think I'll just pack everything up and go home. Call me?"

"I'll let you know the minute I hear anything. If we can find out where this guy is by at least three in the morning, there should be time to go and get him. And that's assuming he's at one of the closer lakes around here. Okay. I gotta run. I've got a few more leads to check out. I'll call you later at home." With that she hung up.

Toni took a deep breath and leaned back in her chair. She allowed herself about five minutes of quiet swearing and cussing at herself before she began packing up her briefcase. The only thing she could do now was memorize these cases and try to come up with a great argument. She left her office and headed for home.

Chapter 5

The woman drove her SUV slowly down an alley on the west side of town. The buildings on either side were mostly abandoned warehouses, but some had been rezoned for future condos. There was a restaurant at the far end of the block, and The Cat's Meow was one street over. She pulled up to one warehouse's large receiving door and hopped out. She unlocked her padlock and opened the door. It was wide enough for her SUV to pull through. Once inside she turned on an overhead light and closed the large door. She then unlocked a smaller door, a pedestrian entrance a few feet away, went outside and resecured her padlock on the receiving door. She pulled on the lock once, twice, three times. Satisfied, she reentered the warehouse through the small door and locked herself inside.

The main floor of the warehouse was practically empty except for her SUV and a few assorted boxes. The warehouse originally was built in the early nineteen hundreds to house a small clothing factory. The bottom floor had been dedicated to shipping and receiving. The second floor had held the sewing machines operated by at least two dozen women, and the third floor was reserved for offices. The building was originally owned by her grandfather and was passed down to her uncle, who'd sold it to her. He now owned several in the area as well as a construction company.

Her father had been disowned by her grandfather many years ago. This happened shortly after her father married her mother, a lady from the wrong side of the tracks. Her father coped with his black-sheep status by drinking heavily and regularly beating his wife and children. The woman's mother died of cancer when she was only six years old. When her father died one year ago, no one was at the burial except for the gravedigger, her and her uncle. Her brother had passed out the night before from his consumption of alcohol to celebrate the death.

She removed a McDonald's bag from the backseat of her car and headed to the stairs. There at the bottom was a bright red welcome mat. It was the only indication that anyone had been in the building over the last twenty years. She carefully wiped her feet and headed upstairs.

The second floor was her beloved loft. The only fully enclosed area was the bathroom. She had spent several months updating the fixtures herself. It was one of the many skills she'd learned from her uncle. He had hired both her and her brother during the summers when they were teenagers to help out on his construction jobs. She knew how to do almost any job, including plumbing and electrical work. Her uncle had sold her the building for a song a few years ago and she was finally making progress. She was able to move in about six months ago after the plumbing was completed. Now she worked on it every chance she had.

Up in her loft she carefully set the bag down on the coffee

table and retrieved a beer from the refrigerator. She returned to the couch and put her feet on the table. It was actually a large wooden crate, but it served well where it was. She closed her eyes and sipped her beer.

It wouldn't be long now, she thought. Just a few more renovations and the place would be ready. She'd had to wait long enough, but she wanted everything to be perfect when Toni saw her new home.

She was halfway through her beer when she noticed the time and flipped on the television. The six o'clock news had just begun.

"A local auto worker was found shot to death in his truck this morning. He was found by a coworker after missing work today. Police say the time of death was most likely sometime Monday evening. He was killed by a gunshot wound to the head. No suspects at this time. We'll keep you updated as more information becomes available. Next on weather . . ."

She smiled and opened the bag. *Was he driving a blue truck?* She laughed out loud. From inside the bag she pulled out her beloved Walther and set it on the table. After carefully unfolding the towel she'd wrapped it in, she stroked the nine-millimeter pistol, a compact model with a three-and-a-half inch barrel. She'd stolen it from her grandfather when she was a teenager and as far as she knew, nobody had ever realized it was gone. It weighed under a pound and was perfect for keeping in a pocket, although she rarely carried it there. It was usually secured under the driver's seat of her SUV. But since she had used it last night, she had wrapped it carefully in a towel and placed it in the McDonald's bag. She wanted to make sure she remembered to bring it inside so she could clean it and return it to its rightful place. Always accessible.

She retrieved her gun-cleaning kit from underneath the sofa. The cleaning was calming, a peaceful ritual. She took pride in her ability to keep her gun in perfect working condition. That was the one trait she inherited from her father. That and her marksmanship. She smiled. For all the beatings and abuse she endured as a child, her father did teach both her and her brother how to shoot. And shoot well. It was the only time her father ever praised her. It was finally paying off. *Thanks, Dad.*

She was amazed at how easy this shot had been. She had followed the blue truck to the outskirts of the city limits. The man pulled into the driveway of his small bungalow house. It looked very much like the house she'd grown up in. His place was located on a corner lot across the street from a church. The main street she was on ran parallel to his driveway. He cut the engine and sat in the truck for a few moments. Once again she recognized her good fortune. She pulled her SUV to the side of the road even with his house and rolled down the passenger side window. She took her Walther from underneath her seat and leveled it at the man's head. He was only about twenty yards away. There was no one else around that she could see. She took a deep breath, exhaled slowly and gently squeezed the trigger. The sound was loud, but not as loud as she expected it to be inside her SUV. She saw him start to slump over and she was shifting into second gear moments later.

Remembering the task, she smiled, a sense of deep satisfaction overtaking her. This jerk had almost killed her Toni and called her names. No one should be allowed to do that. Ever. After cleaning the pistol, she left it on the coffee table. She would return it to her SUV in the morning. She finished her beer and began working on her renovations. She hoped to finish the tiling in the kitchen by the end of the week. She was humming as she worked.

Chapter 6

Toni arrived at the office early Wednesday morning. She had gotten a call from Boggs around midnight with bad news. No one had been able to track down Officer Benson. Boggs had said she would continue to search up until the hearing at ten this morning. Toni had done all she could do, but she was still upset with herself for not making sure Benson was in town.

She was on her fourth cup of coffee and it was only eight o'clock. She had gone over the case law for the tenth time and had practiced her argument ad nauseam. To clear her mind she dug out the morning newspaper from her briefcase. She scanned the headlines, not really reading any story. She was on page seven when a photograph caught her eye. It was a picture of the man who nearly crashed into her on Monday. *My God*, she thought. Someone shot him in the head. She read on. Apparently it happened Monday night. *He nearly crashes into me and then somebody shoots him?* She shook her head. Maybe his attitude had really set someone off. He had one hell of a temper, that was for sure.

Suddenly her intercom buzzed. Startled, she responded quickly. "Yes?"

"Ms. Boggsworth on line three," Chloe, the receptionist, said pleasantly.

Toni smiled. Chloe insisted on calling everyone either Ms. or Mr. "Hello, Ms. Boggsworth."

"Ugh. I wish she wouldn't do that," Boggs said. "Anyway, still no luck finding Benson. Vicky is nosing around, but it doesn't look like we'll find him before the hearing. Sorry, babe."

"It's not your fault." Toni frowned. "I can't believe how stupid I was, not making sure he'd be here for the trial. I really appreciate all you've done. I'll call you when it's over, okay?"

"Sure. Just do your best and everything will turn out fine," Boggs replied. "Don't drive yourself nuts. Under normal circumstances you'd never need Benson. It'll be okay, Toni. Really."

Toni hung up not feeling any better. She kept going over her notes until it was time to head to court.

Less than an hour later Toni was sitting in Anne Mulhoney's office. To say that she was stunned would be a gross understatement. Shell-shocked was more like it!

"I still can't believe Judge Smith granted the motion to dismiss with prejudice," Toni said for the fourth time. Anne just nodded and let her ramble on. "He overruled every objection I made. Even when Butch was blatantly leading the witnesses. I mean, jeez. He was practically testifying for them!"

Anne nodded again. "I know, Toni. I was in the back of the courtroom, remember? Judge Smith was anything but fair and impartial. I know he's dirty, but I'm not sure how far the dirt rises or spreads, if you know what I mean. Let me look into a few things before we do anything else, okay?"

Toni nodded and blinked several times, trying to keep the tears from flowing down her cheeks.

"You did your best," Anne reassured her. "It wouldn't have mattered if it was you or me up there today. Judge Smith would have done the exact same thing. Stop blaming yourself. It's not so bad. The homeowners got all their property back. Now get yourself some lunch and move on to your next case. I'll let you know what's going on as soon as I know." She smiled and gestured for Toni to leave.

Back at her own desk Toni absently munched on some Pringles and sipped her iced tea. She had gotten past being upset with herself and was now just furious at Judge Smith and Mr. Defense Lawyer, Butch Henley. How could the justice system be so corrupt? *Or is it that I'm just too naïve?* Somehow she was able to complete what she needed to do for most of the afternoon, despite being distracted. It was almost four thirty when Boggs appeared at her office door.

"Hey, how ya doing?" she asked.

Toni just sighed and rolled her eyes. "I'm still in a state of shock. And I'm pissed as hell."

"I know," Boggs replied. "I just talked to Anne Mulhoney. She's pissed too. Why don't we just call it a day? Let's grab something to eat, okay? I've been on the road most of the day."

"I guess you're right," Toni agreed. "Want to hit The Cat's Meow again? I would just need to pop home, feed Mr. Rupert and change."

"That sounds great. How about I follow you home and we go from there?"

Toni didn't even respond. She just packed up her briefcase, grabbed her suit jacket and headed for the door.

"I guess that's a yes," Boggs said as she followed Toni out the door.

Chapter 7

Toni and Boggs sat on the patio of The Cat's Meow sipping their beer. It was a warm March evening and it felt good to be outside. The bar was really crowded for a Wednesday—there were only a couple empty tables. They'd already finished their sandwiches and Toni was absently picking at her chips. She had described the motion hearing in detail to Boggs for the second time and now she was getting down to the emotional side of her day.

"It wasn't just the fact that he overruled everything." Toni took another bite. The chips were great. "It was his whole attitude, you know? So demeaning and condescending. More than the average good ol' boy judge, do you know what I mean?" She raised her voice to be heard over the din of other conversations. "And Butch Henley. Ugh. Talk about not playing by the rules. And the way he just sneered at me when he left the courtroom. Slime ball, that's all I can say."

Boggs just nodded as she had through most of the evening. Toni was grateful Boggs was letting her get it out of her system.

"Ugh," Toni finally said. "Okay, enough of this. So, how was your day?"

Boggs described her unsuccessful search for Officer Benson and her drive to the nearest lake. "On the brighter side, I did find a really cool cabin to rent for a weekend. All the furniture is made from redwood and there's a fireplace in the bedroom. It has a small kitchen with a microwave and a mini fridge. Maybe we could go down there this summer."

"That sounds wonderful. Let's plan it." Toni and Boggs chatted for a while longer, then finished their beers and left.

The woman had arrived at The Cat's Meow a little after five o'clock. She had the evening free so she'd planned on drinking a beer and picking up some food to take home. She was anxious to work on her kitchen. The sight of Toni caused a quick intake of breath.

She watched Toni and Boggs make their way to the fenced-in patio and sit at one of the tables close to the outside perimeter. They sat with their backs to her, their view toward the doorway into the bar. Neither looked in her direction. *Why was Boggs with Toni? Is it work related? She better not be trying to move in on my Toni!* She felt her rage growing and her hands tighten into fists. The reaction was immediate, almost unconscious.

Micky, the tattooed and pierced waitress with unfortunate teeth, brushed past her small table. She smiled and said hey, taking her order for a beer and burger to go, before heading to Toni's table. The woman felt herself relax just a bit. She leaned back and lit a cigarette. If she turned her head slightly she could make out their conversation.

Although for her everything was about Toni, she was momentarily fixated on Boggs. After listening for a few more minutes she decided that Toni and Boggs were just friends, discussing the day's events. She felt much better and allowed herself to just listen to the sound of Toni's voice. It both soothed and excited her.

She sipped her beer, realizing how upset Toni sounded. Instead of just being enveloped by the sound of Toni's voice, she now listened to what was actually being said. She felt her anger rising again and again as Toni recounted the awful experience with the judge. She was incensed that anyone, especially a judge, would treat her Toni that way.

She paid her tab and left, even though Toni and Boggs were still there. Back in her loft, she dropped her hamburger on the desk where it sat untouched next to her as she stared at her computer screen. She was researching Judge Smith on her laptop and planning her next move. She was also fantasizing how Toni would react when she finally knew that it was she who did it. *Mmm. She'll wrap her arms around me and thank me over and over in between kisses. And from there she'll just melt into my arms. Yesss. That's my Toni.*

After allowing herself to feel the full effect of her fantasy, she got back to planning. This would be far more satisfying than the truck driver. It would definitely take more research, but the reward would be far greater. She still needed to deal with that defense attorney, but the judge would be first. She unwrapped her takeout burger and got back to her objective.

By the next morning the woman was satisfied that she knew all she needed to know to complete her task. As for Butch Henley, she now knew he had permanent tee times at seven a.m. every Tuesday and Thursday at the Tower Grove golf course. The idiot had listed that information in his bio on his law firm's Web site. That wouldn't be a problem for her. But first the judge needed to be dealt with. She knew that all the judges, as well as most of the high-powered people in city hall, parked in the three-floor garage attached to the Metro Building. It was not completely closed in. It had open space above the concrete exterior walls from about three feet from the floor. The parking garage had reserved spots. At eight o'clock she'd called the parking garage, posing as the judge's secretary. She asked for the number of the judge's reserved spot so that she could tell the mechanic. She explained that he was to check a low tire on the judge's car. Within minutes she had the number of the reserved parking spot. She checked the parking garage's Web site and found a detailed map of each parking level. The judge's spot was on the second level, three spaces down from the elevator, and his space faced the street.

At three o'clock she left her job and drove into the parking garage across the street from the Metro Building. It was six stories tall and was used mostly by downtown workers. The first three levels were reserved for monthly parkers and the remaining levels were open for daily or hourly parkers. She drove slowly through the second level. The majority of the spaces were filled, but she found exactly what she was looking for. Next to one of the back stairwells, on the side facing the Metro Building, was an area just big enough for a small vehicle. It was painted with bright yellow stripes, signifying a no-parking zone. It would be perfect. There was only one more hurdle to overcome. How did she get the judge to go to his car at the right time? It needed to be at a time when there weren't any people around.

She sat in her SUV and smoked a cigarette. Then she smoked another. During that time she saw no one. She didn't even hear a car. It was three thirty on a Thursday afternoon. This would be a perfect time of day. After her third cigarette she had a solution. Although there was some risk, she was pretty sure it would work. It had to work. Toni deserved it to work. She had another thought. She got out and began looking in the surrounding cars. She hit the jackpot on the fourth one. It was unlocked and there, on the front seat, was the parking garage keycard. She pocketed the treasure and got back into her car. She was humming as she drove out of the parking garage.

Chapter 8

It was two thirty on Friday and Toni was ready for the week to be over. She was still upset about the Johnson case and wondering if Anne Mulhoney had made a decision about an appeal yet. Moments later Dorothy, Anne's secretary, called her.

"Anne would like you to stop by this afternoon, Toni."

"I can come up now, if she's available," Toni replied.

"Perfect," Dorothy said. "She asked that you bring the Johnson file with you."

Toni gathered everything she had, including all her research, and headed up to Anne's office. Dorothy smiled and nodded toward Anne's door. Toni knocked softly.

"Come in," Anne said.

Toni was impressed, as usual, with Anne's demeanor. Just her presence exuded such confidence, yet she never made you feel inferior. Toni handed her the file.

"I'm thinking we need to go ahead and appeal Judge Smith's ruling," Anne said. "I'm still looking into the *other* issue, but that's a little tricky. What do you think?"

"I'd love to appeal this," Toni said, more than a little nervous. She had only written one brief in her short career, and that was in law school. Her apprehension must have been evident because Anne immediately smiled.

"Don't worry, Toni," she said. "We'll send it to our appellate folks."

Toni immediately relaxed. "What about the *other* stuff?"

Anne sighed. "I'm having someone I really trust do some snooping. I'll keep you in the loop about what I find out. I'd love to be able to prove what I've suspected for a long time." She adjusted the papers on her incredibly neat desk. "It's been a long week for you, hasn't it? Do you have anything on the docket for this afternoon?"

"No, nothing in court." Toni shrugged.

"Why don't you take the rest of the day off. I know you put in a lot of extra hours this week."

"I'm fine, really. I've got a lot of work I can do," Toni said.

Anne shook her head. "I've never met anyone so unwilling to take time off. But since I'm the boss . . . I'll see you Monday morning." She gestured toward the door.

"Thanks, Anne."

Toni went back to her office and tried to figure out what she could do with this unexpected chunk of free time. She nearly ran into Cindy as she rounded the corner.

"Oh, Cindy. I'm sorry. I didn't see you." She noticed Cindy was carrying a large tote bag. "Are you going somewhere?"

"What? Oh, yes," Cindy stammered. "I've got an appointment. See you later." She hurried down the hall.

That was the first time she didn't try to talk my ear off. This must be my lucky day. Toni went into her office and packed up her briefcase. Although she had no idea what she was going to do, she was anxious to get started.

The woman was ready. It wasn't a foolproof plan, but she truly believed it would work. Everything had gone smoothly so far, and she was convinced it was meant to be. In fact, it was fate and it was time for the judge to die.

When she'd done her research the night before, she'd found a picture of Judge Smith and immediately she had a plan. The first time she'd seen Timothy Smith was in her uncle's home when she was only seven years old. He and her uncle were occasional hunting buddies, but she knew there was much more to the story. Her uncle had been sexually abusing her for over a year the first time she saw Smith. He'd looked at her the same way her uncle did. She knew then, as she did now, that Smith liked little girls. She doubted his taste had changed some twenty years later.

The plan had been quite simple. She called the judge's chambers, the number thoughtfully listed on the court's Web site. After telling his secretary she was returning the judge's call regarding a gift for his wife, she was connected to Smith. She told him she had something he'd really enjoy, a gift from a friend. She mentioned her uncle's name. All he needed to do was go to his car at 3:30 and there would be a large envelope taped to the ledge in front of his car. If he liked what he saw, he could contact her at the phone number inside. If not, she wouldn't bother him again. But she strongly hinted that he would not be disappointed. From what she believed, this son of a bitch would be chomping at the bit to see the photos of young girls. The woman was positive he would make an appearance, and that's all she needed.

She drove into the parking garage a little after three o'clock. In the backseat was a guitar case. She wound her way up to the second level and found the space she had occupied the day before. There was no one around. There were no cameras in this garage, unlike the more secure parking garage the judge parked in. She backed into the space and lit a cigarette. She wasn't nervous; she was excited. This was for her Toni.

After she finished her cigarette she glanced at her watch. It was three twenty. Still no one. She got out and opened the back of her SUV. She opened the guitar case and pulled out her weapon of choice for the day. It was a Springfield Standard M1A bolt action rifle with a tactical scope. It was beautiful. She caressed it for only a moment before she got back to the task at hand. She used the ledge of the exterior half-wall of the garage to steady the weapon, even though she would have done fine without it. The muzzle of the rifle was three inches past the wall. This would help diffuse the sound. Being downtown amid numerous tall buildings, it would be difficult for the average person to determine where the shot came from. She breathed deeply, excited about her deed. She peered through the scope and quickly located the judge's car. She worked the single-bolt action and inserted a single shell. She was ready. She was five minutes early, but she had a feeling the judge would also be early. She was not disappointed. She saw him coming from the elevators toward his car. He was looking around like a kid about to get caught with his hand in the cookie jar. He walked around his car to the ledge. He was directly in the crosshairs of her scope. He looked puzzled. There was no envelope. He didn't look puzzled for long.

The woman took a deep breath and began to exhale slowly. Then she slowly squeezed the trigger. The shot was perfect. She figured the bullet pierced his heart before the sound reached his ears. He looked confused as his hand went to his chest and he fell forward. The red color appeared in the center of his crisp white shirt and begin to spread. That was all she needed. She quickly placed her rifle back in her guitar case. She glanced around the garage and picked up the spent casing and put it in her pocket, then hopped in the driver's seat. She lit a cigarette and headed to the exit for monthly parkers. She used her new keycard. There was no attendant at that exit and no cameras. She drove away without being seen. Another successful mission. Next would be Butch Henley. But for now she needed to work on the loft. She needed it to be ready for Toni.

Chapter 9

Toni heard her phone ring, but she ignored it. It was Friday afternoon and no one knew she was home. *Probably a telemarketer.* She was soaking in the tub with tons of bubbles, so whoever was calling could wait. She couldn't hear the message. Mr. Rupert was sitting on the toilet seat taking a bath of his own. He seemed to enjoy having her home in the afternoon.

"This is the life, isn't it, boy?" She sunk lower into the tub. The water was beginning to cool and she considered adding some more hot water. Her phone rang again. "Who would call me during the day?"

Mr. Rupert seemed to shrug. Then her cell phone rang. There was a pause and it rang again.

"Something's not right, Mr. Rupert," she said as she stood and began to towel off. He jumped down from his perch and trotted to her bedroom. She dried herself quickly, threw on sweats and a sweatshirt and headed downstairs. Mr. Rupert followed her, as if sensing her anxiety. She pushed *Play* on her answering machine.

"Toni? This is Anne. Please call me at the office as soon as you get this message."

There was a pause and the second message played. "Toni? Hey, babe, call me on my cell. Something's up."

Before returning either call, Toni grabbed her cell phone from the table. Another message from Anne and one from Boggs. Toni called Boggs first.

"What the hell is going on?" she asked as soon as Boggs answered.

"Someone shot Judge Smith. He's dead."

"What?" Toni gasped.

"Someone shot him in the parking garage just an hour ago. Judge Carlson found him when she went to her own car. The whole building is going crazy and the press is everywhere."

"I've got to call Anne. She also left me a message. I'll call you back after I talk to her, okay?"

"Sure. No, wait. I'll call you. I need to see what Sam wants me to do." Sam Clark was the chief investigator in the prosecutor's office. "I'll talk to you in a bit."

Toni hung up and quickly called Anne's office. Dorothy put her through immediately.

"What happened, Anne?" Toni asked.

"All we know right now is that Judge Smith was shot in the parking garage. He was pronounced dead at the scene. We've got the best crime scene unit over there now, but it looks like we're going to get 'help' from the FBI or Homeland Security or whomever. Apparently the judge was on some planning committee in Fairfield that dealt with security issues. I wanted to give you a heads-up. I'm sure everyone is going to be questioned, but you just had an unpleasant experience with the man."

"You mean I'm a suspect?" Toni couldn't believe it.

"Of course I don't think so, but you know how the feds are," Anne said tersely.

Toni didn't know how "the feds were," but it didn't sound good. "What should I do? Do you want me to come into the office?"

"No," Anne said. "I just didn't want you to be caught off-guard. The media is swarming around here. You might get a call from one of them. I'll let you know if I hear anything else."

"What should I do if they call me?"

"The safest thing is just don't answer the phone. I'll handle the media on this end. If one of them does get through, just say 'no comment' and refer them to me."

"Okay. Thanks, Anne." She rang off. She was dumbfounded. Just a few months ago she was almost killed by a crazy man and now she might be a suspect in the killing of a judge? This wasn't what she signed up for when she went to law school. She paced around the living room for several minutes, mumbling to Mr. Rupert. Not knowing what else to do, she poured herself a glass of wine and waited for Boggs to call her back.

Boggs hung up from Toni and headed to the chief investigator's office, stopping at the vending machine in the hall. Sam Clark was sitting at his desk with the phone in one hand and a Diet Coke clutched in the other. He was almost as tall as her, but substantially larger around the middle. He kept his gray hair cut short and he always seemed to have a smile on his face. He nodded at one of his office chairs. Boggs sat and waited. After several minutes he disconnected.

"This is a mess," Sam said as he chugged the last of his Diet Coke. He absently tossed the empty can in the trash. It clunked against the half-dozen already there.

Boggs held up the new can. "Give me the dirt and you get your next fix," she said, grinning.

Sam held out his hand, motioning for the Diet Coke. He popped open the new can and took another few slugs, then slumped back in his chair. "Thanks. I just talked to Captain Billings. He said that the crime scene unit is still in the garage, but here's the best part. The FBI is taking over the investigation."

"What gives them jurisdiction over the Fairfield PD? This is a state matter, not federal."

Sam shook his head. "Some bullshit about Judge Smith being involved in Homeland Security or something, according to Billings. He's really pissed, off the record, of course. He thinks there's something else going on."

"It doesn't smell right to me, Sam."

"Me, either, but right now, we're just supposed to cooperate with the investigation. I mean, obviously we, our unit, wouldn't be involved at this stage, but it sounds like we're supposed to be strictly hands-off here. I told the captain you'll be the go-to person in our department when the time comes. But even his people aren't involved yet. The crime scene unit is supposed to basically secure the area and wait for the feds to show up. It just doesn't make sense."

"I know what you mean." Boggs was baffled too. "Well, it's not like I'm shocked that someone killed the bastard. I just don't get the quick involvement by the feds. I've never known them to get involved so fast." She wanted to say more but decided not to. "I know a few feds. Do you know who's heading up the investigation?"

Sam gave her a sly look. He loved having information first. "The special agent in charge is"—he looked down at his notepad—"Agent Johnny Layton, based here in Fairfield. Do you know him?"

Boggs grinned. "No. I don't know *him*, but I do know about a female special agent named Johnnie Layton. Think it's her?"

He shook his head. "Why do you always seem to know more than me?" He laughed. "I'm going home. Betty is making lasagna tonight. Maybe I can impress her with my knowledge of something, since obviously I'm out of the loop here." He patted Boggs on the shoulder as he headed out. "Have a great weekend and call me if you hear anything, okay?"

"Sure," she answered. "Tell Betty I said hi." Sam was a great boss and always kept Boggs involved in the high-profile cases. She was his number one investigator and she considered him a friend as well as her boss. And she adored his wife, Betty. Boggs went back to her own office and wondered how long it would be before Agent Layton called her. She didn't think it would be long. She'd never met the agent, but she heard she was like a dog with a bone when she was on a case. She checked her messages before calling Toni. Nothing yet.

Toni answered on the first ring. "Hello?" She sounded nervous.

"Shit, Toni," Boggs said. "Did you have the phone in your hand, or what?"

"I'm just a little keyed up, that's all," Toni said with a little laugh. "Do you know anything?"

"Not really. Sam said the feds are definitely taking over and Captain Billings is unofficially pissed off about the whole thing."

"I bet. This is his turf. What's the deal?" Toni asked.

"Some national security bullshit," Boggs replied. "But anyway, are we still on for tonight? You still want to meet Vicky and Patty for dinner?"

"Absolutely," Toni said. "I can't wait to pick their brains about all this."

Boggs chuckled. Their friend Vicky, as a detective for the Fairfield Police Department, would for sure be in on some of the details, if there were any. And Patty was a beat cop, so she might know what was being said on the street. "So, you're over trying to fix them up as a couple?"

"Hell, yes." Toni laughed. "After the lecture Vicky gave me last week, I'll wait at least another month before I try to find the perfect woman for her."

Two hours later the four women were seated around a table at Aunt Hattie's. It was one of those hole-in-the-wall places located inside an old warehouse. If you didn't know where you were going, you'd probably never find the place. Inside it was a quaint diner. There were about twenty tables, each with its own candle and mismatched silverware.

A waitress appeared at their table, the same waitress Toni had seen on her first night there with Boggs six months ago. She wore jeans and the same flannel shirt that had apparently been shrunk in the dryer. Again it was unbuttoned dangerously low. This time, unlike Toni's first experience here, she was able to look at the waitress without staring at her cleavage.

"I think I'll have a Miller Lite," she said with a smile.

Boggs and Vicky were a little more discerning in their tastes.

"I'll have a Hefeweizen," Boggs said.

"Make that two," Vicky chimed in.

Patty shrugged. "I'll have whatever's on tap." She had never been there and was busy taking in all the sights, including the waitress.

As soon as the beer arrived, the women ordered the burger baskets.

"These things are so huge, you'll never be able to finish it all," Toni explained to Patty. "We had them the first time we came here. They're to die for."

Vicky laughed. "You were probably too busy drooling over each other to eat." She then proceeded to tell Patty how Boggs and Toni tried to remain "professional" last fall but failed miserably. "It was disgusting. They were all googly-eyed at each other while that maniac serial killer was stalking them."

As she spoke of the killer, Vicky touched the scar on her neck. Toni realized it was probably a reminder of how close to death Vicky herself had come. Toni had never heard Vicky talk about the scar and she didn't think Vicky seemed self-conscious about it. In fact, Toni had never seen her attempt to even cover it by wearing makeup or a scarf. In Toni's mind, it was just who Vicky was, a part of her.

"Of course I'm sure you noticed it yourself," Vicky said, referring to Toni and Boggs's behavior.

Patty chuckled and nodded. "Yeah. It was pretty obvious."

"You're so full of shit," Boggs retorted. "We never let our personal life interfere with work and you know it."

Vicky laughed again. "But that makes the story so dull."

"Well, talk amongst yourselves, ladies," Boggs said as she excused herself to go to the bathroom.

Toni spotted Boggs a few minutes later talking to a woman near the restrooms. The woman had long blond hair and kept flipping it back over her shoulder. She kept reaching out and touching Boggs's arm.

"Who is that woman Boggs is talking to?" Toni asked Vicky.

Vicky turned around. "Oh, yuck." She stuck out her tongue. "That's Tina. She may be nice to look at, but she's about as bright as a box of hair."

"She looks a little friendly," Toni said softly.

"They dated for a bit," Vicky murmured. "But that was ages ago."

Boggs returned to the table.

"How's Tina?" Vicky asked.

"Same as always," Boggs said matter-of-factly. If she had noticed that Toni felt a little uncomfortable, she didn't let on.

By the time the food arrived they were discussing the murder of Judge Smith. Boggs filled them in with all she knew.

"I've met Johnnie Layton," Vicky said. "She worked on a case with us a few years back."

Patty nodded. "I met her on that case. It was when I first came on the force. She was strictly by the book but seemed okay to me."

Vicky agreed. "Totally hard-core on the job." Then she gave a knowing grin, inferring she knew the dirt. "But I hear she's a real softy off the job." All three women looked to Vicky to continue. She put on her innocent face. "What?"

"What have you heard?" Toni asked.

Vicky beamed. "Well, this is not confirmed, you understand." She took another bite of her burger. "But a friend of a friend said she let some woman walk all over her. This apparently happened when she lived and worked in D.C. That was a few years ago, I think."

"That's it? That's all you know?" Boggs snickered. "God, Vicky. I thought you'd have some real dirt her. Or at least a way we could find out what's really going on with the FBI doing an investigation."

"I'll see what I can find out," Vicky retorted.

"What does she look like?" Toni asked in between french fries.

"She's really cute," Patty said immediately. Everyone at the table looked at her with raised eyebrows and grins. Patty blushed.

"Well, that narrows it down." Boggs laughed.

"Well, she is. She's about five foot ten inches with an athletic build. Her hair is light brown, and short, above the collar. Very sexy. Icy blue eyes that can look right through you. Um, let's see. No tattoos or scars that I know of, and her voice is like butter. I could listen to her talk all night." Patty leaned back in her chair and smiled. "Oh, and her drink of choice is rum and Coke, but she also likes beer."

"And you know this how?" Vicky asked.

"When she worked that case a few years ago, I was fresh out of the academy. And in lust, I must say. My job was to be a gopher, so I brought her coffee and stuff. Mainly I hung around waiting for someone to ask for copies or to make calls. I overheard a few things, but I don't think she ever really saw me."

Patty sighed.

"Is she gay?" Boggs asked.

"No confirmation," Patty said, "but I'm hopeful." She grinned at the others.

"Hey," Toni said. "I think I might have met her during law school. A few agents came to talk about the FBI during my first year. The female agent sounds very much like Johnnie, at least the height, hair and eyes. I did talk to her for a while afterward, but I'm ashamed to admit I don't remember her name. We talked about my background and she thought I should look into working for the feds." She actually remembered the encounter more clearly than she let on. "I think I had to leave and go to class, because I don't remember getting any contact information from her or anything."

"Interesting," Boggs said. "So you thought about working for the feds?"

"Not really." Toni shrugged. "In your first year of law school you sign up for a ton of meetings and groups. I signed up for anything within reason as long as we got free pizza and beer. I became a little more discriminating during my second and third year. Anyway, I'll know pretty soon. Anne said that the agents would be talking to anyone who had contact with the judge."

"Well, you sure as hell did," Boggs said. Then she told Vicky and Patty about the hearing with Judge Smith.

"I know that bastard was crooked as hell," Vicky said. "He always treated me like crap when I had to testify. It's no wonder someone shot him."

Toni was shaking her head. "I know he's dirty, but why shoot him? Who'd he piss off?"

"You mean besides you?" Vicky asked.

"Yes, Vicky, besides me," Toni said. "I guess this wasn't a good week for men to cross my path." She told Vicky and Patty about the man in the truck. "Then I read someone had shot him that same night. Kinda creepy, don't you think?"

"Remind me not to piss you off," Vicky said. "In fact, how about I buy your dinner?"

Everyone laughed, but Boggs got serious. "Toni, you know that the feds are going to suspect everyone, right? So don't freak out if they ask you where you were, okay?"

Toni froze. "Are you serious? Would they really consider me a suspect?"

"The feds consider everyone a suspect. I just didn't want you to be caught off-guard."

"That's what Anne told me," Toni said, squirming. "And I don't feel too comfortable with this."

"Just don't tell them you killed the guy in the truck," Vicky quipped. "That might not look too good."

Again everyone laughed and the subject went back to Patty's obvious lust for Johnnie. But Toni worried. She didn't have an alibi for this afternoon, except for Mr. Rupert. And she didn't have an alibi for the night the truck driver was killed. It wouldn't look good.

Chapter 10

The woman awoke Saturday morning with a smile. She was quite pleased with herself. The task of killing the judge went off without a hitch. Her next assignment was Butch Henley, but that would have to wait a few days. She knew he had a standing tee time at seven a.m. on Tuesdays at Tower Grove golf course, so that would give her a chance to scope things out. But now she needed to pick out something to wear today. She knew she would see Toni and wanted to look her very best.

Toni slapped at her alarm clock Saturday morning. She hit the snooze button on the third try, but by then Mr. Rupert was sitting on her chest. She struggled to keep her eyes open.

"I can't breathe, Mr. Rupert," she managed to say.

He meowed several times, no doubt more concerned with

breakfast than her need for oxygen. He seemed to know that his twenty pounds of girth could come in handy in many situations. When she closed her eyes again he began to knead her chest.

She moaned. "Okay, okay." She gently pushed him off and sat on the edge of the bed. Her eyes remained closed. Mr. Rupert pushed his huge head against her, nudging her to get up. She pulled on her sweatpants and padded down to the kitchen, where she dumped way too much food in Mr. Rupert's bowl and made herself an extra-strong pot of coffee. She turned on the coffeemaker before heading up to the shower, mumbling as she went.

By the time Toni got out of the shower, Mr. Rupert was sitting on the toilet seat washing his face. He seemed very pleased with himself.

"Ugh," Toni grunted. "Don't look so happy. At least you had a full night's sleep." She was grinning as she ruffled his fur and got dressed. Even though she had only a few hours' sleep, she couldn't help but smile. After dinner last night she and Boggs had come back here. They shared a bottle of wine and a few stories. Toni resisted telling Boggs that she hoped Johnnie was the agent who had come to her school a few years ago. Like Patty, she had been immediately attracted to the woman, but at the time she was going through a breakup with her ex. For at least a year afterward, Toni had fantasized about the agent. She was sure it had to be the same woman and felt both nervous and excited at the prospect of being questioned by her. The fantasy had been fresh in her mind last night, but instead of telling Boggs, she merely acted it out. Three hours later they were both exhausted but incredibly satisfied. Toni had to get up early this morning so Boggs had reluctantly left her townhouse at three a.m.

Toni was sipping her coffee downstairs and reliving the night before. She caught herself breathing a little heavy when she was interrupted by Mr. Rupert, who jumped up on the table. She nearly spilled her coffee.

"I can't help it, boy," she said. "Damn, that was one hell of a night. I could live with that on a regular basis."

She looked at her watch. It was eight o'clock. She needed to get going. She was attending the monthly meeting of the Community Awareness group at nine. She had joined the group when she was a therapist and had continued attending despite her change of career. The committee sponsored several local events and involved a broad spectrum of women from all walks of life. It was being held at Izzy's, one of the local coffeehouses. Izzy was on the committee and often hosted the meetings. Toni was especially glad it was there this month. Not only did she adore Izzy, but she would need a latté with a couple extra shots of espresso. She grabbed her keys and, jamming her wallet into her jacket pocket, ruffled Mr. Rupert's head as she left.

Johnnie Layton sat in her kitchen and went over her notes. She was glad that she had been assigned as the lead agent in the Judge Smith case. She liked being the one who called the shots. No surprises. She had already done a lot of research on the life of the judge and didn't like what she'd found. He had definitely been a real sleaze, but she needed to follow the proper protocol. He was on the Fairfield Homeland Security Council and so there was the possibility, according to her supervisors, that the murder had been the doing of a terrorist. She knew that wasn't true. His name had also come up tied to several conservative religious groups.

Johnnie looked over her list of regular people to interview. She also needed to do some investigating on the supposed terrorist angle, but she knew that was a dead end. She glanced down at her notepad. She needed to talk with the prosecuting attorney, Anne Mulhoney, to get her ideas about the judge. Of course she needed to talk to all the other judges, but she knew the majority would be a waste of time. She would get a list of all the defendants he had sentenced in the last year or so, and all those who had recently gotten out of prison, just to cover all her bases. She would get around to interviewing all of the staff at Metro, but she was anxious to interview Toni. She never forgot their introduction three years ago. Cute and ambitious, Toni had intrigued her then, and she had been curious what had become of her. But she needed to be very careful.

Johnnie had been with the FBI for a little over ten years now. She had always been cautious and none of her coworkers knew that she was gay. Although some of them might have wondered, there had never been any confirmation. She had been closeted from the beginning, although there had been one close call when she was in Quantico. All of her "relationships" had occurred out of town. It had cost her a considerable amount of money, and many lonely nights, but it was worth it. She needed to remain professional throughout this investigation. Completely by the book. Toni needed to be treated just like any other suspect. Johnnie smiled when she thought about that. It would mean that she would have a lot of contact with Toni and that suited her just fine. She must be careful and remind herself not to cross that line. At least not yet. Once this case was over she'd have her promotion to a supervising agent, and then she could live her life openly. She had made that promise to herself ten years ago. She smiled. Timing was everything. She pulled on her blazer and checked her weapon, snug in its holster located in the small of her back. She opened her black leather messenger bag, making sure it contained all the files and information she needed. She put on her dark sunglasses and grabbed her car keys. Before leaving her apartment she grabbed her pack of Marlboros and put them in her pocket.

Bertha Jane Newton was drinking a cup of black coffee at Izzy's.

"Need a refill, Bertha?" Izzy asked.

She smiled and nodded. Izzy was the only one in Fairfield that dared to call her by her given name. To everyone else, she was Bert.

She had worked pretty late the night before at The Cat's Meow but didn't mind getting up early, knowing this was where the Community Awareness group planned to meet today. She had positioned herself at a table near the front so she could see everyone come through the front door.

Bert had worn her favorite black leather pants and a clean, tight white T-shirt. Her belt was made of leather and silver. Her trucker's wallet was secured to her belt loop with a silver chain. Her black motorcycle boots were well-worn, but shined. She looked good. Before leaving her place that morning she had slicked back her light brown hair. She liked the look. Her black leather jacket completed the outfit.

As she sat at Izzy's she lit another cigarette with her trusted Zippo lighter. Hardly anyone used a Zippo anymore, but she liked how it sounded. She nodded and winked at several women as they entered the coffeehouse. A few times she jumped up to open the door for an obvious femme. She'd been waiting about twenty minutes when Toni arrived. She opened the door for her.

"Hey, Toni," she said. "How you doing?"

"Oh, hey, Bert. Thanks," Toni replied as she stepped through the door. "Just here for some much-needed caffeine and to go to a meeting."

Bert knew the meeting wouldn't start for at least fifteen minutes. She took a chance. "I'll treat you to a coffee if you've got a few minutes."

Toni looked at her watch. "Sure, Bert. I've got time before it starts. But I'll get it. Where are you sitting?"

Bert pointed to her table. She felt uncomfortable allowing Toni to buy her own coffee, but she didn't want to come on too strong. At least not yet. She sat back down at her table and waited.

Toni ordered the biggest latté available with an extra shot of espresso. She waved at Izzy, who was in the back room, and returned to Bert's table.

"What has you up so early?" Toni asked.

"Oh, I've got a lot of errands to run today, so I thought I'd get a caffeine jumpstart."

Toni laughed. "I know how you feel. I think I'm going to need more than one of these to make it through my day." She seemed comfortable talking to Bert. They chatted easily for several minutes before Toni looked at Bert's hair. "You did your hair different." She smiled. "I like it. It looks good on you."

Bert grinned and winked at her. "Thanks."

"Well, I hate to cut this short, Bert, but I've got to go to this meeting. Thanks for keeping me company. See you at the bar?"

"Absolutely." Bert wished she could keep Toni there longer, but this was good enough for now.

Toni wound her way through the coffeehouse to the back room. Crystal Phillips was the president of the group and she was chatting with several other women when Toni entered the room. She spotted Nancy Manford at one of the tables and joined her. Nancy was an activist and a little outspoken for Toni's taste, but she loved her company. She was quick-witted and told great stories. The only drawback was Nancy's blatant disgust for men in general, although she had made a few exceptions over the years. Toni always wondered if Nancy's last name irritated her. Toni thought it was ironic and teased her often.

"Hey, Nancy *Man*ford. How's it going?"

"Well, hello, Ms. Attorney. Glad you graced us with your presence."

Toni poked her in the arm. Everyone had a lawyer joke or dig. "Well, a girl has to make a living," she shot back. "You're looking sharp today. Got a date afterward?"

Before Nancy could respond Crystal started the meeting. They talked about the upcoming Walk-A-Thon for the Alliance for Mental Health and the need for additional volunteers to staff the hotline. Crystal went through the agenda quickly, then asked for volunteers for a new committee she was forming.

"We need to address the impact of violence on our community," Crystal said, "especially now that Judge Smith was murdered. According to the latest state crime statistics, the crime rate for violent offenses in Fairfield has risen ten percent in the last two years."

Several women began talking at once. Nancy leaned over to Toni and whispered, "That asshole got what he deserved, don't you think?"

Toni was surprised. She knew Nancy wasn't fond of men, but this was a little more than her usual banter. "Are you serious? I mean, jeez, the guy was shot in broad daylight."

"Don't tell me you're upset that he's gone," Nancy countered.

"Well," Toni said, "it's not like he was one of my favorites. In fact, he was a real jerk to me last week. But I don't think anyone *deserves* to be killed."

Nancy shrugged. She turned her attention back to the meeting and then actually volunteered for the new committee. After the meeting concluded, Nancy pulled her aside. "Hey, I didn't mean to upset you. I didn't, did I?"

"Oh, hell, no. You're one of my favorites. You're the reason I keep coming to these meetings."

Nancy grinned. "Why don't we get together for a drink soon? We haven't done that for a long time."

"That sounds like fun," Toni said. "Why don't you give me a call next week and we'll set something up."

Nancy nodded as she was being drawn away by another member of the new committee. She kept her eyes on Toni.

Toni waved good-bye and went back to the front counter. She ordered another latté. While she was waiting for her coffee, her cell rang. It was a number from her office. She frowned.

"Hello?"

"Hi, Toni. It's Cindy Brown. Sorry to bother you. Did I catch you at a bad time?"

"Oh, hi, Cindy. No, I was just ordering a latté. What's up? Is something wrong?"

"Well," Cindy said slowly, "I'm here at work. I needed to catch up on a few things." She paused. "You got another one of those letters in yesterday's mail."

Toni shook her head. She'd been getting anonymous letters for the past five months, although this was the first in about a month. They were mostly letters of admiration, all signed "Till We Meet Again." She found them a little creepy, but Anne told her it was common to get letters, especially after she had been on the news. There had been a lot of media attention last fall with that serial killer on the loose. The letters weren't actually threatening or anything. Toni was puzzled as to why Cindy felt it important enough to call her on a Saturday.

"They're no big deal, Cindy," she said.

"This one is a little different," Cindy explained. "It's in a huge envelope and it isn't flat. It just doesn't look right to me, so I thought you should know."

"Okay." Toni rolled her eyes and paid the cashier. "I'm only a few minutes away from Metro. Are you going to be there for a while?"

"Absolutely," Cindy said. "I'll be waiting for you."

Toni walked in Metro fifteen minutes later, waving to the weekend guard, Wilbur. She wound her way around the halls. She saw Cindy sitting at her desk drinking a Coke from the vending machine. She was wearing tight blue jeans and an even tighter sweater. Toni couldn't help but notice. Cindy had a nice figure and she was beaming, as usual.

"Hey, Cindy. You look nice today. So where's the letter?"

Cindy pointed at a large manila envelope with the familiar

handwriting on the outside. The envelope looked lumpy, just as Cindy had told her.

"Let's open it up," Toni said. Cindy handed her rubber gloves from the closet and she slit open the end with a letter opener and emptied out the contents. Several miniature Snickers candy bars fell onto the desk. Toni extracted the letter from the envelope and scanned the handwritten note. It was basically the same as all the others, the writer telling Toni how wonderful she was. This time it was signed TWMA, instead of the longer version, Till We Meet Again. She shook her head. "I guess he's moved up a notch with the candy."

"Maybe you should tell Anne," Cindy suggested, frowning. "This is beginning to creep me out."

"I guess you're right," Toni said. "I'll talk to her on Monday."

Cindy retrieved a copypaper box from the supply closet. It had Toni's name printed on the side. "I've kept all of them, just in case." She watched Toni put the candy and the letter back in its envelope and add it to the box. She moved closer to Toni and whispered, "Aren't you a little afraid?"

Toni could feel Cindy's breath on her face and felt instantly uncomfortable with the proximity. She took the box from Cindy and deliberately placed it between them, creating a little distance. "I don't think it's anyone dangerous, just a little nutty," she said. "But I'll let Anne know, just in case."

"Let Anne know what," a voice said from the hall. Toni glanced up, surprised to see Anne Mulhoney. She was accompanied by another woman. Toni knew instantly it was Johnnie Layton. She felt her face flush.

"Toni's been getting letters from some guy for the last five months," Cindy explained. "This last one had little candy bars inside."

She showed the box to Anne, who peered inside and shook her head. "It's probably nothing, but let's give it to Sam and see what he comes up with, okay?"

64

Toni nodded but said nothing.

Anne turned to the other woman. "Agent Layton," she began, "this is Toni Barston, one of our attorneys. And this is Cindy Brown, one of our secretaries."

Johnnie first looked at Cindy and nodded. "Pleased to meet you." She then looked at Toni and smiled, her hand outstretched. "I think we met once before, Ms. Barston."

Toni was flustered but thought she covered it well. She shook the agent's hand. "It's been almost three years, I believe." She hoped her voice sounded normal. It was hard not to recall the old fantasies she'd had after they first met. The handshake lasted a fraction of a second longer than normal. *Maybe she really is gay.* Not that it mattered. She was happy with Boggs. *But damn, there is something about her.*

"I'd like to speak with you later, Ms. Barston," Johnnie said. "If you're available I'll stop by your home later this afternoon. Would three o'clock be convenient for you?"

Toni was more than a little taken aback as several things went through her mind at once. Why, for example, would she want to come to her home instead of talking to her in the office? *Am I really a suspect? Should I say no?* She couldn't do that; it'd look suspicious. *Oh, my God. She's coming to my house? I need to get home and clean. I bet she can tell I'm nervous. Can she tell I'm attracted to her. Jeez!*

"Ms. Barston? Would that be okay with you?" Johnnie asked again.

Toni stammered just slightly. "Um, that would be fine."

"See you then," Johnnie said. She nodded good-bye to Anne and Cindy and walked away.

Anne smiled at Toni as if sensing her nervousness. "It's fine, Toni," she said. "Just routine questions. She talked to me for about twenty minutes. She seems very professional and by the book. Don't worry about it. Now, tell me again about these letters."

Toni felt a little relief. This was all routine, after all. She told Anne about the content of the last letter, then took the box over to Sam's office. She left him a detailed note and headed home. She had some cleaning to do before Johnnie arrived.

On her drive home, she called Boggs and told her that she was going to be interviewed at three o'clock by the infamous Johnnie. "I'll call you as soon as she leaves," she said. "You're still coming over tonight, right?"

"Oh, yeah. Try and stop me," Boggs said. "How about me bringing over some Chinese food?"

"That would be wonderful. I've got the wine covered. I'll call you later."

Boggs hung up the phone and sat at her computer for several minutes. She didn't feel right about all this, the interview at Toni's home in particular. She picked up her phone and called Vicky.

"I don't like this," she confided to Vicky. "Why not question her at the office? They were both there. Why go to her home? Doesn't that sound odd to you?"

"Not if she thinks Toni's a suspect," Vicky said blandly. "If it were me I'd want to see where the person lives. Look around as much as I can, try to get a feel for the person. But as soon as she realizes that Toni's not the person, she'll leave her alone. Sounds like you're a little jealous of Patty's dreamy agent."

"Oh, shut up. But I guess you're right about the interview. I suppose I'd do the same thing. But Toni sounded weird to me. Maybe she's just nervous about being questioned. I'll find out more tonight when I go over there. So, what are you up to tonight?"

Vicky laughed. "Nothing as exciting and lustful as your evening, I'm sure," she said. "Anne had asked me to look into Judge Smith before he was killed. There is a lot of really bizarre stuff with this creep, may he rest in peace. I'm going to keep digging. You know how I am—once I get something, I can't let go."

"That's one of the things I love about you," Boggs said fondly. "Keep me in the loop, okay? And something else." She hesitated just a moment. "Keep this just between us for now, okay?"

"Sure, what do you need?"

"Well, Toni's been having this feeling that someone is watching her, or following her," Boggs explained. "Maybe she's just being a little paranoid after all that happened to us last fall, but it wouldn't hurt to keep an eye out. Do you know what I mean?"

"Hopefully it's just a feeling," Vicky said. "But to be on the safe side, I'll keep an eye out. But I think we should let Patty in on this. She's a good egg, and she sees and hears stuff on the street. You know we can trust her."

"Okay," Boggs agreed. "Let's just not let Toni know for now, okay? I don't want her to stress about it right now, but if we can assure her in a week or so that everything is fine, maybe that will help."

"Done," Vicky said. "Now, I've got some digging of my own to do. Besides looking into Judge Creepo, I want to see what I can find out about Johnnie. If you guys get bored later, I'll be at The Cat's Meow, hopefully with some hot chick."

Boggs was chuckling as she hung up the phone. She sincerely doubted she and Toni would get bored tonight. After last night, she was just hoping she could keep up with Toni's libido. The thought made her smile. Maybe she should take a nap this afternoon.

Chapter 11

Toni finished vacuuming and straightening the living room in record time. She had already changed the sheets and started a load of laundry. She was dusting in her bedroom when Mr. Rupert meowed loudly.

"I'm just doing my regular weekly cleaning."

He didn't seem convinced.

"The bedroom cleaning is for Boggs, not the FBI," she explained. "And why am I telling you this? Nothing is going to happen with Johnnie. I'm probably just nervous."

Mr. Rupert didn't seem to believe a word she was saying. He jumped up on the bed and stretched out. Being a rather large cat, he took up a good portion of the bed.

"You can stand guard if you like," she informed him. "I know you like Boggs. Don't worry. No one but her is coming up here today."

With that he appeared satisfied. Toni wondered why she was so jittery. But instead of dwelling on that, she decided it was time to clean the bathroom. She still had over an hour before Johnnie would arrive.

After all possible cleaning was done, Toni took a quick shower and stood in her walk-in closet naked. For the life of her she couldn't decide what to wear. After almost fifteen minutes she decided she'd better pick something or freeze to death. Probably her best option, she thought, was to appear incredibly casual. Just wear her normal, "around the house" outfit for a Saturday afternoon. She chose faded jeans and her favorite denim work-shirt. She would keep it buttoned high until Johnnie left, then unbutton it much lower after Boggs arrived. Her funky red tennis shoes completed the look.

The doorbell rang at exactly three o'clock. Toni looked through the peephole even though she knew it would be Johnnie. She took a deep breath and opened the door. "Good afternoon, Agent Layton." She motioned Johnnie inside.

Johnnie entered and looked around the living room. She was dressed the same as she was earlier in the day and carried a black leather messenger bag. "Thanks for seeing me, Ms. Barston."

"I'm happy to cooperate," Toni replied. "And please, call me Toni."

"Okay, Toni. Call me Johnnie."

Toni blushed. She felt like a teenager with her first crush. Johnnie seemed to always be in total control. Patty was right, she thought. Johnnie had a voice like butter, and it made Toni want to melt. Why hadn't she remembered that? Well, it had been three years, after all. Toni tried to shake away any unprofessional images from her mind.

"Have a seat," she said, noticing that her voice cracked. "Can I get you a soda or coffee?" *Quick recovery, Toni. You sounded like an idiot.*

"No, thanks," Johnnie said. "I'm good for now." She smiled

and then let her gaze go to the couch.

"Have a seat," Toni said again. She watched Johnnie slowly go over to the couch and sit on the far side, facing the front door. It was a large sectional couch that curled around the corner. Toni chose to sit at the opposite end because aside from the dining room table, there wasn't any other place to sit. She didn't want to be too close to her. Or rather, she knew she shouldn't *want* to be too close to her.

Johnnie opened her bag and took out a small notebook. She smiled at Toni. "Just a few routine questions." She clicked her pen. "How well did you know Judge Smith?"

"Well," Toni said slowly, "I really didn't know him at all. I had my first court appearance before him just a few days ago. It was a suppression hearing."

Johnnie didn't say anything, just kept looking at her.

"I lost," Toni stammered.

Again Johnnie said nothing. She jotted something down on her notepad and looked back at Toni, who shifted uncomfortably on the sofa. She was just about to open her mouth again when Mr. Rupert entered the room, announcing himself with a loud meow. He jumped up on the back of the couch between Johnnie and Toni.

Johnnie flinched just a bit. "My God, that cat is huge!"

Toni laughed. "No, he's just big-boned. Johnnie, meet Mr. Rupert."

To emphasize his introduction, Mr. Rupert looked directly at Johnnie and meowed. She grinned broadly and put her hand out for him to sniff. He took the offer and seemed satisfied with the guest. He positioned himself on the couch squarely between the two women.

As Toni reached out to scratch his head, she realized that Johnnie had been using a common technique for interviewing someone. She had employed it hundreds of times herself as a psychotherapist. All you needed to do was ask one question and wait. If you remained silent, the person often felt uncomfortable with the silence and continued to talk or explain. It usually worked very well. Toni was surprised she'd fallen into that trap. Now that she'd figured this out, she just continued to pet Mr. Rupert and smile at Johnnie.

The two sat quietly for some time, until apparently Johnnie realized Toni was unmoved by the silence and asked, "Had you heard anything about the judge before you were before him in court?"

Toni thought for a moment. "No, not really." She smiled again.

"When was the last time you saw him?"

"When I left the courtroom around eleven Wednesday morning."

"Where were you between three and four o'clock yesterday?"

"I was here with Mr. Rupert."

Johnnie wrote a couple more things in her notepad and then seemed to relax a bit. "So, Toni, any thoughts about working for the FBI?"

This threw Toni for a loop, but she countered nicely, if she did say so herself. "Not really. I'm really enjoying working for Anne Mulhoney. The experience has been great. You've been with the agency quite a while now. How do you like it?"

Johnnie put her notebook away and sighed. "Well, the first few years were hard. You really have to prove yourself. It's still a good ol' boy kind of place, even though there are a lot of women. I'm sure it's the same with you."

Toni laughed. "That's the truth. It's not nearly as bad as it was years ago, I'm sure. But it's still in the undercurrent. Are you stationed here in Fairfield now?" She couldn't remember where Johnnie was working when she came to the law school three years ago.

"Yes. I'm about ready to move up a slot in the department and I've been told I can stay here now, so this is my home. The first few years you get moved around a lot, but I'm hoping I can really put down some roots now. I have some big plans for the next chapter in my life."

Toni waited for her to add more, but she didn't. She realized that the uncomfortable feeling she'd had earlier had vanished. In fact, she felt at ease with Johnnie. "Are you sure you don't want something to drink?"

"No, thanks. How about a rain check? I really need to finish interviewing people."

"What do you think about this murder? Any leads, or is that off limits to me?" Toni asked.

Johnnie laughed. "Well, you don't have an alibi for it, so technically you're still a suspect."

Toni's eyes grew wide.

"But I really don't think you killed him, if that helps," she said. "But for the record, do you own a gun?"

Toni shook her head. "Nope, sure don't."

"Well, I guess that does it for now," Johnnie said as she stood up. "It was great seeing you again and talking to you. I really enjoyed it. I'll probably be talking to you again, as well as most of the other people at Metro."

Toni walked her to the door.

There was an awkward pause for just a moment, then Johnnie extended her hand. "See you around, okay?"

"Okay," Toni said as she shook Johnnie's hand. She watched Johnnie walk down the sidewalk and out of her view before she shut the door. She sat back down on the couch with Mr. Rupert. "Well, that wasn't what I expected," she told him. "She actually seemed pretty nice, although I'm not thrilled with being a suspect." She guessed she should call Boggs and fill her in.

Boggs answered on the second ring.

"Well," Toni confessed, "I'm not under arrest, so I guess we're still on for tonight."

"So I don't have to worry about getting bail money?" Boggs

teased.

"At least not today." Toni filled her in on the short interview. "She was actually pretty nice. She said she was going to settle down here in Fairfield. But now on to more important things. What time are you coming over?"

"How about six thirty? I'll pick up our dinner and a couple movies. Is there anything you want to see?"

"Six thirty sounds perfect. Maybe something funny or romantic. Nothing scary. I get enough of that in the real world. Unless, of course, you're thinking of stopping at a more, um, specific type video rental place? Then I'm up for anything that drops your socks."

"Well, there's an offer I can hardly refuse," Boggs said. "How about one regular movie that we can watch while we eat, and a special one, or two, for dessert?"

"Nothing too kinky, and I'm all over that." Toni smiled. "See you soon, honey. And you may want to bring your softball stuff. I don't think you'll be leaving before noon tomorrow."

Toni hung up the phone feeling almost giddy. There was something about Boggs that she felt soul deep. A real connection. Add to that the fact that she thought Boggs was incredibly hot and it made a great combination. She made sure there was white wine chilling in the fridge as well as a couple bottles of water. Then she went upstairs to inspect the bedroom and made sure everything was ready. She planned on keeping Boggs in bed as long as she could.

Chapter 12

The next day Toni sat on the small bleachers at the softball field clutching a huge latté. She had on gray sweats and a red Chiefs sweatshirt with an old blue baseball cap pulled down low. Her eyes were shaded by dark sunglasses. At her feet was a cooler that held soda and water. She felt like she could literally fall asleep while she sat on the bumpy metal bleachers. Boggs was warming up with the other players, and Toni wondered how she had the energy to walk, let alone jog around and throw the ball. They couldn't have gotten more than three hours of sleep.

"You look like hell on toast," Vicky announced as she tromped up the bleachers toward her. "Did you have a rough night?" she asked politely.

"Go to hell," Toni growled. "I can't believe Boggs is out there. This is my second latté and I'm not even close to functioning." She paused a moment, realizing that Vicky wasn't wearing a uniform. "Why aren't you playing?"

"I'm too old for this shit," Vicky muttered. "I'd much rather sit here and watch the cute girls run around in their shorts. At least that's what I'm telling myself now. We'll see how I hold up as a spectator once the season progresses."

"I can't believe they're already playing," Toni said. "It's just the end of March. My God, how long is the damn season?"

"It goes through July, and then there's the fall league in August," Vicky replied. "This is a hard-core co-ed league, although a lot of the guys have seen their day. Those are the ones who should never wear shorts. Metro has a pretty good team because we take kids from the Metro Police Academy. I prefer to watch women's softball, but I need to show my support. How come you're not playing?"

"I prefer being a fan and supporting my team," Toni said. "And I suck."

Vicky laughed. "Nuff said."

Toni drained her coffee, took off the top and peered inside.

"Want a refill?" Vicky produced a huge thermos from her backpack. "It's spiked," she confided.

"As long as it has caffeine, I want it." Toni held her empty cup out. Vicky poured in just a bit.

"Try it first. I'd hate to waste any if you hate it or something."

Toni tentatively took a sip and coughed. "Jeez, Vicky. Is there any coffee in this?" She took another sip. "But, damn. It's good." She put her cup out for more and Vicky filled it to the brim. Toni replaced the lid and sipped the steaming brew of coffee-laced brandy. "Now, this is the way to watch softball on a cool day." She sighed.

The two women watched the other side's players trot to the benches as the game was about to start. Boggs waved at them from shortstop. Toni grinned like a schoolgirl and waved back.

Vicky groaned. "You guys are sickening. Hasn't the lust worn off yet?"

"Hardly," Toni said with a grin, remembering last night.

Halfway through the game Toni began to notice that Boggs was chatting with a woman from the other team each time she came off the field. By now the brandy had kicked in and Toni felt a twinge of jealousy. It happened again and she poked Vicky in the arm. "Who is that woman that Boggs keeps talking to?"

Vicky looked down at the field. "That's Pam Cooper, or Copeland or something. She works at City Hall. Why?"

Toni just shrugged. "Did Boggs go out with her?"

"Probably," Vicky replied.

Toni didn't say anything.

"Oh, hey, Toni. That was years ago. Boggs has dated a lot, you know."

"I know," Toni said. "I just didn't think I'd see two of her old girlfriends in two days." After a few minutes she decided to change the subject. "Oh, by the way, you are cordially invited to my parents' house for Easter dinner, three weeks from today."

"Wow," Vicky said sarcastically. "That sounds like so much fun, but I don't think I have an appropriate Easter dress, and my Easter bonnet is at the cleaners."

Toni shook her head. "Oh, it's not like that at all. Every year my folks invite everyone and their dog over. It just happens to be on Easter; there's no religious tone about it. Everyone brings a dish, or a bag of chips or something, like a potluck. We eat until we're stuffed and then we have an Easter egg hunt. Actually, that's not even true. We just hide candy."

"No eggs?" Vicky asked.

"No. Everyone is required to bring one bag of candy. Then my favorite aunt, my cousin and I dump all the candy together. We mix it all up and then put it in bags, mark each bag with a name. It started off as little bags, but now we use gallon-size. It is ridiculous, actually. Then my cousin and I hide the bags outside and you have to find the one with your name on it. It doesn't matter if you're three years old or ninety-eight. Everyone gets a bag. We hide a few in 'special' places. Last year I put my uncle's on the roof of the house."

"Well," Vicky said, "that actually sounds like fun. Can I let you know? But isn't this something you should ask your girlfriend to go to?"

"I told her about it last night. She said that she wasn't sure because her mother has been asking her to visit."

Vicky hesitated just a moment. "Can I let you know? I'm hoping to be in bed, recovering from Easter eve."

"What?"

"Easter eve," Vicky said, a coy smile on her face. "I go out to the bars the night before Easter and I'm usually pretty good at finding a wonderful woman to accompany me back home. That's my Easter tradition and I'd hate to alter it."

"You can let me know, or just show up. All you have to do is bring the bag of candy with you. I'll give you the address."

The two continued to watch the game, cheering when appropriate. Toni was beginning to feel the effect of her "coffee."

"I'm going to have to take a nap after this," she announced. "I can't handle booze in the morning after only a few hours' sleep. I'm not as young as I used to be. And I told my folks I'd come over for dinner tonight. Boggs has to interview some people tonight for a trial tomorrow. Elizabeth is trying a drug trafficking case. I guess she wasn't able to catch up with them until now."

Again Vicky hesitated. "Ah, an investigator's work is never done" was all she said.

After the game was over, Boggs came over to the bleachers and took a bottle of water from Toni's cooler.

"Great game, Boggs," Vicky said. "I can hardly believe you guys won without me there."

"It was tough." Boggs chugged down half the bottle of water. "We barely squeaked it out, ten to one." She turned to Toni. "Are you heading home?"

"Yeah. I think I'll take a nap before heading over to the folks' house. I'm a little tuckered," she said with a wink. "I'll give you a call when I get home tonight, okay?"

"Absolutely, babe."

"See ya, Vicky. Thanks for the java," Toni called as she went to her car.

Boggs watched her walk away. Exhausted, she wished she could sleep the rest of the day.

"What the hell is going on?" Vicky demanded as soon as Toni was out of earshot.

"What?" Boggs asked sheepishly, knowing Vicky was about to come down on her.

"You know damn well what. You have to question some witnesses tonight? I don't buy that for a second unless it's some new info that Elizabeth just found out about. And what in the hell is this shit about visiting your mother? She's been asking you to visit for years. What's the rush all of the sudden?"

"She wants to see me," Boggs answered meekly. It was actually true.

"But you can't stand her or your stepfather. Don't tell me you're actually considering going up there?"

"Actually, yes," Boggs insisted. Her mother and stepfather lived in Wisconsin. "I haven't seen her for almost three years. I thought maybe it was time. Maybe things would be different. Anyway, my brother is going to be there."

"I still don't buy it, Boggs. What's going on?"

Boggs sat on the bleachers and downed the rest of the water. Why did everything have to be so hard? She'd dated more women than she could count and had never run into this before. After almost five minutes of silence, she said, "Seriously?"

"Yes," Vicky snapped. "Seriously, what's going on?"

"I'm scared," Boggs said, just above a whisper. It was hard to admit.

Vicky leaned closer and put a hand on her shoulder. "Scared of what, honey?"

Boggs sighed. "She wants me to meet her family. She asked me to go there for Easter."

"And?"

"And nothing."

"So she wants you to meet her folks. So what? She asked me to go to the Easter thing, too."

"Really? Maybe it's nothing, then," Boggs said. Maybe the lack of sleep had blown things out of proportion.

"What were you thinking? That there was more to it?"

"Well, yes," Boggs said, feeling overwhelmed. "I've never met anyone's parents before. What does that mean? Does this mean we're moving to the next step? Moving in together or something? I'm not good at this, Vicky. Anyway, what if her parents hate me or something?"

"For one thing, her folks won't hate you. You're too cute to hate," Vicky teased.

"I'm being serious. Regardless of her parents—even though I am scared about meeting them—what does this all mean? Is she expecting me to ask her to move in together? I've never lived with anyone before. I'm a kinda short-term-relationship person. I usually only date someone for a few months then just fade away. I'm freaking out here."

"Slow down, Boggs. This doesn't have to mean anything. But first, how do you feel about Toni? Do you love her? Have either or you said 'I love you'?"

"No. Neither of us has said that. I don't know, Vicky. I don't think I even know what love is. You've known me for a long time. I've always been a player. I date who I want, when I want. I've never even considered being tied down to one woman before."

"And now you're thinking about it," Vicky said. "And that's got you scared?"

"I'm not sure what I'm thinking about." Boggs finished the water and threw the bottle at a trash can. She missed. "Damn." She walked over to retrieve the bottle and put it in the barrel. "All I know is that I'm scared out of my mind. I think I'll need some time to sort this out. I know that she drives me crazy. Hell, we've been dating for five months and I still fantasize about making love to her."

"Okay," Vicky said, laughing. "Too much information there. But what about just spending time with her? Do you like to just be with her?"

"Well, yes. I think so. Hell, I don't know anything anymore," Boggs said, flustered.

"Do you want to date anyone else?" Vicky prodded.

"No. At least I don't think so. God, Vicky. I'm not sure what I'm feeling."

"Well, you need to figure it out, girl," Vicky insisted. "Maybe you need some soul-searching. We've been friends for a long time. I want whatever you want, but I really like Toni. I don't want to see either of you get hurt. Figure out how you're feeling then talk to her about this. Maybe you're going too fast. Maybe she has no idea you're feeling this way. Maybe she wants you to propose or something, and maybe she's happy just dating. Talk to her, okay?"

"I will," Boggs replied, dreading a heart-to-heart with Toni. "But not yet. I'm not ready yet. I don't know what I want. Maybe I'll just back off a little until I figure out what the hell I'm doing."

"Do you want to talk about this some more?" Vicky asked. "I was just going to do some snooping this afternoon, but I can put it off for a while."

"No, go ahead. I think some time alone will be better. But thanks for the offer."

"Anytime, hon," Vicky said. "Just keep me posted, okay?"

"I will," Boggs said as she got up and headed to her car. "See ya." She sat in her car for fifteen minutes before starting the engine. Things had been so much easier when she was younger. She dated more than one woman at a time and never had a problem. When she was in the air force she was considered quite the catch, but never got too involved with anyone. Now here she was feeling overwhelmed from a stupid invitation to an Easter dinner. She was dreading the conversation she knew she needed to have with Toni. Maybe she could avoid it all together. At this moment she didn't know what to do or where to go, so she just drove home.

Chapter 13

Thursday morning. Toni groaned as she hit her snooze button. It had been a long week already. Her days had been busy with preliminary hearings, pleas and sentencings. She had picked up another felony burglary case and it looked like it might go to trial. Ordinarily she would have been excited, but this week was different. She hadn't seen Boggs outside of work all week. In fact, she had only seen her intermittently while at work. She knew that Boggs was busy, but something didn't seem right. Even during their phone calls, something was missing. Boggs was still flirty and suggestive, but it didn't seem as intense as it had been. Toni wondered if she'd said or done something wrong. What the hell had happened?

She tried to remain optimistic on her drive to work. They had a date tomorrow night and she'd know then, or at least that's what she told herself. She looked at her watch. It was nearly nine o'clock and she was just pulling into the garage. She rarely came into work this late, but she just couldn't seem to get going this morning. At least there was nothing on her docket until that afternoon.

When she walked into her office she sighed and rolled her eyes. She had forgotten her coffee travel mug on her kitchen counter. This was going to be one hell of a day if that was any indication. Cindy appeared before she even set her briefcase down.

"Are you okay?" Cindy asked.

"Just having one of those days. I forgot my coffee at home." Toni turned on her computer, not really up to chatting.

"I was just heading down to the cafeteria. Want me to get you a cup? Two creams, right?"

"That would be wonderful, Cindy." Toni smiled at her and then began fishing inside her briefcase for her wallet.

"No. It's on me today," Cindy said. "I want this to be a really good day for you."

Cindy left before she could respond. Toni smiled. It really was so sweet of her. She should do something special for Cindy to let her know she appreciated all she did, even if she could be really annoying at times.

Cindy returned with an extra large cup of coffee for Toni and one for herself. "I got the special blend for both of us. I figured we could both use the treat."

"That was so sweet of you." Toni held up her cup. "Here's to us, then. Let's have a fabulous day."

Cindy returned the gesture, a big smile on her face, and went back to work.

A few minutes later the receptionist buzzed. "Ms. Barston, there is a Ms. Manford on line three for you."

"Thank you, Chloe." She punched the button. "Hey, Ms. *Man*ford. What's up?"

"I was just sitting here sipping some coffee and I thought of you," Nancy said. "How about meeting me for dinner tonight? I feel like celebrating and I thought of you."

"What's the cause for celebration?" Toni took a sip of her cafeteria coffee.

"Oh, we just won a small battle at city hall, but any victory there is worth a drink or two. What do you say? We could grab a bite at The Cat's Meow. That seems to be the hot spot lately."

Toni knew she wouldn't be seeing Boggs. What the heck. It would make the evening go by quicker. "Sounds good to me. What time?"

"Six thirty?"

"Perfect. Then I'll see you there." Toni hung up the phone feeling a little strange. It wasn't like she was going on a date or anything. Just having dinner with a friend. Why did it feel weird? She shrugged it off. She had a lot of work to do.

Bert Newton came into The Cat's Meow earlier than usual. It was barely nine thirty. She unlocked the door and quickly put on a pot of breakfast blend coffee. It was her favorite and it always tasted better when she fixed it at work. She had already had a productive morning and was ready for a break. She couldn't keep her mind off Toni this morning, so she'd decided to come in early. She was hoping that Toni would stop by for dinner. She hadn't seen her for several days and that was hard. She was getting a little anxious. Soon she would be ready to make her big move. Not quite yet, but soon. Bert grinned and flipped open her Zippo to light a cigarette while the coffee brewed. Soon.

Johnnie Layton pulled up to the drive-through window at Starbucks. She ordered a venti latté and told the young woman at the window to keep the change. She was feeling good this morning. The investigation was going well, as far as she was concerned. She knew that the only reason the FBI had jumped on the case was politics. They wanted it known that they were on top of things when it came to homeland security. It was all bullshit. No one upstairs at the Bureau seriously thought that a terrorist had killed the judge, but it looked good for them to step in and it justified their budget allotment for Fairfield. Once that angle was cleared she could easily close the case and give it back to the Fairfield PD, where it really belonged. She didn't want to do that just yet. She wanted to make sure that she questioned all the right people and followed any and all leads. Even if it were just for political show, she never wanted to be accused of sloppy work. And best of all, it gave her a legitimate reason for being around Toni. That was enough for her. She thought Toni was one of the sexiest women she'd ever encountered. Johnnie sipped at her latté as she drove to Metro. A few more rounds of questioning would be perfect.

Fifteen minutes after her first sip of coffee, the woman took her last. There was nothing like a good cup of coffee in the morning. It was one of her favorite things. And Toni was another one of her favorite things. This had been a great morning so far. The only thing that would have made it better was if she could have shared everything with her. But that would have to wait just a little bit longer.

The woman had completed another brilliant task. She had completed her research on Butch Henley over the weekend by calling the golf club and verifying his tee time. Then, on Tuesday morning, very early, she had driven out to the golf course. She knew he had a standing tee time at seven, so she arrived at six fifteen. There was no one else there. Of course there wouldn't be. According to the club's Web site, the seven a.m. tee time was the first of the day. She had scoped out the course and could not find any appropriate place for her business. She knew Butch would be golfing with his law partner and probably two others. She was frustrated for a while, but her drive to succeed was intense. She hated Butch and she loved Toni. She had to find some way. Any way.

Her anger began to grow when she realized that there was no way she could kill Butch while he was golfing. She had imagined just blowing them all away, but that seemed too messy. And what if Toni got upset? The other men hadn't hurt her, only Butch. There had to be some other way.

She had driven away from the clubhouse parking area slowly that morning. There was still no one around. She drove over to the maintenance building not far away and parked. Nobody there either. Good, she thought. She got out of her car, leaned against the hood and lit a cigarette. She felt a familiar emptiness inside her. It had always been with her from the time she was a child being abused by her uncle. It never went away. In the past she had tried to fill the hole with lovers, anonymous sex, alcohol and even drugs. It worked for a short time, but it was never really gone. But now she had Toni. Toni could fill the hole. Once the loft was completed and her tasks were done, she would be whole.

Her attention came back to the task when she heard a car pull into the clubhouse lot. It was Butch and he was alone. She watched him from her vantage point and lit another cigarette. She wasn't concerned that he would see her. He got out of his car and began stretching. He went through a little routine and she chuckled to herself. It was slow and almost calming to watch, like a slow ballet. She chuckled again. He looked like such a girl. She hated him. Hated how he had treated Toni.

Butch slowly stretched for almost fifteen minutes, then he retrieved his golf clubs from the trunk of his car and glanced at his watch. He took out his cell phone and made a call. Another ten minutes passed. It was now fifteen minutes to seven. He was still alone. She smiled. This would be perfect. A little dangerous, sure, but perfect. The danger excited her anyway.

She got back in her SUV and drove around the back of the maintenance building. She had studied a map of the golf course over the weekend and knew there was a maintenance road that would lead her out of the golf course. She wasn't sure if there would be any locked gates, but she could handle that if it came up. She followed it as it wound around for about a half-mile or so, finally ending up on a side street that surrounded the course. She encountered no barriers and quickly turned onto the main road. She had been back at her loft by seven twenty.

She had awakened early this morning, knowing that today, Thursday, was the day. She retraced her route to the golf course and arrived again at six fifteen. This time she had her guitar case with her. Once she was parked by the maintenance building she opened the case and retrieved her rifle. Butch arrived about ten minutes later and parked in the same spot. He was beginning his little stretching routine as she leaned over the hood of her SUV. She could see him clearly in the crosshairs of her scope. This was almost too easy, she thought. She worked the single-bolt action. She took a deep breath and slowly exhaled, gently squeezing the trigger. He seemed to fall in slow motion. She could see that her shot was perfect, as usual. His lime green golf shirt was covered in red as he fell forward. She replaced the rifle in the guitar case and looked for the spent casing. She didn't see it at first. Then she noticed a glint of brass on the hood, near the windshield wiper blade. She reached for it and it fell through the gap between the hood and the windshield, but not all the way to the ground. She couldn't take a chance on opening the hood right now, so she just got in her SUV and drove away. She would deal with that later. She saw no one as she'd wound her way around the maintenance road and back out to the main road.

All that was a memory now, and the coffee had been her special treat. She couldn't wait until the time was right and she would be able to tell Toni all about her accomplishments. *I know she'll love me even more than she does now. Once I tell her everything*

I've done for her, for us, she'll love me forever and ever.

She continued going about her normal routine, but she put a star on her calendar for Thursday. This would always be a special day.

Chapter 14

It was nearly noon on Thursday when Dorothy buzzed Toni. "Anne would like to see you, Toni. Can you come up now?"

"Absolutely, Dorothy," Toni said. "Is this about a specific case? Should I bring a file?"

"No, just you, honey." Dorothy rang off.

Toni wondered what was up. Maybe Anne wanted to talk to her about the appeal in the Johnson case. Toni pulled on her blazer, ran her fingers through her hair and sighed. She needed to get her hair cut this weekend. It was out of control. Maybe she'd take the leap and get it cut shorter. That would certainly shave at least fifteen minutes off her mornings. She wondered if Boggs would like a shorter cut on her. She'd ask her tomorrow.

By the time she decided on an updated hairdo, she was standing in front of Dorothy's desk.

"Go on in, Toni. She's waiting for you."

Toni tapped lightly on Anne's door, then opened it and went in. She was surprised to see Detective Frank Parker sitting in one of the chairs. He was dressed impeccably as usual in his "detective garb," as she thought of it, pressed khaki slacks, crisp white oxford shirt, brown print tie and a brown blazer. Although it was the standard-issue uniform for Fairfield detectives, his was tailored. He looked more like a *GQ* model than a cop, with his year-round tan. He was one of the best detectives in Fairfield and he knew it. He was also one of the most arrogant and sexist men she knew. Toni had disliked him from the moment she met him, but her opinion of him had softened considerably after her brush with death last fall. Still, he was forever an arrogant son of a bitch.

"Hello, Frank," she said and then smiled at Anne, who motioned for her to take a seat. Frank barely nodded to her and then looked at Anne. Toni sat as instructed and waited. Something wasn't right.

"Frank just came from the Tower Grove Golf Course," Anne began. "Butch Henley was killed this morning."

"What?" Toni said in disbelief. "What happened?"

"Shot," Frank answered coolly. "Same as the judge."

Toni looked from Frank to Anne, then back to Frank. Her mind was racing. Who would kill Butch? Same as the judge? Did that mean Butch was involved in Homeland Security stuff too? What the hell was going on? *Wait.* Why the hell were they telling her this? Here in Anne's office and not with the rest of the staff? *Shit.* Did they think she was a suspect? *Oh, God.*

"Toni?" Anne said. "Are you okay?"

Toni blinked several times and stared at Anne. "I just can't believe this. What . . . um, I don't know what to do," she confessed.

"Where were you?" Frank asked, glaring at her.

"What?"

"I said, where were you?" he repeated.

"When?"

"This morning. About six until seven o'clock."

Toni sighed deeply, closed her eyes for a moment and shook her head. "I was at home, Frank."

"Alone?"

"Yes, Frank. Alone. Unless you can verify that with Mr. Rupert, I was alone." She looked at Anne and shrugged. "I don't have an alibi, if that's what you're asking."

"Frank," Anne said with a hint of disgust, "you could have been a little more subtle about this." She turned to Toni. "Frank has the case and this is just routine for the file," she explained.

Frank grinned at Toni. "Yeah, Toni. Just routine. Sorry. I didn't think you shot the asshole, but I had to ask for the file, just like Anne said." He laughed. "It's not like I think you could whip out a rifle and shoot the guy. You probably couldn't even hit the side of a barn."

Toni didn't even respond to that. She couldn't. If that arrogant son of a bitch only knew, she thought. Instead, she looked again to Anne for guidance. "What does this mean? Am I a suspect? Will the FBI get involved in this case, too?"

"I'm not sure, Toni. Ballistics aren't back yet, of course. We'll know more then, but Frank thinks it looks like the same type of hit. Captain Billings has called Agent Layton to let her know, just in case. Anyway, Frank knew he had to get a statement from anyone who had any sort of contact with Butch that was, well, unpleasant. So he came to me. That's why I asked you here."

Toni didn't feel too reassured. In fact, she felt like she could be sick.

Anne smiled broadly at her. "Toni, we don't think you killed anyone." Her voice was confident and comforting.

Even Frank seemed to soften a bit. "Really, Toni," he said, "I don't think you killed him or anything. Honest."

Toni relaxed slightly and tried to smiled. "Thank you, both. Really. What should I do now? Wait for Agent Layton to call me and question me again?"

"I think so, Toni." Anne nodded. "Just go about your normal routine, okay?"

"All right." Still shaky, Toni stood to leave.

"We've got our best crime scene unit out there now," Frank offered as he rose and brushed past Toni toward the door. He nodded to both women before leaving.

"Toni," Anne said. Toni turned back toward her boss. "Don't fret about this. And don't fret about those anonymous letters. Sam sent everything to the lab and he's looking into that for us."

"Okay," Toni said. "Thanks, Anne." She left the office feeling overwhelmed. Now Butch was dead. She had been quite vocal last week about how much she couldn't stand the man, and now he was dead. And she had no alibi. Did people really think she killed two men? *Oh, my God. Oh, my God.*

It was lunchtime, but she sure didn't feel like eating. She knew she should, but the thought of food actually made her stomach turn. She went to the bathroom and stood in front of the mirror, just staring at her reflection.

She couldn't believe this. Just routine? It felt like more than that. And they didn't even know about the man in the truck. What would they think if they knew about him? Was someone trying to set her up? She needed to see Boggs. She needed to talk to her about this. But Boggs had seemed so distant lately. Did she think she was really a cold-blooded killer? Who could she talk to? She didn't think she could make it through a dinner with Nancy tonight. She needed to figure this out. Vicky. She'd call Vicky. She'd know what to do.

After a few minutes, Toni felt better. She ran a paper towel under cold water and patted her neck. It reminded her of the last time she did that and Boggs had come into the restroom. Yes. She definitely needed to talk to Vicky. Maybe she'd know what was going on with Boggs. Toni glanced in the mirror one more time. She had to get to get her hair cut. Something short and sexy.

As she left the bathroom she literally ran into Cindy. "I am so sorry. I wasn't paying any attention."

"Are you okay?" Cindy asked. "You were in there a long time. I was just going to check on you."

"I'm fine, thanks." Toni ran a hand through her hair. "I've just decided I need to change my hairstyle, something shorter and maybe a little sexier. What do you think?"

"Ohhh . . ." Cindy murmured. "That would look really good, something just a little shorter, but not too much."

"No, not too much," Toni said. "Do you really think it would look good? I mean, be honest. Really. I want to know what you think."

Cindy beamed. "I think you'll look even better than you do now. And that's no easy feat."

Toni blushed and looked away.

Cindy seemed a little nervous, almost embarrassed at her own comments. "Maybe you could look at some of the magazines in the lunchroom," she suggested. "That would give you an idea to tell your hairdresser."

"That's a great idea," Toni said. "Thank you, Cindy. I'll do that."

Toni went in her office and shut the door, something she rarely did. She needed time to sort all this out. Even though she desperately wanted to talk to Boggs, to hear her voice, her first call was to Vicky. She was relieved when Vicky picked up on the second ring.

"Carter."

"Vicky, it's me, Toni."

"Hey, girl. What's up?"

"Um, did you hear about Butch?" Toni asked.

"Yeah. Frank has the case. Are you okay?"

"Yes. Well, no," Toni confessed. "I could really use someone to talk to. By any chance could you spare some time for me tonight? If you're busy I totally understand."

"No plans with Boggs tonight?"

"No. We're going out tomorrow. She's been busy."

"Then how about I stop by your place around six? I'll even bring a couple burgers and some French fries for Mr. Rupert."

"That would be wonderful, Vicky. Are you sure it's not interfering with something?"

"Not at all, hon. I'll see you then. Make sure you have beer." Vicky disconnected without saying anything more.

Toni felt much better. Talking to Vicky would help. She called Nancy and left a message canceling their dinner. In a long apology, she stretched the truth a bit and said she needed to do some last-minute work on a case. She felt bad, but she knew she couldn't make it through a carefree dinner tonight. Her next call was to Boggs. She got her voice mail.

"Hiya, Boggs. It's me. I don't know if you heard, but someone killed Butch this morning. This is really getting weird. Anyway, just thought I'd touch base with you. I'm having a bite with Vicky tonight. I can't wait to see you tomorrow night. I miss you."

Toni hung up the phone and just stared at her calendar. She had a preliminary hearing at one thirty and a plea at two. There was nothing else on the docket today for her. She had worked through lunch every day this week. Maybe she could take off work at four today and squeeze in a haircut. She quickly called her stylist, Anthony. She was in luck. He would take her at four fifteen. She told him she wanted a new cut, something a little shorter and sexy. He giggled and told her he'd have several pictures for her to look at when she arrived. She felt better as she gathered her files and headed to the courtrooms.

Chapter 15

Toni was in a little bit of shock when she left Anthony at five o'clock. She had never had her hair this short. It was now above her collar with bangs just above her eyebrows. Anthony had shown her how to wear this style for court and she agreed it looked good. Still professional, but a lot more stylish. Anthony insisted on giving her the "date" look before she left and he slathered on a ton of gel to produce a wild spiky 'do. She blinked several times in the mirror when he spun her chair around. It would take some getting used to, that was for sure. Anthony sent her on her way with a bag full of mousse and gels. A quick glance at her watch told her she still had time to stop by the grocery store before Vicky arrived at six.

She found a parking spot right in front of the store. She dug her wallet out of her briefcase, which was secured in the trunk of her car. Even though she was only going to pick up a six-pack of beer, Toni grabbed a shopping cart on the way inside and headed toward the cooler in the back of the store.

She should get at least two six-packs, she thought. The weekend was coming up. She noticed that there were several brands on sale. She decided on two of Hefeweizen and two of Miller Lite. Both Boggs and Vicky liked German beer. Well, that should hold them for a bit. And maybe she should pick up another couple bottles of wine, just in case. After finding what she wanted, Toni made her way to the front of the store through the chips aisle and impulsively threw in two bags. *Ooh . . . Fritos!* She loved those. They were perfect with beer. She had almost made it to the checkout when she saw the pastry display. She couldn't decide between the apple strudel or the cream cheese thing. She took both.

She was shaking her head as she walked back to her car with her bags. When would she learn not to go to the grocery store when she was hungry?

By the time Toni opened her front door it was a quarter till six. She would barely have time to put the beer in the fridge and change her clothes. She dropped her briefcase on the floor and kicked the door shut. Mr. Rupert followed her to the kitchen and waited patiently by his bowl. He was still staring at her. Toni fed him before putting the food away. When she finished he was staring at her.

"What?"

He meowed loudly and kept staring.

"Oh, my hair. Do you like it, buddy?"

He stared a bit longer and then rubbed against her leg.

"Thank you. It'll look different once I shower, but no time for that now."

Toni rushed upstairs and stripped off her suit. She pulled on her faded jeans and an old blue plaid flannel shirt. She didn't bother to tuck it in. She was washing her face when the doorbell rang. She glanced in the mirror. The sight of her hair almost startled her. This was going to take some time. She sure hoped Boggs liked it. She wondered what Vicky would say.

Boggs called Vicky, who was on her way to Toni's townhouse. She begged her to find out what Toni's intentions were.

"I'll try and find out what she's thinking," Vicky said calmly.

Boggs felt desperate. She needed information. "Don't just ask her point-blank, okay? Be subtle, for God's sake. I'm freaking out, remember?"

"I know. I know. You've told me that a hundred times today." Vicky sighed. "I'll see if she's happy just dating . . . you know. I'll just use my skillful ways to get all the info out of her. Are you sure you want me to tell her you're working?"

"Yeah," Boggs said. It was partially true. She just couldn't face her yet. "Tell her I'll pick her up tomorrow night at seven. We're still all going out together, right? That should give me enough time to figure out what to do. But don't forget to call me as soon as you leave tonight, okay?"

"Yeah, yeah. Whatever. And yes, we're all still going out. You know it should be you over here tonight, not me. She's pretty upset."

"I know. I'm a real creep." Boggs wondered if all this stress was worth it. "Maybe I'm not good enough for someone like Toni."

Vicky sighed loudly. "Take it easy, Boggs. Let me find out what's going on before you throw in the towel. God, you're such a pain in the ass. Okay, I'm here. I'll call you later."

Toni opened the door after looking through the peephole. "Hey, Vicky," she said, motioning her inside.

Vicky took one step inside and froze. "Damn." She whistled while blatantly giving Toni the once-over. She shook her head

97

and went to the kitchen with her bag of burgers. After setting the food on the counter, she turned and looked at Toni again.

"Do you like my hair?" Toni asked timidly. "I won't wear it like this for work or anything. Anthony was just showing me how to fix it for a date," she stammered. Vicky wasn't saying a word. "Does it look okay?"

"Damn, girl," Vicky said, eyeing her. "Didn't you even look in the mirror?"

Toni was embarrassed, and her hand went immediately to her hair. "Is it that bad?" she asked quietly, afraid to hear what Vicky thought.

Vicky smiled and leaned against the doorway to the kitchen. "Toni," she said softly. "You look incredible. Really."

Toni relaxed and grinned sheepishly. "Are you sure? I've never had it this short."

"Oh, yes." Vicky paused. "I'm *so* sure. Don't take this wrong, okay? I'm not hitting on you or anything. But, damn. The hair is great. Very sexy. And the shirt. Well, I think you'd better button it up a little more."

Toni's face burned as she quickly reached up and buttoned her shirt almost to the very top. "I'm sorry." She felt like an ass. "I was getting dressed when you rang the bell."

Vicky laughed. "Boggs is one lucky woman, that's all I've got to say."

Toni smiled. "Do you think she'll like it?"

"Oh, I wouldn't worry about that. Nope. Don't worry about that," she said, still grinning. "And by the way, I talked to her earlier. She said that she's working, but she'll pick you up tomorrow night at seven."

"Okay." Toni nodded. "But, don't tell her about my hair or anything, okay? I want to surprise her. I doubt I'll see her at work tomorrow, and it would look different anyway. I sure hope I can make it look like this again."

"Me, too," Vicky mumbled.

Toni brushed past her to get to the refrigerator. "Do you want wine or beer? I stopped and got some Hefeweizen."

"Beer, please," Vicky said as she dug the burgers and fries out of the bag. "Got any paper plates?"

"Right up there." Toni pointed to the upper cabinet. "Need a glass for this?"

"Nah," Vicky said. "Bottle's fine."

They settled on the couch, eating their food in silence. Mr. Rupert joined them and immediately took a fry off of Vicky's plate.

"I got these just for you, handsome," Vicky said to him. "Need to keep up your strength." She rubbed his head as he munched on his prize.

"Need another?" Toni asked as she rose to get a beer.

"Not yet, thanks. Am I slow tonight? I don't ever remember you finishing a beer before me."

"Rough day." Toni returned with a fresh bottle, wondering how to broach the subject of the latest murder. "Did Boggs tell you that I feel like someone is watching me?"

Vicky glanced at her. "Well, yes. She did."

"She probably thinks I'm crazy or something, huh?"

"No." Vicky shrugged. "She doesn't. In fact, she asked me to snoop around. And we don't think you're crazy, by the way. We know what it's like to have a gut feeling or a hunch."

"Find anything?" Toni asked, curious.

"No. Not yet. But we're still checking things out."

"We?" Toni raised an eyebrow. "Meaning you and Boggs?"

"And Patty," Vicky replied. "We were all in that crap last fall, remember. We look out for each other."

Well, that makes me feel a little better, Toni thought. At least for the moment. She sighed deeply. "Frank asked me where I was this morning, between six and seven."

"He was just doing his job, Toni. But he can be a real asshole about it."

Toni took several more gulps of beer. "I know. And then he said something like, 'You couldn't hit the side of a barn anyway,' and I didn't answer."

"He's an ass," Vicky stated simply. "Good detective, but an ass nonetheless." She finished off her burger. "What else?"

"What do you mean?"

"What else happened?" Vicky said. "There's something you're not telling me. What is it?"

Toni grimaced. "I can hit the side of a barn."

"Huh?"

"I can hit the side of a barn," Toni repeated. "In fact, I can hit almost anything at one hundred yards." She looked squarely at Vicky. She was proud of her marksmanship, but it was stressing her out right now. "With a rifle or a pistol," she added.

Vicky's eyes widened. "You're, um . . . a good shot?"

"Yes."

Vicky nodded. "Maybe I'll have that next beer now." Toni went to the fridge and brought her out another beer. "So that's what has you scared, huh? No alibi for either shooting and the fact that you're a really good marksman?"

Toni nodded as she curled up on the end of the couch. "And the fact that the man in the truck that almost hit me was killed. No alibi for that night either. They don't even know about that." She finished the beer and got herself another one.

"Slow down, Toni."

Toni returned to her spot on the couch. "It's not like I'm driving anywhere tonight." Suddenly feeling overwhelmed, she wiped a tear from her eye. "Do you think I did it?" she murmured.

"Oh, honey," Vicky said, reaching out to touch Toni's arm. "Of course not. I don't care if you can shoot the balls off a gnat at three hundred yards, I know you didn't kill those men."

"Thank you," Toni whispered. She took another gulp of beer. "I think maybe Boggs has her doubts, though."

"Oh, no, Toni," Vicky said. "I hardly think she believes you've done anything wrong."

"But she's been so distant this past week. I think she might be wondering." Toni wanted to cry.

"I really don't think so," Vicky said, gathering up their paper plates. "You really like Boggs, don't you?"

"Oh, God, Vicky. I do." Toni could tell her speech was beginning to slur a bit. "She is wonderful. She's strong, and she's funny. I love her sense of humor." She continued to ramble. "And the sex is incredible!"

"Whoa," Vicky said, holding up her hand. "Way too much information here." She was laughing. "I mean, I'm glad for you and all, but I don't want to hear the details, okay? It's been a little slow for me lately in that department and I don't think I could take it tonight."

Toni laughed too. "Okay. Nuff said. But it's true."

"So," Vicky said tentatively, "is it serious?"

Toni closed her eyes and smiled, reliving a particularly gratifying moment with Boggs last weekend. "Yeah," she said, opening her eyes again. "I think, maybe." She took another few swallows. "Unless she thinks I'm some murdering crazy paranoid person, then no. She can go to hell."

"I don't think she thinks that, Toni. Really."

"Then why has she barely talked to me all week? What else could it be?" Toni asked, feeling more than a little tipsy.

"I don't know," Vicky replied, shaking her head. "I'm sure it's just work or something. You'll see her tomorrow night. Don't worry about it."

She was trying to sound reassuring, Toni thought. And it was mostly working. Before she could think of anything to say, the doorbell rang. Both women jumped.

"Are you expecting anyone?"

"No," Toni said as she attempted to get off the couch. Slightly woozy, she fell back down.

"How about I get that," Vicky suggested. She went to the door and looked through the peephole. "It appears to be Agent Layton. Should we let her in?" She came over and whispered to Toni, "Don't say anything about the truck driver or your ability to shoot, okay?"

Toni nodded, wishing this would all just go away.

Vicky opened the front door. "Hello, Agent Layton," she said with a smile. "May I help you?"

"Oh, it's Detective Carter, isn't it?" Johnnie replied. "I stopped by to talk to Toni. Is she here?"

Toni groaned to herself. This was the last thing she wanted to do tonight.

"Why, yes, she is," Vicky said rather sarcastically. "Won't you come in?"

Toni didn't get up. From her end of the couch, drinking a beer, she watched as Johnnie glared at Vicky and strode toward her.

"Hi, Toni. New haircut?" Johnnie stood looking down at her.

"Yup. Like it?"

"It's stunning," Johnnie replied. "I hope I didn't interrupt anything."

"Nah." Toni remembered her manners. "Wanna beer, Johnnie?"

Johnnie raised an eyebrow at Vicky, obviously looking for a little help. Vicky returned the look with a grin. "We're just having a little dinner with our beer," she said with a nod toward Toni. "Have a seat, Agent Layton. Can I get you something?"

"Um, no, thanks, Detective. And call me Johnnie," she said, smiling. "It's been a few years, hasn't it? As I recall you did a really good job on that case we had."

"It's Vicky. And thanks, so did you. What brings you over tonight?"

"I'm assuming you both know about Butch Henley?"

Vicky nodded. Depressed, Toni looked at her beer. She'd let

Vicky handle this.

"Well," Johnnie continued, taking a seat on the couch, "the preliminary ballistics match those of the judge. So for the moment I'm now looking into both murders."

"Any leads?" Vicky asked.

"Nothing solid. I'm just taking statements and such."

"Still think it's a terrorist?" Vicky asked.

Johnnie smiled slightly. "Officially, we are looking into that possibility."

"Unofficially?" Vicky countered.

Toni's ears perked up, but Johnnie just shook her head. She pulled a notebook from her jacket pocket.

"Both of us were at our respective homes, alone," Vicky offered. "And neither of us killed the man."

"Any idea of who would want to kill them?" Johnnie asked.

"Nope," Vicky answered.

Johnnie looked at Toni.

"Nope," she parroted Vicky.

Johnnie closed her notebook. "Good enough for me."

"That's it?" Toni asked, relieved.

"Yup. Just doing my job, ladies."

"Wanna beer?" Toni asked again.

Johnnie glanced at Toni, then Vicky again, as though sizing up their relationship. Vicky just shrugged.

"Sure, why not?"

Toni was already up. She pulled three beers from the fridge and handed one to Johnnie through the opening from the kitchen.

"How about some of those chips to soak up the beer," Vicky suggested.

Toni complied and brought two bags of Fritos. Somehow on her short trip to the kitchen one of the top buttons on her shirt had come unbuttoned. She was vaguely aware of it, but both Johnnie and Vicky seemed to notice. As Toni leaned down to put the chips on the table, she caught Johnnie oogling her cleavage, but that bit of information quickly left her.

"Well, that answers that question," Vicky mumbled.

Toni had no idea what Vicky was talking about. She sat cross-legged at the end of the couch, then grabbed a bag of Fritos and set them in her lap. "So, Johnnie, what do FBI agents do for fun?"

"I think most of them sit around talking about how wonderful they are," she said.

Both Toni and Vicky laughed. If there had been any tension in the room, it was gone, for which Toni was very grateful. Vicky and Johnnie talked about the case they'd shared years ago and made fun of one of the agents they both knew. Toni laughed along with them, but mostly just listened to the sound of Johnnie's voice. She knew she was buzzed, but she had to remember to tell Patty she was right. Johnnie's voice was amazing, like butter. And there was no question she was attractive. Not like Boggs, but there *was* something about her. Toni thought about that long-ago fantasy she'd had about Johnnie in law school.

Vicky stood up. "I must use the facilities, ladies."

As soon as she left the room, Johnnie moved to the vacant spot on the couch and reached for the bag of Fritos on the table. Toni shifted slightly. Johnnie was within touching distance. She looked deep into her eyes, then let her gaze trail down to Toni's open shirt. Her gaze met Toni's again and she smiled. Toni was speechless.

Johnnie leaned over. "You're not a suspect," she whispered.

Toni closed her eyes for a moment and let out a deep breath as relief washed over her. She opened her eyes again and touched Johnnie's arm. She could feel the heat of Johnnie's skin against her fingers. "Thank you," she whispered back. She let her fingers linger just a moment before pulling away. It looked like Johnnie was about to say something when Vicky returned.

She noted the change of positions and frowned. "I guess it's getting late for a school night," she said lightly. "Maybe we should break this up and go home and do our homework." She remained standing.

"I guess you're right," Toni answered. "We've all got to work in the morning." She got up and swayed just a little. Johnnie reached out to steady her. Toni felt the heat of her hand on her leg. "Whoa," she said. "Guess it's a good thing I'm not drinking. I mean driving." She giggled.

"No doubt," Vicky quipped. "Here, I'll help you clean up."

"I can help," Johnnie offered.

"No, that's okay," Vicky said quickly. "I've got it. You head on." Vicky locked eyes with Johnnie for just a moment. "It was great seeing you again, Johnnie. We should all get together again."

Johnnie took the hint. "That would be great. I'd love that." She smiled at Toni. "I'll see you soon, Toni." She looked at Vicky. "See ya." Johnnie left.

"She's really nice, don't you think?" Toni helped Vicky carry bottles to the kitchen.

"Yeah," Vicky said. "I think so. And I don't think there's a question about her being gay."

"Really?" Toni had wondered but still wasn't positive despite the heat she'd felt from her touch. "Did I miss something?"

"Well," Vicky said as she pointed to Toni's shirt. "She was sure enjoying the view."

Toni looked down and gasped. "Oh, shit." She quickly rebuttoned her shirt. "How long has that been like that?" She thought she'd buttoned it up before.

"A while." Vicky laughed. "I don't think either one of us minded, though."

"God, Vicky. I'm so embarrassed. I know I'm buzzed, but I had no intention of flashing you two."

"Oh, I know, honey," Vicky reassured her. "But at least now

we know. No straight woman would have stared at you like that. And I think she creamed her jeans when she saw your hair, along with that outfit. It was perfect. Another mystery solved."

They finished cleaning up.

"Vicky, I really appreciate you coming over tonight and talking to me. It means a lot to me. I do feel better."

"My pleasure, honey," Vicky said. "And try not to freak yourself out about Boggs, okay?"

"I'm still not sure what's going on with her, but okay. So, we're going to Gertrude's Garage tomorrow, right? A little dancing and, ugh, drinking?"

"Absolutely," Vicky said. "You better get to bed now so you'll be up for that. Remember, Boggs said she'd pick you up at seven. Patty and I will meet you guys there. And no, it is not a date. Patty and I are just friends, got that?"

"Yes, yes. I've got that," Toni said. "I'm not even considering hooking you up with anyone, honest."

"Well, I wouldn't go that far. If you know any available women, I'm always open to suggestions. Get some sleep. I'll see you tomorrow." Vicky grabbed her jacket and headed for the door. "Are you going to be okay?"

"Yeah," Toni said. "I'll be fine. Mr. Rupert and I are going to crawl into bed as soon you leave."

Vicky glanced at her. "Hey, can I make a suggestion?"

"Sure," Toni said, a little puzzled.

"Do you know what you're wearing tomorrow night?"

"No," Toni said truthfully. "I hadn't really thought about it. Did you have something in mind?"

Vicky grinned. "I think Boggs might faint if you wear that white button-down, brushed denim shirt. You wore it over a T-shirt a few weeks ago, remember? But this time just wear it, not the T-shirt."

"I know which one you're talking about," Toni said. "But I usually wear it over another shirt, because, um, it's a little tight

106

when it's buttoned."

"I figured that from looking at it," Vicky said with a grin. "But is it really too tight? Especially if it's unbuttoned a bit?"

Toni blushed. "No, I think it would be okay, but it might look a little . . . oh, I don't know. Can I try it on real quick? You tell me the truth, okay? I don't want to look slutty or anything."

"Sure," Vicky said. "Run up and change right now." She waited by the door.

Toni ran upstairs, threw it on and came back down two minutes later.

Vicky whistled again. "It looks fabulous," she said. "It's not too tight, just right. Is it comfortable?"

Toni moved her arms around and then mimicked dancing. The buttons strained just a little. Unbuttoning one more helped. It felt okay. She grinned. "Thanks, Vicky. I'll wear this and maybe Boggs will do more than faint on me."

"Excellent. I'll see you tomorrow."

Vicky left and Toni bolted the door. Mr. Rupert was standing beside her. "Let's hit the sack, boy."

As she got ready for bed, Toni replayed the night in her mind, wondering if Boggs thought she was a suspect. Was that why she was pulling away? Johnnie didn't think so, thank God. She couldn't believe she'd reacted so strongly to Johnnie's touch. What the hell was she thinking? She berated herself. That was an old fantasy. Or was it? If she didn't have Boggs, would she go for it? She wondered how Boggs would react tomorrow night when she saw her new hair and the shirt Vicky picked out.

It was just too much to think about tonight and her head still buzzed from the beer. Toni crawled into bed with Mr. Rupert and pulled the covers up to her chin. Tomorrow was another day and she had a date with Boggs. She would think about all this tomorrow. She was asleep within minutes.

≪≫

Boggs had spent Thursday night at home, alone with her fish. She'd tried to busy herself by cleaning the fifty-five-gallon tank. It didn't work. She spent over an hour on her computer, returning e-mails and surfing the Net. Nothing helped. If she could just make a decision. She'd dated more women than she could count, but none had created this effect in her. She was scared. She might even be in love, but what did that mean? She couldn't imagine spending the rest of her life with just one woman, but she couldn't imagine not being with Toni. *Shit. What the hell am I going to do.* She stared at the phone, willing it to ring. Vicky should have called by now. Finally, it did.

Boggs answered on the first ring.

"My," Vicky said. "A little anxious, are we?"

Boggs rolled her eyes. Vicky always seemed to call her on shit like that. "Shut up. What happened?"

"You missed a very interesting evening," Vicky teased.

"What did she say?"

"Well, first of all, she got a bit drunk."

"Drunk? Are you serious? Toni?" Boggs had seen Toni a little tipsy, but never drunk.

"Yes. Toni. She's pretty freaked about being a suspect. In fact, she thinks that you're avoiding her because you think she killed those guys."

"That's ridiculous," Boggs said. That thought had never even crossed her mind. "You told her I don't think that, didn't you?"

"Yes, but it doesn't help hearing it from me. And you are avoiding her. What was I supposed to say? That you're a big chickenshit?"

"You didn't tell her anything about, you know . . ." Boggs's voice trailed off. She couldn't even bring herself to say it out loud. This mushy love kind of feeling was foreign to her.

"No, Boggs. I didn't say a word about that. But there's more."

"What?"

"It looks like the preliminary ballistics match the judge's.

Same gun. So it's someone who knows how to shoot."

"And so? What's that matter?" Boggs didn't see the connection. What did this have to do with Toni and why would it bother her?

"Did you know Toni can shoot?"

"So maybe she's been to the range before or something. What's that got to do with it?"

"According to Toni," Vicky explained, "she can hit anything at one hundred yards. Pistol or rifle. And it's scaring the shit out of her. And they don't even know about the crazy truck driver. I think she's really worried that the feds are going after her."

"You've got to be kidding. Oh, my God. She must be going crazy. Does she think someone's trying to set her up or something?"

"I don't know. But add to that the fact that she believes someone's watching her, and you can just imagine. She's beginning to wonder if you think she's some crazy person and that's why you're backing off."

"Oh, God," Boggs said again. "I don't think that, but I can see how she'd be upset. I don't think anyone knows she's ever held a gun before. And if they knew she could really shoot, well . . . that might cause some eyebrows to raise." Boggs was quiet for a moment, wondering if Toni actually owned a gun. "So she really thinks that's why I've been avoiding her?"

"Yes. She has no idea you're a chickenshit," Vicky said. "Have you figured out how you feel about this yet?"

"No," Boggs answered honestly. "I wish I had."

"Well, you better hurry up." Vicky paused. "There's more."

"Now what?"

"Well, there's good news and bad news," Vicky said. "The good news is that I've solved the mystery of whether or not Johnnie Layton is gay. The bad news is that I figured it out because she was checking out Toni's boobs all evening."

"What the hell are you talking about?" Boggs demanded, her

anger rising. "Why was Johnnie there?"

"She came over for statements, or so she said," Vicky answered. "I told her that both Toni and I were home alone this morning and that neither of us killed Butch. Then Toni offered her a beer and she accepted. Oh, did I mention that Toni was quite drunk by then?"

"And Johnnie was checking her out?"

"No question."

"Why didn't you do something?" Boggs screamed into the phone. This was the last straw.

"Hey," Vicky snapped. "I'm on your side, remember?"

"Sorry," Boggs said, struggling to regain her composure. "But you know the rumors. Johnnie is smooth."

"Yes, I'm the one who told you. And I did do something."

"What?"

"Well," Vicky explained, "I went to the bathroom and when I came back, Johnnie had taken my spot on the couch. Next to Toni. She was leaning over. She must have said something to her because I saw her reach out and touch Johnnie. I think she said something back, but I couldn't hear."

Boggs groaned. Even though she wasn't sure how she felt about Toni, she sure as hell hated the idea of her being with anyone else.

"So, friend that I am," Vicky continued, "I immediately announced that it was very late and we should all go home. Johnnie tried to stay around and I had to almost push her out the door. You can say thank you now."

"Thank you," Boggs said obediently. She could just picture Vicky ushering Johnnie out the door. "Do you think Toni likes her?"

"I don't know. I just don't know. I do know that Toni really likes you, but if you keep avoiding her, well, like I said, I don't know."

"Shit."

"Feast or famine, huh, Boggs? Anyway, aside from Johnnie leering at your girlfriend, she's actually a lot of fun. I almost invited her to go with us tomorrow night."

Boggs's jaw dropped. "You're kidding, right?"

"Pretty much," Vicky said. "I'm not quite sure about her yet. She's fun, but I don't know if she's playing us or not. I'll have to do some more digging. Oh, and I did tell Toni you'd pick her up at seven. Dress nice."

"Why?" Boggs asked, puzzled. "Aren't we just going to Gertrude's?"

"Yes, but dress nice anyway. Just in case you decide you're not a chickenshit, you may have competition."

"Very funny," Boggs said.

"And carry."

"Why? Anyway, I always do."

"That whole thing about Toni feeling like someone is watching her. I don't like that. I'd feel better knowing that we're all armed, that's all. I'll make sure Patty is carrying."

"Okay," Boggs said. "You're right." She laughed. "Anyway, Toni thinks it looks sexy when I wear my shoulder holster."

"Ugh," Vicky replied. "You're such a butch. I'll see you tomorrow.

Chapter 16

Toni awoke to her alarm clocking screaming at her. She knocked it over in an attempt to turn it off. Mr. Rupert was staring at her. As she sat up her hand went immediately to her head.

"Ugh." She groaned. "I think I'll pass on beer for at least a month."

Mr. Rupert meowed loudly and several times, making her already pounding head hurt even worse.

"Shh . . ." She put her finger to her lips and motioned for him to follow. She made her way downstairs with her eyes barely open. She missed his bowl when she tried to dump in his food. She didn't care and apparently neither did he as he hungrily munched away. She somehow fixed her coffee and headed for the shower. She let the warm water cascade over her body for several minutes before she was able to open her eyes fully. What the hell was she thinking, drinking that much. *Ugh. Never again*. She laughed out loud. How many people had said that before?

As she washed her hair she felt the strangeness of how short it was. She was hoping desperately that it would turn out okay this morning. Anthony had shown her how to blow-dry it, but seeing him do it and doing it herself were two different things. She toweled off and stood in front of the mirror. The reflection still startled her. She pulled out her hairdryer. *Here I go.* For the first five minutes it looked like hell, but as she maneuvered the round brush, it began to take shape. By the time she finished it didn't look half bad. Not as good as when Anthony had done it for her, but still, not too bad. She quickly dressed in navy slacks and an ivory blouse, taking a blazer from the closet as she headed down to the kitchen. Mr. Rupert was sitting by the coffeepot.

"Did you make sure it brewed properly?" she asked him as she rubbed his head. She rinsed out her to-go cup that she had left on the counter yesterday and filled it, adding a touch of milk. She sat at her dining room table and sipped the steaming brew. She fished some aspirin out of her briefcase and downed four. *This should help.* By the time she finished her second cup she was feeling much better. She refilled her cup once more and patted Mr. Rupert on the head. "See you after work, boy. Don't go crazy and order a bunch of stuff from the shopping channel."

Toni grabbed her briefcase and keys, then checked her wallet for cash. She'd need to get some more before tonight, but she had enough for a bacon, egg and cheese biscuit.

Twenty minutes later, she took the last bite of her biscuit as she pulled into a parking spot in the garage. Normally she'd have waited to eat it at her desk, but she was famished. Luckily she hadn't dropped any on her slacks, which was a feat in and of itself. She'd never gotten the hang of driving, eating and shifting. The day was going better than she expected.

She got a few looks and smiles on her stroll to her office, but it didn't occur to her that people were looking at her new hairstyle until she saw Cindy.

"Wow!" Cindy said. "You look great, Toni. I love it!"

Toni blushed as she set her coffee and briefcase down on her desk. "You really think it looks okay?" She was feeling unsure about the drastic change.

"Oh, yes. More than okay." Cindy winked. "Very sexy."

Toni's eyes grew wide. Was this the kind of look she wanted for the office?

"But still very professional," Cindy added.

Toni relaxed. "Okay." She self-consciously touched her hair then smiled. "Thanks, Cindy. Anything new?"

Cindy was just staring at her as though she was lost in her own world.

"Cindy?" Toni repeated. "Anything new? Any filings?"

"What?" Cindy said, blinking several times. "Uh, no. No filings this morning and none from last night."

"Okay, thanks." Toni removed her blazer and sat down at her desk. Cindy hovered in the doorway for about two minutes before disappearing to her own workstation.

Toni was working on a file two hours later when Cindy reappeared.

"You got another letter," she said, dangling it in the air for her to see. Toni noticed she was wearing latex gloves. The envelope was large, like the one before.

Toni cleared a space on her desk. "Got an opener?"

Cindy produced one and slit open the end. Again several miniature Snickers bars fell out. The letter only said, "SOON," and was signed TWMA.

Toni nodded to Cindy and she put the contents back inside the envelope. "Would you mind taking that over to Sam's office?"

"No problem," Cindy said. "Creepy, huh?"

"Really creepy," Toni said. "But it's probably nothing to worry about." Even to her own ears, she sounded much more confident than she felt. What next? she wondered.

Thankfully she made it through the rest of her day without incident. By the time five o'clock rolled around she was more than ready to go home. Cindy was standing at the elevator when she got there.

"Have a good weekend, Cindy," she said cheerfully.

"Thanks. You, too. Got anything special planned?"

"Not really." Toni shrugged. "A few of us are going to Gertrude's tonight for a bite and I may help my folks do some spring cleaning, but that's about it. How about you?"

Cindy grinned. "I'm just going to do some work around the house."

"That doesn't sound too fun," Toni commented.

"Oh, but I really enjoy it, and it will be worth it in the end, you know."

The elevator arrived and they rode to the garage in silence. Toni waved to her as she went to her car.

Back home, Toni dropped her briefcase on her table and scooped up the mail. Mr. Rupert pushed against her leg.

"I'm feeling much better now. Thanks for asking." She ruffled his fur. "How about some dinner?"

He beat her to the kitchen. She washed out his little food dish before dumping a half a can of wet food inside. He ate while sitting on the counter. Then she noticed the floor and cleaned up the mess she'd made this morning when his food had landed on the floor instead of his dish.

"Sorry about that, buddy." She filled his other dish with dry food. As soon as he finished the wet food he jumped down to inspect what she'd put in the other dish. He took one bite and walked away. "I know. Boring." She laughed.

She grabbed a bottle of water from the fridge and cut a few chunks of cheese for herself. She wasn't about to have a drink before eating something. Not tonight. She figured the cheese and a few crackers would tide her over until they had dinner, and she'd made sure she had a decent lunch. She ate quickly and then took her water with her upstairs.

She peeled off her clothes and carefully hung up her slacks and blazer. The blouse went into the dry cleaning pile. She would need to go tomorrow. She looked in the mirror at her hair. Still a little strange, but she was getting used to it. She showered quickly and toweled off. Standing in front of the mirror, she looked at the products on the vanity and tried to remember exactly what Anthony had done to create her "date" hair. Conditioner? No. She should have used that this morning in the shower. Oh, well. Mousse? No. Gel? Yes. He'd put some in his palms and rubbed his hands together. Then put it on her hair, pulling it up and out. She tried to mimic his actions. It wasn't going too well. She closed her eyes and tried again. Maybe looking in the mirror had been messing her up. When she opened her eyes she was both shocked and pleased. It was quite the transformation. Her hair looked almost identical to last night. She grinned. *Not too shabby, Toni.*

Satisfied with her hair, she went to her closet and pulled out her white denim shirt. She grabbed a bra from the drawer, then stopped. It was plain and well, ugly. Practical, but ugly. She fished around in her drawer and found what she was looking for. It was the color of her skin, plunged low and supported her C-cup breasts beautifully. There was just a hint of lace on the edges. It was perfect. She pulled on her faded bootcut jeans and a pair of cowboy boots and tucked her shirt in. A wide brown leather belt and gold earrings finished the look. She stared at her image in the mirror and grinned again. She hoped Boggs would like it. She sprayed on some perfume and headed back downstairs.

She still had over a half-hour to kill before Boggs arrived, so she thumbed through the day's mail. Mr. Rupert took his station on the dining room table and waited patiently. Bill. Bill. Junk. Crap. Credit card offer.

"Oh, here you go, Mr. Rupert," she said, handing him an

envelope. "It looks like you've been approved for a home mortgage." He chewed on the corner.

She looked at the remaining pile. Another psych thing? Why was she still getting this? She needed to call them and get off the mailing list. No sense in wasting trees on her account. It was for a workshop on personality disorders. That had been her specialty when she'd been a psychotherapist, so she took it and her water to the couch. Hell, it was something to read while she waited for Boggs. One of the workshops was dedicated to borderline personality disorder. That was one of the toughest to treat, Toni recalled. Medication was rarely prescribed and the only help came from hours of therapy. A few cases were severe, but most functioned within society. In fact, most of their relatives and coworkers didn't even know they had an actual mental illness. They had difficulty with relationships and changed jobs often. They either hated you or loved you. There was usually no in-between for them. They were also plagued by an intense feeling of abandonment and a huge sense of emptiness. Toni frowned at the memory of one of her clients. Sue had been so hard to help, yet so desperate for help. She had ended up using drugs and alcohol. Toni wondered whatever happened to her after she left therapy. Mr. Rupert interrupted her train of thought.

"Hey, boy. Finished eating your mail?" He was sitting on the coffee table, washing his face. Toni looked at her watch. Boggs should be here in a few minutes. She went into the little bath downstairs and checked her hair once more. It still looked good. As she fiddled with it some more, she noticed that her shirt was pulling a bit. She remembered that Vicky had suggested she unbutton one more than usual. Normally she kept her shirt buttoned high except when Boggs was coming over and they were planning on staying in. She went ahead and unbuttoned her shirt. Then she moved around while looking in the mirror to make sure it wasn't too revealing. It was close, but you couldn't really see anything unless she bent down. She would remember that. The doorbell rang. She took a deep breath. *Here I go. God, please let Boggs like what she sees.*

As always, Toni looked out the peephole before opening the door. It was a little distorted, but she could tell Boggs was wearing black jeans, a white T-shirt and a soft black leather jacket. She looked incredible to Toni and she found herself biting her lower lip in anticipation. She opened the door and looked into Boggs's green eyes.

Boggs started to take a step inside and froze. Her mouth opened, but no words came out. She just stood there staring at Toni.

"Are you coming in?" Toni asked, thrilled at Boggs's reaction. She'd noticed.

Boggs blinked several times and then stepped inside. "Holy shit, Toni."

Toni kept her eyes locked on Boggs's and took a small step toward her. "Do you like it?" she whispered.

Boggs nodded several times. Then for the first time Toni saw Boggs's gaze trail down to her chest. A smile formed on her lips. Toni saw Boggs swallow hard. Toni took Boggs's hands in hers and pulled her closer. Not close enough to touch, but just close enough for Boggs to get a great view down her shirt.

Then Toni leaned in and whispered in her ear. "You're looking pretty sexy tonight, hon." She could feel Boggs sway a bit.

Boggs regained her composure and stepped back. She took her time looking Toni up and down, then said, "My God. You look unbelievable. I love your hair. I mean, I've always loved your hair, but this is a whole new look. And I'm afraid we won't be able to go out tonight." She pulled her close. "I don't think I'm even going to let you out of this room before I take you." She kissed her ear and breathed in her perfume. "God, I've missed you," she whispered. She pulled Toni even closer. Then she slid her hands below Toni's waist and squeezed.

Toni moaned as Boggs kissed her lightly. She drew back and looked deeply into her green eyes. Her hands cupped each side of Boggs's face. "I missed you, too," she said softly. She kissed Boggs again, but more passionately this time.

Their mouths opened and Toni hungered for that closeness. Her hands went under the leather jacket and she felt the shoulder holster. She pushed the jacket off and let it fall to the floor.

"Mmm . . ." Toni had pulled the T-shirt from Boggs's pants and was attempting to unbuckle her belt when the phone rang. "Ignore it," she said, kissing Boggs again.

Then Boggs's cell rang. A moment later Toni's rang. Toni sighed and stepped back. It was still ringing so she grabbed it off the dining room table and answered. It was Vicky.

"I'm assuming that she liked what she saw?"

Toni was still breathing hard. "Yes, I believe she did."

"Figured if I didn't call, you guys wouldn't show."

"It's Vicky," Toni said to Boggs, who just rolled her eyes then began kissing Toni's neck.

"Tell her we're busy and we'll see her in a week or so," Boggs said, apparently loud enough for Vicky to hear.

"Listen, you two," Vicky said sternly. "You need to take a breath, okay? You can do that later. We need to talk."

The seriousness of Vicky's tone got Toni's attention. She put a hand up to stop Boggs. "Did something happen?" she asked Vicky.

"No, but we all need to put our heads together here, okay? I'm not kidding. Get your butts over here. Patty and I have a table in the back by the dartboards. We'll see you in fifteen minutes."

"What's going on?" Boggs asked when Toni hung up.

"Vicky sounded really serious. Said we needed to talk. Maybe she knows something."

Boggs furrowed her brow in thought. "Okay. I don't think she'd interrupt us for real if she weren't serious." She sighed.

119

"Can we continue this? Later?"

Thrilled, Toni hugged her. "Absolutely. Try and stop me."

They put themselves back together and looked each other over.

"You are really hot," Toni said.

"Me?" Boggs replied. "Hardly. I'm really going to have to keep my eye out tonight. There are going to be women falling all over you."

"But you'll protect me?" Toni asked coyly.

"I'll shoot anyone who gets between you and me."

"I appreciate the gesture." Toni kissed her lightly on the lips. Her intention was just a quick kiss before walking out the door, but her passion overrode her senses. She kissed her again. And again. Her tongue found Boggs's and her entire body began to tingle. She moaned and urged Boggs even closer.

Minutes passed. Toni had once again eased up Boggs's T-shirt and was caressing her breasts. Boggs had already unfastened Toni's belt. In one quick move she turned Toni around. Toni's back was now against Boggs's chest. Boggs used one hand to unbutton her blouse while her other hand dropped below her waist and held her tight. She kissed the back of Toni's neck. Once the buttons were no longer an obstacle, Boggs reached inside and cupped her breast. A loud moan followed.

"Not fair." Toni gasped. "I . . . can't . . . touch . . . you."

Boggs didn't answer. Instead she slid her hand inside Toni's jeans. Toni tried to protest, mumbling something again about fairness, but actually she was in heaven and was moaning softly. Soon her moans became louder until she could no longer contain herself.

"Oh, my God" was all she could say. She could barely stand.

Boggs finally released her hold and Toni turned to face her. Boggs was grinning. Toni grabbed her hands and pushed her full weight against Boggs, pushing her back against the front door.

"It is *so* my turn, now," Toni said thickly, desire coating her words.

She had just leaned in harder and began kissing Boggs when her cell phone and home phone began ringing at the same time. She ignored both. Then Boggs's cell started. Then the home phone again. Then the cell. Finally she gave up, frustrated at the interruption.

Boggs answered her cell. "Okay, okay," she said, then snapped the phone shut. "This is just the appetizer, babe," she said. "Let's make it a quick dinner so we can get back here, okay?"

"You're right. If we don't go now, Vicky and Patty will show up here. And Vicky's got a key. Let me try to put myself back together, okay?" Toni went into the bathroom on shaky legs. She returned minutes later and Boggs whistled.

"God, I want you," she said as she grabbed Toni.

"Let's get out of here . . . so we can hurry up and get back," Toni whispered.

They reluctantly left the townhouse and headed out the door.

Chapter 17

Boggs had her arm at Toni's back and with a light pressure, she guided her through Gertrude's. Toni liked the feeling. The feeling that she and Boggs were a couple. Vicky waved at them from a table in the corner, where she and Patty were already halfway through a bottle of wine.

Patty poured some wine into the two empty glasses. "You look great, Toni. Love the 'do."

"Thanks," she said with a smile. "Hey, Vicky."

Vicky looked directly at Toni's cleavage then met her gaze and winked. Toni blushed.

"This better be good," Boggs said as she took a sip of wine and opened her menu.

They chatted a while, and Toni finally decided on a grilled chicken sandwich and a small salad.

A waitress appeared and took their order. "Want another

bottle of wine, Vicky?" she asked.

"With the food, I guess, Cheryl. Thanks."

Boggs chuckled. "Another one of your conquests?"

"Very funny." Vicky shot her a look. "She's a sweet kid. I've known her for years, from back on my days as a street cop. Anyway, let's get down to business. I've filled Patty in on everything I know." She glanced at Toni. "Everything."

Toni nodded.

"First, I found out some info about the missing cop, Jack Benson."

"Was he really at the lake?" Toni was still upset with herself for not making sure he was available for trial.

"Yep. Sure was. He and his wife were staying at that lieutenant's condo at the Lake of the Ozarks. No cell service there. Benson had no idea he'd have no service. I chatted with him for just a bit, not letting him know what was going on. Anyway, he said the lieutenant offered the condo, almost insisted he take some lost time. I don't think Benson had a clue, but I'd bet money that damn lieutenant is dirty."

"That's crap," Toni said, shaking her head. "Did you tell Anne?"

"Absolutely," Vicky said, taking another sip of wine. "She thinks this is somehow connected to the judge and Butch. She wants me to do more digging."

"Excellent," Boggs said. "But what's going on now that was so damn important?"

"Okay, to recap," Vicky began, rolling her eyes at Boggs, "we know that we've got three dead guys. Two were killed with the same gun. The truck guy was killed with a nine-millimeter. So far there's no physical evidence to speak of—no casings, no prints, nothing. The judge and Butch had law in common, and maybe some dirty politics. The truck driver was an asshole and regularly pissed people off, but no ties to the judge or Butch that we know of so far. And the judge"—she stopped and looked

123

around the table. "This is just between the four of us, remember?"

"Absolutely," Toni said, and they all agreed.

"Okay." Vicky took a sip of her wine. "From what I've been able to dig up, the judge was not only dirty, he was a disgusting pervert. Anne's had me looking into him, ever since he dismissed Toni's case. Anyway, it looks like there's a possibility he was involved in kiddie porn, little girls. At least that's what one of my street sources said. I don't have any evidence."

"Sick bastard," Boggs muttered.

"Anyway, unless Butch and the truck boy were into kiddie porn too, the only thing these guys seem to have in common—and I mean all three of them—is Toni."

"But I didn't do anything," Toni pleaded.

"We know that, babe," Boggs said. She put her hand on Toni's back and smiled at her. Toni felt a heavy weight lift from her shoulders and she threw her arms around Boggs's neck and hugged her fiercely. After a minute Vicky cleared her throat loudly.

Toni sat back and stuck her tongue out at Vicky. "Sorry, Vicky. Go ahead."

"So at first I thought maybe someone was trying to set you up. Make you look like a killer or something." Vicky nodded at Patty. "That's where Patty comes in."

Patty started to speak then stopped when the waitress appeared with their food. After she left the food and another bottle of wine, Patty said, "Last night my sister came over for dinner with her friend Cathy. And no," she quickly explained, "my sister's not gay."

"Which is a real shame," Vicky commented.

"Anyway, they were looking at the Halloween pictures from that party you guys went to last fall. Vicky had left them at my house."

Boggs raised an eyebrow at Vicky.

124

"And no," Vicky said, "it's not what you're thinking."

Everyone tittered.

"Can we get you to keep your minds out of the gutter for just one evening?" Vicky scowled.

"Not really," Boggs replied. "But go ahead, Patty."

"When they saw the picture of Toni dressed in her Halloween costume, they laughed at first, but then Cathy was just staring at it for a long time."

"But she's not gay?" Boggs laughed.

"Well, yes, Cathy is," Patty said. "But it wasn't that. She's a psychic and my sister is a medium. I don't know if you guys believe in that, but I do."

"Oh," Toni said quickly, "I absolutely believe. One of my roommates in college had several psychic experiences. I was skeptical at first, but not now."

Boggs nodded. "There's a woman in St. Louis who is a psychic. I worked with her on a case. But what's the difference between a psychic and a medium?"

"Short answer is that a medium can converse with those who have crossed over and has the trifecta, but I'll get into that another time." Patty took a bite of her salad.

Tony, Boggs and Vicky, all glued to Patty, barely touched their food.

"Back to Cathy," Patty said. "She asked me how well I knew Toni, so I told her. Then she said that she was getting some really negative energy."

"From me?" Toni was disheartened.

"No, from around you," Patty explained. "The way she described it to me was that it was as though someone wanted to possess you, and not in a good way. That's all she could get. I knew that you had felt like someone had been watching you, so I called Vicky."

"Okay," Boggs said. "So I'm not sure I get it. If someone wanted to possess her, then why kill these guys?"

Toni thought for a moment. "Okay, hear me out on this. Bizarre coincidence, but I just got a flyer on this in the mail today. There's something called borderline personality disorder. But it doesn't mean what it sounds like. This type of person can be very possessive of someone they love and then if they're somehow disappointed, the intense love turns to intense hate. Anyway, they often believe that someone is in love with them and that person has no clue. Actually, they have no real relationship with that person at all, or at most just friends. The love part is just something fabricated in their mind. And I can see where they'd try to 'protect' the one they love and maybe even 'right any wrongs' that were done to the object of their affection."

"God, Toni," Vicky said. "No wonder you got out of psychotherapy and went to law school. How do you deal with someone like that?"

"Most of the time there's no danger for anyone," Toni explained. "It's pretty rare you run into the type I just described. But if this is what's going on, it's going to be tough."

"Any ideas who it could be?" Boggs asked.

"Not off the top of my head." Toni shrugged. She realized she'd stopped eating so she took a healthy bite of sandwich. "Of course, there is that guy who's been sending letters and now candy bars to me at the office."

Boggs filled in Vicky and Patty. "Sam's looking into that. I'll talk to him about it more tomorrow."

"Okay," Vicky said. "That's one angle we have. Some nut job is killing off people that he thinks might have harmed Toni."

"Or she," Toni added. "This type of disorder is more common in women."

"Or she, right." Vicky finished off her mozzarella sticks. "I had another thought on this, just in case we're going about it all wrong. Who benefits from all this?"

"What do you mean?" Patty asked.

"This may sound crazy—"

126

"Not any crazier than our other theory," Toni replied.

"Well, I'm a little suspicious of Johnnie," Vicky stated plainly.

"No way," Patty said, immediately coming to Johnnie's defense.

"Listen," Vicky continued, "almost everyone in Metro has been questioned by the FBI, right?"

"She left me a voice mail," Boggs offered. "I haven't talked to her yet."

"I checked with a lot of people. She's talked to most of them, but she talked to them all in their offices."

"Not me," Toni volunteered. "I saw her there last Saturday, but she said she was coming over to my house. Then she showed up last night."

"Exactly," Vicky said. "And it was pretty obvious she was totally checking you out, Toni."

Toni blushed. She remembered the feeling she had when Johnnie touched her.

Boggs clenched her fists. "Not that it doesn't totally piss me off, but remember, Vicky, we talked about this. Both of us would absolutely go to a suspect's home to get the feel of things when we question them."

"Sure, maybe the first time." Vicky took another sip of wine. "But what about last night? And *nobody* else has seen her in their homes. Only Toni. And she did stay for a beer. What's that all about? All I'm saying is that she might be a little nuts or some-thing. I checked her background at Quantico and she's an expert marksman, by the way."

"So you're saying that this woman killed two men and made it look like Toni could be a suspect so that she could get in her pants?" Patty was clearly shocked. "That's a little far-fetched, don't you think?"

"At this point I think anything is possible," Vicky said. "The only thing we really know about her is that she showed up for this investigation. We haven't seen or heard about her for years and now here she is with an obvious crush on our girl here. Aside from the fact that we know she's been a good investigator and has a voice like butter, what do we know?"

Boggs looked at Toni. "Could she have borderline personality disorder?"

Toni thought for a minute and took another sip of wine. The idea hadn't occurred to her. "I don't know. It's hard to imagine that, since she's been on the job for ten years. I can't really see a borderline being able to keep an intense job like that for that long. But you never know. I'd need to talk to her more to be sure."

Vicky got out a notebook and started to jot things down. "Whichever theory we go by, this person would be attracted to you, right?"

"Well, yes. I guess so. But it wouldn't necessarily be apparent. God, this is unbelievable. Are you guys sure about this?"

"I am," Patty said. "I would have been only half on board before Cathy, but now I think there might be someone out there with designs on you, one way or another."

"Okay," Vicky said. "Let's write down anyone—and I mean anyone who's shown an interest in Toni."

"That's half the bar," Boggs said, grinning. "I mean, look at her, for God's sake."

Toni shoved her away. "Be serious, now."

"The bartender at The Cat's Meow," Boggs said. "She's definitely got a crush on Toni. Always gives her more wine than me."

"Maybe she just doesn't like you, Boggs," Vicky teased.

"No," Toni said. "She's right. If we're going to do this, let's consider anyone and everyone and then narrow it down from there. Bert may be interested. I even shared a coffee with her last week when I was waiting for my meeting to start."

"Is she on that committee?" Boggs frowned.

"No, she was just having coffee at Izzy's when I walked in. She opened the door for me and offered to buy me a cup of coffee while I waited."

"Okay," Vicky said as she scribbled in her book. "Bert, the anonymous letter guy, Johnnie . . . Who else? Try to think of anyone who has popped up lately or seems to show up at places that you're at, like Bert did. Or someone who's called you lately to see you."

"Nancy Manford called me and asked me to dinner yesterday," Toni said.

"Who's that?" Boggs asked.

"She's on the committee with me. We talked on Saturday and she called yesterday and wanted to celebrate some victory at city hall. I said yes, but I called later and cancelled because of the news about Butch."

"Do you think she's interested in you?" Vicky asked.

"I don't think so," Toni answered. "I've known Nancy for a number of years. But she did make a remark, about the judge deserving to die, that I thought was odd."

"Nancy Manford. I'll mark her down. Anyone else?"

"Cindy, one of the secretaries at Metro," Boggs offered.

"You're kidding, right?" Toni said. The idea of Cindy being that violent didn't seem right.

"No." Boggs shook her head. "You said she's always going into the bathroom when you go in, and she did kinda walk in the other day, remember?"

Vicky giggled. "Did you guys get caught in the ladies' room?"

"No." Toni sneered at Boggs. "Almost, but no."

Patty and Vicky made a few colorful remarks. Toni reached over and touched Boggs. She leaned over to kiss her then stopped dead in her tracks.

"Oh, my God," she whispered.

"What?" Boggs, Vicky and Patty said in unison.

Toni felt the blood drain from her face. She just stared at Boggs.

"What, babe?" Boggs asked. "Did you see someone?"

"No." Toni gulped. "It just occurred to me. If this person really did kill these men because he or she thinks they hurt me . . ."

"Yes?" Boggs prompted.

"Well," Toni continued softly, "then they would think nothing of hurting someone who they thought was interested in me. Or that I was dating. Competition. They'd think they were the only one 'right' for me and, well, eliminate any other."

Everyone looked at Boggs.

"I can handle myself," she said defiantly.

Vicky shook her head. "No way, hon. This person took out a judge in broad daylight and a lawyer. And maybe some crazy truck driver. You wouldn't be safe driving across town." She looked at Toni. "Who knows that you're seeing Boggs?"

"We've kept it pretty quiet, for the most part," Toni said slowly. "At the office, well, let's see. Sam knows and Anne knows. Others may suspect, but I've never said anything and we keep it turned off at work."

"Except in the ladies' room?" Vicky snickered.

"Just that once and no one saw us. Cindy walked in, but the door bumped Boggs. By the time the door opened I acted like I was just coming out of a stall."

"What about at the bars?" Patty asked.

Toni thought about that.

"From what I can remember," Boggs said, "most of the time we go out with others, like you guys. Then we go back to Toni's. There have only been a few times we've gone out by ourselves."

"Were you all over each other or kissing or something?" Vicky asked, her pen poised above her notepad.

Boggs glared at her.

"I don't think so, Vicky," Toni said, hoping to placate Boggs. "The last couple times we just grabbed dinner at The Cat's Meow and talked. Then we went back to my place. We never danced or anything that I remember." She stared at Boggs.

"I think she's right."

"Good," Vicky said. "Until we figure this out, I think it's best if you guys keep your hands to yourselves when you're out. And try not to go out too much alone. If you're in a group like this and the crazy person sees you, he or she might just think you're friends. But if you keep looking at each other with those stupid googly eyes, well . . . Boggs, you could be in danger."

"I think you're going too far," Boggs said flatly.

"I don't," Toni countered. She started to reach out but stopped. "I don't want anything to happen to you, honey. I'm serious." She pushed her chair a few inches farther away from Boggs.

"So how do we narrow the field here?" Patty asked.

"Well," Toni said slowly, "if I knew a little more about them"—she pointed to Vicky's list—"I could rule some out for sure. I would need them to open up a little to me, get them talking about their past. I might be able to know that some are okay and maybe see red flags for others I suppose. There are some indicators that I should be able to spot."

"So," Boggs said, "in order for us to figure this out, I've got to first keep my hands to myself, which is very difficult at the moment. Second, I've got to let you hang out with a variety of women who are lusting after you to see if one is crazy enough to kill me?"

"That sounds about right," Vicky said. "It's not like we're going to send Toni out on dates with these women. And the anonymous letter writer will be handled by Sam, right?"

"I guess I could do that," Toni said. "As long as I'm always in a public place." She was feeling a little frightened.

"This reminds me of last fall," Vicky said. "I think we should meet regularly to share information."

"Patty," Toni said. "Do you think Cathy could come over tomorrow night? Maybe she could get a little more by seeing me."

"I'll call her now." Patty pulled out her cell phone.

"Let's all meet over at my place tomorrow night, with Cathy, okay? I'll call Nancy and see if she wants to meet me for lunch tomorrow." A few minutes later Toni put her phone back in her pocket. "I'm meeting Nancy tomorrow at Izzy's. Eleven thirty."

"What about the others?" Vicky asked.

Toni thought about her work schedule for the next week. "I can ask Cindy to lunch on Monday at work. And maybe after work I can stop by the bar and talk to Bert."

Vicky nodded. "Patty and I will do some background checks on all of them, and, of course, I'm still going to pursue the angle that maybe it's the dirty politics for Butch and the judge and the truck driver is a coincidence. There's also still the kiddie porn connection. Might as well keep all our options open. But what about Johnnie?"

Patty closed her phone. "Cathy can come over tomorrow night. And I don't think we have to worry about setting something up with Johnnie. She just walked in."

Boggs clenched her fists again. "See how I'm not turning around and going after her? Remember that, okay?"

Vicky looked at Toni. "Remember, Toni, you're not dating anyone, so act as though any sexy butch has a chance with you. If she asks you to dance, do it. I'm going to ask her to join us."

"I'll try not to hit her," Boggs said through clenched teeth.

"You absolutely won't hit her," Vicky said sternly. "In fact, I'm assuming she'll jump at the chance to sit with us, and you are going to shoot some pool."

"Are you serious?"

"Dead serious," Vicky responded. "Toni needs to be able to talk to her, and with you sitting there it won't work."

"But you can sit here?" Boggs asked, clearly pissed off.

"Yes. Patty and I will whisper and giggle together. We'll act like you two. If we notice that Toni and Johnnie are having a deep conversation, we'll excuse ourselves to the dance floor. Or maybe the ladies' room. Are you up for some acting, Patty?"

"Sure, it might be fun."

"But remember, Toni," Vicky said seriously. "We won't let you out of our sight. Boggs will try not to stare from the pool table. Patty and I will keep an eye on you from wherever we go. Are you okay with this?"

"I think so." Toni gave herself a pep talk. This was just work. "Sure. I'm just talking, that's all. I was a psychotherapist, for God's sake. Just never in a bar. Go ahead, Vicky. Ask her over." She winked at Boggs. "We're still going home together, remember that," she whispered. "We have some unfinished business."

Vicky left the table and Toni took a deep breath and a long swallow of wine. Vicky returned alone.

"No luck?" Patty asked, obviously disappointed. "I was kinda hoping we could eliminate her quickly and then go from there."

"Still got that crush?" Vicky teased. Toni saw Patty kick her under the table. "She's coming over. She asked what we were drinking."

Johnnie appeared a few minutes later with a bottle of wine and another glass. Instead of her usual FBI garb, she was wearing blue jeans and a light blue oxford shirt. Toni wondered if she was carrying her weapon in an ankle holster. Vicky had pulled a chair from another table and placed it between her and Boggs.

"Hey, Johnnie," Vicky said, taking the wine and filling Johnnie's glass. "Have a seat. This is Patty Green. You might remember her from that case a few years ago."

Johnnie smiled warmly at Patty and shook her outstretched hand. "Of course I remember you, Patty. You were fresh out of the academy. Good to see you again."

Patty was clearly speechless. She just nodded. Toni thought Patty would melt and she couldn't help but smile.

"And this is Boggs. She's an investigator at Metro."

Again Johnnie smiled and shook hands. "I've heard a lot of good things about you, Boggs. We've been playing phone tag. Good to meet you."

"Really nice to finally meet you, too. I've heard many things about you," Boggs said.

Vicky glared at Boggs, who, Toni could tell, got the message.

Boggs said easily, "That murder down in Atlanta about five years ago. I followed that. Great collar."

"Thanks," Johnnie replied. "But it was more luck than anything."

"And of course you know Toni," Vicky said finally.

"Hiya, Toni," Johnnie said. Her gaze locked on Toni's and held it for a moment. She picked up the bottle of wine and refilled Toni's glass. Then she glanced around the others and held up the bottle. The rest pushed their glasses forward for refills.

"Are you here for business or pleasure?" Vicky asked.

Johnnie laughed. "Well, I guess it doesn't matter anymore." She laughed again. "Pleasure," she said. "Definitely pleasure. I've been pretty closeted at the Bureau, but I decided when I hit the ten-year mark I'd come out. I hit that milestone a couple months ago."

"I wondered a few years ago," Vicky said. "Still pretty rough at the Bureau?"

"It's getting better." Johnnie shrugged. "But I wanted to be straitlaced and by the book, so to speak. Now that my promotion is coming up in a couple weeks, I feel more comfortable. And people know my record, so it doesn't matter as much."

"So is this going to be your home base, or station or whatever?" Toni asked.

"Yeah. Once you hit a certain level you can pretty much stay in one place. It costs too much to move agents around like they used to."

"That's great," Toni said, smiling at her.

Boggs looked like she was going to say something but caught another glare from Vicky. Toni pretended not to notice.

"I think I'll play a round of pool, if no one minds," Boggs

announced.

"Give 'em hell," Vicky said with a grin.

Boggs snatched a quick look at Toni before getting up. "I'll be back in a bit."

The busboy appeared and cleared away the dishes. Toni grabbed the remaining french fry from her plate. Johnnie stood to give him more room. When she sat down she took the chair Boggs had been sitting in. At that point Vicky began her acting stint. She leaned in close to Patty and whispered in her ear.

Toni couldn't hear what she said, but Patty playfully pushed her away and giggled nervously. Vicky scooted her chair closer and rested her arm on the back of Patty's chair. They continued to whisper in each other's ears, pretending to totally ignore Toni and Johnnie.

In response, Johnnie pulled her chair closer to Toni. "You look stunning tonight, counselor."

Toni blushed as she saw Johnnie's eyes drop to her unbuttoned shirt. "You look pretty fine yourself, Agent Layton." *She is smooth.* God, what was she doing? She needed to find out her story. Johnnie could be a dangerous woman. "Tell me about yourself."

Johnnie leaned back in her chair and took a sip of wine. "I was born and raised here. I went to college at the University of Kansas with a degree in criminology. I wandered around for a year after graduation and then joined the Bureau."

"Girlfriend?"

"Not at the moment." Johnnie winked at her. "You?"

"Um." Toni hesitated. "No one special, no."

"And your life story?"

Toni gave a brief history, careful not to reveal too much. She spoke of her parents. "I'm pretty lucky in that department." She smiled. "How about you? Do you get along with your parents? Do they know you're gay?"

"My mom died when I was still pretty young," Johnnie

replied. "But I get along great with my brother. Everyone knows I'm gay. Never had a problem there."

"Yeah," Toni said. "I've got some friends who were basically thrown out when they told their parents."

"My ex had that problem," Johnnie confided. "Karen and I were together for about three years. Her parents treated her like shit and, of course, they hated me. I think they thought I 'turned' her gay." She laughed. "I was her first serious relationship."

"What happened?"

Johnnie sighed. "We were both in the Bureau and neither of us wanted to be out . . . at least not at work. It took its toll. We had to keep separate apartments for appearance's sake, or so we thought at the time. Then she was transferred to D.C. That was the beginning of the end. I tried to make it work, but the distance was so hard. She ended up meeting someone there."

To Toni, that didn't sound like someone with borderline personality disorder. "I'm so sorry," she said sincerely. "That must have been hell."

"It was hard, but that was years ago. She's doing well. She quit the agency and teaches up there. We exchange Christmas cards every year." She smiled sadly and Toni figured she was remembering another time, another place.

Unless her therapy skills had completely failed her, she didn't think there was any way in hell that this woman was the crazy person. She seemed too introspective and balanced. Toni decided she'd let the gang know tomorrow what she thought.

Johnnie leaned in close. "How about a dance?" she murmured.

Toni glanced at Vicky, who had obviously overheard the invitation. She was nodding slightly.

"Sure." Toni could hear the music from the next room. It was a fast song and she actually liked the beat. As she stood, Johnnie grasped Toni's hand in hers and led her to the dance floor. Toni couldn't see Boggs but she could feel her watching them.

Once they hit the dance floor the song ended and a slow one started. Johnnie pulled her closer and they began to sway with the music. Toni could feel Johnnie's lean muscular body as her hands rested on her shoulders. She could smell her musky perfume and feel her breath on her neck. Johnnie was a graceful dancer and Toni matched her movements effortlessly. Johnnie caressed Toni's back as they moved around the floor.

"You wear that blouse very well," Johnnie whispered.

Toni felt her whole body react when those lips touched her ear. She remembered her long-ago fantasy. Closing her eyes, she momentarily forgot about everything but the music and the arms around her. The song ended just as she felt Johnnie bend closer, her lips only inches away. Toni opened her eyes and looked up at her. This was too confusing. She wished she knew how Boggs felt about her. Was she just another woman, or did she really feel something for her? Toni knew she'd always been a player, but she didn't know now. Everywhere they went it seemed like she saw another of Boggs's ex-girlfriends, still lusting after her. *Shit.* Would that be her in a couple months, an ex-girlfriend? She pulled away from Johnnie and grabbed her hand, leading her back to their table.

Johnnie stopped her halfway there. "Too fast?"

"A little, yes." Toni squeezed her hand, then let it go. They went back to the table. Boggs had returned and was sitting back in her chair.

Toni sat down next to her and took a big gulp of wine. There was no question that she was attracted to Johnnie, but was that because of an old fantasy and this sudden attention? Or was she just suddenly aware of all the women Boggs had dated and was feeling like another conquest? Well, she was definitely aroused. But that didn't mean a damn thing. She had practically torn off Boggs's clothes earlier that evening, and they'd left without finishing what she started. No wonder she was horny as hell. *Jeez.* Who wouldn't be? She should go home and be with Boggs. She could figure out the rest later.

Toni took another drink, then looked at her watch. Everyone else was talking. She had learned what she needed from Johnnie. Unless Vicky and Patty gave her conflicting information, there was no way Johnnie was a suspect. Now not only did she need to find out who the crazy person was, but she needed to know if her feelings for Boggs were one-sided or not. She desperately did *not* want to be just another notch on her belt. After their brief tryst earlier that evening, she certainly didn't feel like a notch on Boggs's belt.

Boggs was at the moment deep in conversation with Johnnie and Vicky. The three of them were laughing and exchanging war stories. Even though Johnnie's voice was like butter, Boggs's voice was deep and sexy. Over the last few months she had come to cherish the time they spent together. She felt comfortable and safe with Boggs. They could talk for hours. And the sex, well, she just couldn't get enough. But in the last week or so Boggs had definitely become more distant. Was it really work, or was she just getting bored with Toni? She didn't know. But she did know that she was falling in love with Boggs. And she was still in lust with her. Toni smiled as she remembered the moments before and just after Vicky had called that evening. Her body had reacted quickly. She knew now what she wanted to do.

"Hey, everyone," Toni announced. "I know it's still early for a Friday night, but I've had a long day and I can hardly keep my eyes open." She shrugged in apology. "I'm going to head out."

Boggs clearly had no trouble following that lead. She looked at her watch. "I think I'm going to hit the road, too. I've got to get up at the crack of dawn."

"Cool," Toni said. "Can you drop me off? I rode in with these two," she said, pointing to Vicky and Patty. She stood up and put her hand on Johnnie's shoulder. "It was great seeing you tonight, Johnnie. See you soon?"

"Absolutely," Johnnie said, grinning. "See ya, Boggs."

Boggs said her good-byes and then kept her arms to her sides rather than putting her arm around Toni as she usually did when they left the bar. They both kept their distance as they got into Boggs's car. Once inside Boggs started to lean over. But Toni, sticking to her guns leaned away.

"Start the car and drive," Toni said, keeping her tone emotionless.

Boggs did as she was told, her brow furrowed in concern. "Are you okay? Did something happen?"

"Just get me home, Boggs," she answered, moving even farther from Boggs and leaning against the passenger door. "If you don't get me home as fast as you can safely drive," she continued, "I'm going to make you pull this damn thing over and rip your clothes off."

Boggs grinned. "Yes, ma'am." She floored it, and they were back at Toni's in less than ten minutes. Neither had spoken the entire drive.

Toni broke the silence as they approached her front door. "I'm warning you now," she said just above a whisper, "I'm not going to be a good hostess. I'm not going to offer you anything to drink or eat." She had the key in the lock. "As soon as this door closes behind us, I'm going to the bedroom. I'm not going to stop and kiss you first, because if I do we'll never make it upstairs. Understand?"

"More than you know," Boggs said huskily.

True to her word, Toni shut the door behind them and headed for the stairs. She didn't even reach out for Boggs. At the top of the stairs she stopped and took Boggs's hand in an attempt to guide her into the bedroom. They only made it about two feet before Toni pushed her against the wall and leaned into her, pushing her leg between Boggs's. They both moaned and again Toni slid the jacket off of Boggs. She had already pulled the T-shirt from her pants and was fumbling once again with her belt when Boggs gently pushed her away. They were both breathing heavily. Toni looked at Boggs, wondering why she'd stopped.

"I need to secure my weapon, babe." Boggs guided Toni into the bedroom, and Toni watched her remove her shoulder harness and place it on the dresser.

Toni's breath caught. *Oh, my God. This woman is my fantasy.* Boggs sat Toni down on the waterbed and pulled off her cowboy boots. Toni leaned back, propped up on her elbows, and watched as Boggs took off her T-shirt. She grinned and started to get up, but Boggs pushed her back and undid Toni's jeans, inching them slowly down her legs. Next she pulled off her panties, then removed her own bra. Toni was admiring Boggs's lean torso and exposed breasts when she suddenly felt herself being pulled to her feet. Boggs touched Toni's face then let her hand trace downward, stopping at the first button. She opened the blouse and let it fall to the floor. She leaned down and kissed the skin near the edge of her lacy bra while her hands worked the hooks in the back. The bra loosened and Boggs let it fall to the floor before returning her mouth to Toni's breast. Her warm, wet mouth made Toni moan.

Toni managed to loosen Boggs's belt and quickly pushed her remaining clothing to the floor. As they fell onto the bed, Toni let herself remain in the moment. No thoughts of crazy people. No thoughts of the future. Her only thoughts were of her and Boggs, together in the here and now. And for a time, that was all she needed.

Chapter 18

On Saturday morning, Toni arrived at Izzy's a little before eleven and ordered a triple-shot latté. Another night with very little sleep, she thought. Not that she was complaining. In fact, she still had a grin on her face. But she wasn't as young as she used to be, and operating on five hours of sleep was tough. She sipped her coffee and tried to concentrate on the task at hand. She needed information.

Nancy joined her at the back table around eleven twenty and Izzy appeared moments later.

"Hiya, ladies," she said. "Can I get you something to munch on?"

"Your famous chicken salad on a croissant for me," Toni answered.

"Me, too," Nancy said. "And an iced tea. Thanks."

Izzy looked at Toni and winked. "Another shot of leaded,

hon, or do you want to switch to tea?"

Toni grinned. "I think iced tea. If I find myself faltering I'll order another latté on my way out." After Izzy left them, she settled back in her chair with her half-finished latté. "I'm so sorry about having to cancel on you Thursday. Sometimes I get overwhelmed."

"Oh, that's okay. I understand."

Nancy, Toni noted, was dressed as if she had just come in from jogging.

Toni smiled and fell into her "therapist" mode. She needed information. "So, Nance, tell me about the city hall thing."

As Nancy filled her in on the resolution passed that would put severe restrictions on absentee landlords, Toni listened while taking in her nonverbals. It was an old habit that came back to her quickly and easily. She asked several open-ended questions and kept Nancy talking about her work until the food arrived. Once they started eating their lunch, Toni decided to check out Nancy's whereabouts during the time when Butch was killed.

"Hey," she said. "Did you see that early-morning news show on Thursday?"

Nancy stopped chewing for a minute. "No, I don't think so. Why?"

Toni evaded the question. "I thought you told me you get up at the crack of dawn every day?"

"I do," Nancy replied. "And I usually watch the news, but I think I missed it. Was there something good?"

"There was a chef on that made pizza," Toni pretended to think about it. "I can't remember what restaurant she works for, but I thought you might've seen the show." She was pleased with herself that she had remembered hearing some of the secretaries talking about it at work.

"Ah, no, sorry," Nancy said. "I must have been doing something else and didn't turn it on."

Well, no clear alibi there. Next subject. "Are you still seeing

Rachel?"

"Are you wondering if I'm available," Nancy said with a coy smile.

"Just making conversation." Toni laughed, feigning innocence.

"I haven't seen the bitch for months," she growled. "And she better hope I never lay eyes on her again."

Toni hid her true feelings well, she thought. Years as a therapist had taught her not to show any physical reaction to a client's outbursts. She was surprised at the immediate and intense hatred from Nancy. Her fists were clenched tightly and her eyes were narrowed.

"Gosh, Nancy," Toni said quietly, offering a frown of concern. "What happened?"

"The bitch said she needed space or some crap like that," Nancy spat. "But I know she was cheating on me. She had to be."

"Just like that, huh?"

"Yeah," Nancy said. "Everything was perfect and then *boom*."

Not a good sign, Toni thought. Love them one minute and hate them the next. She needed to ease her into a different subject. "I'm really sorry. If there's something I can do, let me know. Oh, that reminds me," she said quickly. "How's the new committee going? The one on community violence?"

Almost immediately Nancy's posture changed and she smiled again. "It's got a good start. A few more people joined yesterday. I guess they're riled up because of that lawyer. But that's just asinine. Did you know that bastard represented Marlene's ex-husband?"

"Marlene? The one who was nearly beaten to death?"

"Yeah. The bastard got him straight probation. Can you believe that? Marlene was scared to death. She moved back to Chicago to live with her mom, she was so frightened. She told me that Butch shook hubby's hand and then just grinned at her when he walked out of the courthouse. Son of a bitch wasn't even worth the price of a bullet, if you ask me."

"I guess Butch wasn't the most loved guy in the city," Toni conceded.

"Hell, no," Nancy shot back. "I heard he was a real asshole to you last week."

Toni was surprised that Nancy knew about that. She was going to ask more but just then Izzy reappeared.

"Can I get you ladies any dessert?" she asked. "I've got a great raspberry cobbler."

"Ooh, I'd love that," Toni said.

"Me, too," Nancy added. After Izzy left she leaned back in her chair and smiled at Toni. The anger and bitterness were gone as quickly as they had come. "I'm really glad we're having lunch today. I wish we could spend the afternoon together, but I've got a few errands I really have to do this afternoon."

Toni was taken aback at this remark. There had been no mention of anything but lunch. "Well," she said, "maybe we can do lunch again sometime soon. Just give me a call."

When the dessert arrived, both women moaned as they took their first bite.

"Oh, my God." Toni sighed. "This is so good it should be illegal." The top was crunchy and sweet and the raspberries delectable.

"I'll remember how much you like it," Nancy said as she took another bite. She winked at Toni.

Toni nodded as she continued to eat. Nancy was again talking about her work at city hall, but Toni was feeling more and more uncomfortable. There were several red flags here, she thought. How could she have known Nancy all these years and never seen it? Could Nancy be the one? Her intense reaction to Rachel was almost a classic textbook case.

"Toni?" Nancy said.

"What?" Toni blinked, realizing she had been in her own world for a moment. "I'm sorry. I guess I zoned for a sec."

"Is something wrong?" Nancy looked a little upset.

"No, not at all, Nance," Toni reassured her. "I apologize. I was just thinking about work. I've got a trial coming up. How rude of me. What were you saying?"

"Nothing important," Nancy said, smiling. "Just blathering on about city hall."

"Well, I apologize again. Sometimes something just pops in my head and I start to worry. I'm still so new at this job, it freaks me out a little."

Nancy put her hand on Toni's. "Don't worry, hon. You'll do just fine. I have confidence in you."

Toni thanked her and pulled her hand away, disguising her uneasiness by reaching for her iced tea. "That's so sweet of you." She glanced at her watch. "Oh, I'm going to have to get going. I've got a bunch of things to do this afternoon also."

Nancy gestured to Izzy, who appeared with the check.

Nancy tried to pay for it, but Toni insisted on picking up the tab. "Hey, I mean, I'm the one who asked you, right?"

Nancy finally agreed. After a quick hug at the door and a promise to call, Toni was heading back to her car. She needed to write all this down so they could try to make sense of it later that night. She wondered what Vicky and Patty would come up with on the background checks. Even though Nancy had a lot of red flags, Toni just couldn't believe it was her.

Toni returned home and plopped down on the couch with Mr. Rupert and the mail. He had gotten a special invitation to a car sale at the local dealer. He didn't seem too thrilled. The rest of the mail was just as fascinating. She tossed it on the coffee table and told Mr. Rupert about her morning. He seemed curious about the raspberry cobbler but lost interest in the rest.

"But now on to more important things," she said. "What about Boggs, huh? Do you think she really likes me and wants a real relationship? Or am I just a fling? Vicky asked me who knew about us and I realize now that hardly anyone does. My folks don't. None of my old friends know. Why is that?"

Mr. Rupert stopped washing his face long enough to look at her. He turned his head sideways and meowed.

"How do I feel about her? Well, if I'm really honest—and I'm always honest with you, buddy—then I think I might be falling in love." She shook her head and sighed. "I don't even know what love is anymore, Mr. Rupert. I was still so young when Sadie and I first got together. And that didn't end too well, did it?"

Mr. Rupert climbed in her lap and began kneading her leg.

Toni leaned back and scratched his head. "Of course, the best part of that was that I got you in the bargain. Best thing that ever happened to me, that's for sure. I sure do love you, boy."

She stretched out on the couch and pulled her tiny twenty-pound cat toward her. They snuggled together.

"I have to let Boggs know how I feel," she mumbled. "Then we'll see what happens from there. One thing at a time, right?" Before Mr. Rupert could answer, Toni drifted off to sleep.

Chapter 19

Toni was jarred awake by the sound of the phone. She was still blinking the sleep away as she fumbled for the handset. "Um, hello?"

"Gee, did I call at a bad time?" It was Vicky.

Toni looked at her watch. It was almost five o'clock. *How could I have slept so long?* "No, in fact, if you hadn't called I'd probably still be asleep when you guys showed up. What's going on?"

"Trying to catch up a little? Not enough sleep last night?" She giggled.

"Just enough," Toni countered.

"How did things go with Nancy?" Vicky asked. "Wait. Don't tell me until tonight, when everybody can hear. Anyway, I'm thinking of stopping at Subs R Us and getting food for tonight. What do you want?"

"Oh, that sounds great, Vicky. I'll take turkey, bacon, cheese and lettuce on honey wheat. Don't worry about chips. I've got those here. And I'll run out and get us some beer and soda."

"Perfect. I'll see you around six thirty, okay?" Vicky hung up before Toni could respond.

"We've got to hurry, boy," she said to the still dozing Mr. Rupert. She cleaned off the coffee table then grabbed her keys and headed to the corner market for supplies.

When she returned with the loot, she took a shower. Dressed in jeans and a sweatshirt by six o'clock, she went back downstairs and made some notes from her lunch with Nancy. Boggs arrived a few minutes later. She was carrying a large gym bag that Toni knew contained her softball uniform for tomorrow. Toni raised an eyebrow and grinned at her.

"Just in case," Boggs said a little sheepishly.

"Excellent idea," Toni teased her. "I mean, gosh." She looked at her watch. "The game starts in only twenty hours. There's a good chance you won't be able to make it back to your place in such a short amount of time." She reached around Boggs and pulled her close. "I love having you here," she whispered. "All the time."

Boggs stiffened just the slightest bit, but Toni noticed. They were long overdue for a serious talk. How obvious was that? One mention of something that could even hint at a real relationship and she freaked. Or was it because Boggs still had doubts about her being a crazy person? But now was not the time, she told herself. The others would be here soon.

"Did you put in your order with Vicky?" she asked instead.

Boggs cocked her head. "No, what order?"

"She's stopping at Subs R Us."

"Perfect. I love that place. She'll know what I want." Boggs went to the kitchen and got herself a beer.

As if on cue, the doorbell rang. Toni peered through the peephole. All she could see was a large white sack with the logo emblazoned on the front. "Either that's Vicky or the place delivers. All I see is a sack." Her hand on the doorknob, she asked, laughing, "Who is it?"

There was no response.

Boggs pushed her aside and looked. "They don't deliver," she said quietly. She pulled her gun from her ankle holster and held it behind her back as she stood by the door. She opened the door slightly and looked outside. The sack lowered and Vicky just grinned. Boggs shook her head and holstered her gun. "What the hell, Vicky? Why didn't you say something?" Boggs growled.

Vicky was chewing. She swallowed and bowed her head slightly.

"Sorry. I took too big a bite. My mouth was full." She pushed her way past them and went to the kitchen. "That was stupid of me. Sorry."

Toni helped Vicky unload the sandwiches. "No, I was the stupid one. It didn't even dawn on me that it was anyone else," she admitted. "Thank goodness I've got you guys. I'm serious." She hugged Vicky.

Vicky responded with a big bear hug. "We're a team, okay? No worries."

The doorbell rang again.

"That should be Patty and Cathy," Vicky said. Boggs nodded and went to the door. She confirmed it was them before ushering them into the living room. Patty made the introductions.

"Thank you so much for coming, Cathy," Toni said as she shook her hand. Cathy's hand was soft and warm. Toni felt immediately at ease and smiled. She took their coats and piled them on the dining room table. "If no one minds, let's eat over there," she said, pointing to the wrap couch. "What would you all like to drink? We have beer, wine, water and soda."

"Beer is good for me," Patty piped up.

"I'll start with water," Cathy said, going to the couch. "My, my . . ." She spotted Mr. Rupert and she put out her hand for him to sniff, which he did immediately. "I don't believe we've met." He sniffed again and then licked her hand.

"That is Mr. Rupert," Toni said proudly. "He owns the building and he's my best friend."

Cathy gently stroked his head. "Very nice to meet you, Mr. Rupert." She smiled and nodded to the giant cat. "He sure does love you," she said to Toni.

Toni beamed. "The feeling is mutual."

Vicky was in the kitchen fixing drinks for everyone. "Should we eat first?" she asked of no one in particular.

"It would probably be better if we weren't stuffed to the gills," Cathy responded.

Toni put the sandwiches in the fridge and helped Vicky pass out the drinks as everyone got settled on the couch. Since the couch wrapped around the corner, there was room for all of them with space to spare.

"What would you like us to do?" Toni asked Cathy.

"I'm going to take just a moment to relax and say a prayer," Cathy said. "If you all would just close your eyes for a moment and try to relax." She paused. "Just think of something calming and soothing."

Everyone did as instructed.

A few minutes later Cathy spoke again. "Excellent." They opened their eyes. "I never know what, if anything, I'm going to get. I'm just going to say what I hear, see or feel. Don't give me any information. I may ask if something makes sense to you. Just tell me yes or no. I'm just going to concentrate on the topic at hand. You guys can sort things out later, okay?"

They all agreed. Patty pulled out a notebook to take notes.

Cathy began. "Again, I feel a negative energy around Toni. There's a feeling of entitlement, sort of like they believe she belongs to them. There's also a sense of great sadness or emptiness, but it's overshadowed by anger. I'm also getting a sense of a large room or space. It feels like a warehouse, but not quite. And I smell smoke. Cigarette smoke, not smoke from a fire. The only other thing is, well, it's pretty strange. I'm not sure if it actually fits into this topic because it's being shown to me by another energy. It's a sound. It reminds me of a small tin bell. I know that's odd, but it sounds like someone ringing a small tin bell—*ting, ting, ting.*" She was quiet for several minutes. "There are other energies as well, mostly those of love and light. I'm sorry. That's all I'm getting right now. At least on this subject."

"Thank you so much, Cathy," Toni said. "Any advice for me?"

"Well," Cathy said, "I can't tell your fortune, if that's what you're asking. Just trust your gut."

"I will. Thank you."

"Just in general," Cathy said, "I feel a lot of good energy around this group. You seem to have a really strong bond."

They nodded vigorously. "We've been through a lot in the short time we've known each other," Toni explained. "So, anyone hungry?"

Vicky hopped up and went right into the kitchen, making herself very much at home. She had located paper plates and was getting the sandwiches out of the refrigerator by the time Toni joined her a moment later and got out the chips.

She tried to push Vicky out of the kitchen. "Vicky! Go sit down. You're a guest, not hired help."

"How rude," Vicky said. "I think of myself more as family. Now shut up and hand these out," she instructed. Toni did as she was told. After trading a few plates to get the correct sandwiches, the women ate and chatted. Mr. Rupert nibbled at the pile of assorted meats and cheeses that everyone had put on the corner of the table for him. When they finished, Toni gathered the plates.

"I hate to see, eat and run," Cathy said with a smile, "but I've got another appointment."

"How much do we owe you?" Toni asked.

"Not a thing," Cathy said. "I wish I could have given you

151

more. But I would like to take something personal from each of you. Maybe I'll get something later."

"Like what?" Vicky asked.

"Oh, anything. Maybe something that you wear a lot, or carry with you."

Vicky removed her pinky ring and handed it over. Toni gave her her class ring and Patty took off her necklace.

Boggs looked at her hands. She wore no rings. "I'm not sure what I can give you," she said to Cathy. "I don't have any jewelry. The only thing I always have on me is my gun, and I don't think that's a good choice."

"Although that could be quite entertaining." Cathy laughed. "I think there might be a better idea."

Boggs thought for a while and finally grinned. "I've got it," she said as she pulled her wallet from her pocket. Tucked in the back was a silver dollar, which she handed to Cathy. "Now be very careful with this," she warned. "I've carried this since I was sixteen years old."

"I'll be very careful," Cathy replied. "But if you're not comfortable we can use something else."

"No, this is the right thing," Boggs assured her.

Cathy smiled and put all the items in a small leather pouch, which she put in her purse. "How about if we meet again in a week?" she suggested. "I'll give you back your things and let you know if I've gotten anything from them."

"Sounds good." Toni walked her to the door. "And thanks again for your help."

Cathy took her hand gently and smiled. "It will turn out okay, Toni. This and the other." She waved at the group and was out the door. Toni wondered what "the other" was, but let it go for now.

Since Patty and Vicky were in the kitchen refilling everyone's drinks, Toni sat next to Boggs on the couch and squeezed her leg. "So, what's the story on the silver dollar?"

"You'll probably think it's stupid," Boggs said.

Toni shook her head.

"Well, my dad gave it to me when I was sixteen," Boggs explained. "He told me that if I always kept this with me, I'd never be broke. He was right. It's been close sometimes, but I've always managed to do okay."

"I don't think that's stupid at all," Toni said. "In fact, I think that's a wonderful way to look at things." Boggs smiled but Toni could feel the underlying sadness. "You still miss him very much, don't you?"

"Yeah," Boggs said quietly. "It's been almost thirteen years, but I still miss him. Sometimes I can feel him around me, though. Like tonight."

Toni nodded. "Maybe because of Cathy. She seemed to raise the psychic energy. I kept thinking of my granny. It felt good."

"It did feel good," Boggs agreed. "You know something? I've never told anyone about feeling my dad around me. I figured they'd think I was nuts."

"You're not nuts," Toni said. "And thanks for sharing it with me." She kissed her on the cheek.

Vicky and Patty came back with the drinks.

"Hey, no smooching, you two," Vicky said. "I'm going through a dry spell."

"You're always in a dry spell," Boggs said. "Okay, ladies. Let's get down to business."

Everyone got out their respective notebooks.

Boggs went first. "I was with Sam today. We've got nothing to work with back from the lab on the anonymous letter guy. Postmark is here in Fairfield. I've got feelers out to other departments to see if he has sent letters to anyone else. Basically I came up dry. Sorry. Oh, I also asked Dave to check some things out for us. He is going to look into medical records."

"Medical records?" Toni asked. "First, isn't there something called confidentiality? And second, how can that help us?"

"I don't know," Boggs confessed. "But I figured any info we can get would be better than none."

"Me, next," Vicky said. "I ran everybody for priors. Bert first. She has an assault second degree ten years ago. It was a bar fight. Big surprise. Then she had a disturbing the peace, knocked down from a domestic abuse charge about eight years ago, and then a few speeding tickets. The most recent was last fall."

"Assault is not a good sign," Toni said. "Nor is domestic abuse. That keeps Bert on the list."

"Next is Johnnie," Vicky continued. "No surprise there were no priors. Next is Nancy. She's had two DWIs and six disturbing the peace convictions. There was also a stalking charge that was dropped last fall."

"Sounds like a fun date." Patty laughed. "Fatal attraction?"

"Maybe," Toni said. "I'll fill you in later on my lunch today."

"Okay." Vicky glanced at her notes. "Last, but not least, is Cindy . . . the bathroom girl. She's got no convictions."

"That's good," Toni commented.

"But she's got one hell of a juvie record," Vicky said. Although juvenile records were sealed to the public, law enforcement always had access. "Seven hits for shoplifting, four for underage drinking, three for drunk as a skunk in public and, my very favorite, lewd and lascivious. Apparently at age fourteen she got caught giving some guy a blow job in a public park. Isn't that precious? And she did a stint in juvenile detention."

"Jeez," Toni said. "How am I supposed to look at her at work and not get that lovely visual? But seriously, all those things are red flags in my book. The only positive is that she's had nothing really since she became an adult. Maybe it was just a rough adolescence."

"Maybe," Boggs said. "But we shouldn't assume anything. She's definitely on the list. Now, tell us about lunch with Nancy and anything about Johnnie from last night."

Toni filled them in on Johnnie. "So I don't think she's our

girl," she concluded. "Unless you guys come up with something else, nothing leads me to believe that she's got issues."

"Except for the fact that she's hitting on you," Boggs said.

"Well, yes. Except for that," Toni said, grinning. "But Nancy has some issues." She told them about her conversation with Nancy and by the end, Vicky was nodding.

"I think she's a real possibility. The intense hatred and the fact that she's been calling you. Maybe we should put a tail on her for a bit, unofficially, of course. See what she's up to."

"Good idea," Patty said. "I'll take that on this week, okay?"

"Done," Vicky said. "And we'll find out more when Toni meets with Cindy and Bert on Monday. Now, what else can we do?"

"What about the things that Cathy said?" Patty looked at her notes. "She talked about a warehouse-type place. We need to think about that. And she talked about cigarette smoke. Do any of our people smoke? I remember seeing Johnnie smoke, but that was years ago."

Toni thought for a moment. "Well, Bert smokes for sure, and she uses a Zippo. And if I'm not mistaken I thought I smelled cigarette smoke when I hugged Nancy at lunch. I know she used to smoke, so I guess she still does. I don't think Cindy smokes. At least I've never seen her smoke. And I have no idea about Johnnie."

"Well," Boggs said. "Check on the smoking thing when you have lunch with Cindy. About the big loft or warehouse thing, that could be where the crazy person lives, or works, or anything really. I'll check out property that they all own, okay?"

"That sounds good," Vicky said. "Any ideas about the tin bell sound?"

"Maybe it's an alarm, like on a watch, or when you arm some-thing," Patty suggested.

"You mean like arming a bomb?" Toni asked.

Patty nodded.

"That's a possibility," Vicky said. "Let's not rule anything out. Just because our crazy person has shot everyone in the past, doesn't mean she, or he, wouldn't try something else. Now, is there anything else we can do?"

"I guess nothing for now," Toni said, feeling like they'd made some strides.

"I don't like you going to see Cindy and Bert alone," Boggs interjected. "How about one of us being wherever you go with Cindy for lunch? And maybe one of us get to the bar before you do?"

"I'll be fine." Toni tried to brush away her concern.

"No," Vicky said. "I think Boggs is right, but not for the same reason." She winked at Boggs. "Maybe we'll see something that you don't. And there's also the fact that we're talking about a possible crazy person, duh."

"I'm off Monday," Patty volunteered. "I can be at both places. Where are you going for lunch?"

"Probably Phil's Deli. It's across the street from Metro."

"I know," Patty said. "What time?"

"I guess around noon, but I'll call you when I know for sure, okay?"

"Perfect," Patty said with a sly grin. "I love sleuthing."

"What if Johnnie calls Toni for another date and—"

"Wait a sec," Toni said, interrupting Boggs. "What do each of you think about Johnnie, now that we have more info?"

"I like her," Patty said. "I mean, aside from my obvious lust thing, I think she's an okay person. I really don't think she's some crazy woman, and I think we can trust her."

"I'm with Patty," Vicky added. "Now that we know she doesn't fit any of the characteristics, except maybe smoking, I think she's okay. She seems to be a good agent, and she's, well, fun to talk to. We chatted quite a while after you guys left last night. I say we bring her in on this."

"Are you serious?" Boggs's jaw dropped. "She's obviously got the hots for Toni, and you want to bring her in?"

"Let's just put that on hold for a couple days, you guys, okay?" Toni said, hoping to soothe Boggs's anger. "Let's see what happens on Monday and then see if we should take her in our confidence about this. If we decide she can help us out, then maybe we'll do it. But for now, let's just stick to the four of us, okay?"

They all agreed, and when Vicky got up to get more beer, Toni didn't protest.

Lost in her own thoughts, she realized that Boggs was genuinely upset with the idea of Johnnie asking her out. Did that mean Boggs had real feelings for her? More than just a short-term thing? God, she wished she had the answer.

For the rest of the evening the four of them bounced different ideas off one another and then branched off into more ordinary topics such as who was dating whom and what movies were coming out. As the evening wound down and Toni was busy in the kitchen, she could see that Vicky and Boggs were deep in some sort of conversation. She wondered if they were talking about her.

When she returned to the living room, Boggs and Vicky suddenly went silent. Maybe they had been talking about her.

Patty was standing near the front door. "I'm taking off, you guys."

"I'll walk out with you," Vicky said as she retrieved her coat from the dining room table. "It's been delightful as always, ladies," she said to Toni and Boggs. "Keep your thinking caps on, okay? We'll figure this thing out sooner or later."

After Vicky and Patty left, Toni thought about bringing up the subject of how Boggs felt about her, but she could feel the tension in the air. She desperately wanted to know, but the fear of rejection was more powerful at the moment. *God, you're such a chickenshit*, she told herself. She should just start talking and get it over with. But what if Boggs told her she just wanted to keep things the way they were? How were they exactly? She'd just try to feel things out tonight. Skip the heavy discussions. With all this other crap going on, she couldn't deal with losing Boggs right now. And if they had some heavy conversation and it ended with them being "just friends," she would feel like she'd lose her mind.

"Hey," Boggs said. "Are you okay?"

"What? I'm sorry," Toni apologized, snapping out of it. "I guess I was zoning out a little. This whole thing has me rattled, I guess."

"Want to watch a movie or something?" Boggs said agreeably. "Something to take our minds off everything?"

"That would be great." Toni sighed. "Want some popcorn?"

Boggs flipped on the television and was checking the listings. "Hey, that sounds pretty good. And a soda maybe?"

"Done. And if you don't find anything on TV, we can watch one of my videos. I don't have anything too exciting."

"We have two choices for movies that start in a few minutes," Boggs called as Toni put the popcorn in the microwave. *Murder on the Orient Express* or *Sleepless in Seattle*. Either sound good to you?"

"I think I've had enough murder for one week," Toni said from the kitchen. "*Sleepless in Seattle* sounds better to me."

The movie was just beginning when Toni came in balancing a giant bowl of popcorn, a can of Coke and a can of Sierra Mist. She snuggled up to Boggs with the bowl between them. Throughout the movie they made comments on the characters and laughed at their own insights on relationships. The conversation came easily and she noticed how comfortable she felt with Boggs. So perhaps it wasn't just lust, she thought. She was really falling for her. She just loved being with her, no matter what they were doing. And Boggs seemed to feel the same way. Or did she?

By the time the movie ended Boggs had fallen asleep. Toni watched her for several minutes before gently waking her.

"Let's go upstairs and get some sleep," she whispered.

"Hmm?" Boggs said, barely awake.

Toni shook her lightly. "Come on, hon. Time for bed."

Boggs blinked several times and looked at the television. It was off. "I'm sorry," she said. "I guess I fell asleep. I didn't realize I was that tired."

"I'm tired too," Toni replied. "Let's get some sleep."

She guided Boggs up the stairs, grabbing her overnight bag on the way. She pushed Boggs into the bathroom and deposited her bag on the floor. By the time Boggs appeared in the bedroom, Toni had pulled down the covers and had changed into a T-shirt.

"My turn," Toni said. "Climb on in. I'll be there in a sec."

When Toni returned a few minutes later, Boggs was sound asleep and Mr. Rupert was lying on the foot of the bed. She rubbed his head.

"I could get used to this, Mr. Rupert," she whispered. "What about you?"

He stretched out and put his head on Boggs's leg.

"I guess that means you could, too." She slipped under the covers. Boggs didn't even move as the gentle wave of the waterbed accommodated Toni.

Chapter 20

Boggs opened her eyes Sunday morning and saw Mr. Rupert staring at her. The spot next to her was empty. He climbed on her chest and sat down.

"Uh, you're a little heavy there, boy," she said.

He meowed loudly and began kneading her chest.

"Ugh," she said with a little difficulty. "Are you trying to tell me to get my ass out of bed?"

"I think he is," Toni called from the hall. "The coffee is ready and I'm making scrambled eggs with cheese. Does that sound okay to you?"

Mr. Rupert jumped off Boggs and headed downstairs. Obviously it sounded good to him.

"That sounds wonderful. What time is it?" Boggs looked around for the alarm clock.

"It's almost nine. I figured you'd want to get up soon, so I sent

Mr. Rupert up to wake you."

"He completed his mission." Boggs laughed as she climbed out of bed.

Toni kissed her lightly on the cheek. "I'll go start the eggs."

Boggs watched her walk away, dressed only in a T-shirt. That was one beautiful woman. She looked even better in a T-shirt than she did in a suit. Boggs smiled. Could she get used to waking up this way every day? Sharing a bed? An apartment? Their lives? Last night was wonderful, just watching television and eating popcorn. She couldn't remember ever falling asleep and being so comfortable like that before. Even when she'd dated someone in the past, she always felt the urge to get up and go home. No matter how late it was, she always preferred to wake up in her own bed. And if she did spend the night she was anxious to leave the next morning. She didn't feel that way with Toni.

But could she do this on a permanent basis? *Do I love her?* Could she commit to a real relationship? And never sleep with another woman? Never play the field again? Never do whatever the hell she wanted whenever the hell she felt like it?

She began to panic. She had never been in a relationship that lasted more than a few months at most. Even though her parents had remained married until she was in high school, they fought constantly and seemed to hate each other. She didn't want that.

Maybe it would be easier if she just got out now. It would save her one hell of a lot of heartache later, of that she felt sure. Better safe than sorry.

That was her attitude when she pulled on a pair of sweatpants and went downstairs, but when she saw Toni standing in the kitchen, her heart melted. There was a fresh cup of coffee and two plates on the dining room table, along with napkins, salt and pepper. The Sunday paper lay next to her cup. Toni had obviously read part of it.

"It's almost ready," Toni said. "Have a seat. I'm out of juice, but I've got milk if you'd like."

"Uh, no," Boggs stammered. "The coffee is just fine. Thank you."

Toni came in carrying the skillet and scooped eggs onto each plate. She returned a moment later with toast and sat down with her own cup of coffee. "There was an article in the paper about a memorial service for Judge Smith on Tuesday," she said in between bites. "The mayor is making it a big production and it sounds like a few senators are going to show."

"Think we should go?" Boggs asked as she took her first bite of eggs. "God, Toni. These are great! What did you do to them?"

"Cooked them." Toni laughed.

"No, really," Boggs said. "I'm serious. They taste . . . different, but incredible."

"Why, thank you very much," Toni said, her cheeks reddening. "I just grate a bunch of Gouda cheese into them before they're cooked and then slowly scramble them. Haven't you ever done that?"

"No," Boggs replied. It had never occurred to her. "When you said scrambled eggs with cheese I figured you meant melted cheese on top of the eggs. But these are really something. Thank you."

Toni was smiling broadly. "Wow. I've never had anyone so appreciative of my cooking." She gave a quick bow. "But back to your question. I'm pretty sure that Anne will want us to go to the memorial. I think it said it was at two o'clock, so I'm sure the courts will be closed down. Just like last fall."

"Yeah, I bet you're right. It might be interesting to see who goes. And maybe to see who comes up and talks to you," Boggs said, the killer never far from her mind.

Toni thought for a minute. "I think you're right. I'll try to keep my eyes open. Maybe one of our suspects will be there, or at least maybe try to contact me shortly thereafter. That might help us figure things out, don't you think?"

"Maybe." Boggs shrugged. She was loving those eggs. She was chewing as she spoke. "I wish we had more to go on."

"Me, too. I keep trying to tell myself that we're all blowing this thing out of proportion. That it really has nothing to do with me, but then I think of Cathy and what she told us."

"I know," Boggs said. "I think I could put it out of my head if it weren't for that. I really believe in mediums and psychics. And I think that gives us a leg up. If it weren't for her we'd probably have already moved on."

"Except for the fact that the FBI questioned me and then Frank asked me for an alibi," Toni said quietly.

"They were just doing their job, Toni," Boggs explained. "And anyway, I know you didn't kill those men."

"Are you sure?" Toni asked, looking like a hopeful child.

"I'm positive."

"Did Vicky tell you that I can shoot?"

"Yeah," Boggs said.

"And didn't that make you wonder a bit?"

"No," Boggs answered truthfully. "It just makes me feel more comfortable that you know how to handle a weapon. Especially since I always carry one."

There were tears in Toni's eyes. "Thank you. I can't tell you how good that makes me feel. That you believe me."

Boggs went over and put her arms around her. "I believe in you, babe. We'll figure this thing out. Don't worry."

Toni leaned back into Boggs and put her arms over hers and squeezed. "Thank you," she said again.

Boggs kissed her neck. "It's okay, babe." She gave her another squeeze. "Want some more coffee?"

Toni nodded and brushed the tears from her eyes. When Boggs returned with their cups, Toni had regained her composure.

"Sorry," Toni said. "I was really worried that you thought I was the crazy person or something."

"Well," Boggs said, grinning, "you are something, that's for sure."

They finished their breakfast and perused the paper, each offering tidbits from articles they were reading. At ten thirty Toni announced she was going to take a quick shower.

"That will still give you enough time to get ready for your game, right?" she asked.

"Oh, sure. Are you coming to the game?"

"I wouldn't miss it," Toni said. "As Vicky says, 'Nothing like watching women run around in shorts,' you know."

Boggs just shook her head. "Maybe you're hanging around Vicky too much." She laughed. "You're really beginning to sound like her."

"I'll take that as a compliment," Toni said as she disappeared upstairs.

Boggs poured herself another cup of coffee and returned to her chair, determined to get a better handle on how she felt. On the one hand, being with Toni felt so comfortable and right. But on the other hand she'd never been able to stick with one person for more than a few months. What if she told Toni she wanted to be with her and then freaked out? Boggs suspected it'd hurt her even worse than never committing. What the hell was she going to do? She'd told Vicky the night before that she went absolutely nuts at the thought of Toni seeing someone else. And Vicky had given her some garbage about "maturing" and "making a decision." This was driving her crazy. Maybe she needed to talk to Vicky again.

Later that day at the softball game, Toni found herself again sitting next to Vicky and drinking spiked coffee.

"You seem to be in a good mood," Vicky commented.

"Pretty much, yeah." Toni smiled and took a sip of her coffee.

"Boggs told me she believed me. That I didn't kill those men. That meant a lot to me."

"We're on your side," Vicky said compassionately. "You are surrounded by friends. Remember that."

"I know," Toni said, giving her a quick hug. "And that means more to me than you can ever know. And maybe if we can figure this thing out soon, no one else will get hurt."

"It will be okay, Toni. Really. It will be okay."

They watched the remainder of the game and congratulated the team on yet another victory. Toni went home to catch up on some much needed laundry and ironing. And to think about how she would broach the subject of her relationship with Boggs.

After Toni left, Boggs sat with Vicky sipping a beer.

"Have you figured things out now?" Vicky asked.

"I thought I'd made a decision to just cut my losses and move on." Boggs sighed. "Then she fixed breakfast for me and I realized how comfortable I was just being with her. So, I'm back to square one. I have no clue."

"Great. I'm telling you that you need to make a decision. And I mean now. Toni *is* going to bring it up. Now that you've told her that you don't think she's a cold-blooded, crazy killer, there's no reason why you should be avoiding her. She's going to think that you're backing off the relationship because you don't love her. The question is, do you?"

"Damn it, Vicky. I don't know. Sometimes I think I do, but then I just get scared. That would mean I'd never be with another woman. Ever. I've never even thought like that before."

"But you're thinking about that now." Vicky said, taking another sip of her spiked coffee. "And that should tell you something, don't you think? I mean, have you ever even considered that before? With anyone else you've ever dated?"

"No. Never even came close," Boggs admitted. "Maybe

you're right."

"Of course I'm right," Vicky said. "And just because you move to the next step doesn't mean you immediately buy a house with a white picket fence. Just take it one step at a time. Ask yourself these questions: Do you want to date anyone else? Do you want her to date anyone else? Do you like being with her, aside from the whole lust thing? Do you love her?"

"I know," Boggs said, downing the rest of her beer. "I know."

"So go home and think about these things, okay?" Vicky picked up her backpack and headed down the bleachers. At the bottom she turned and looked back at Boggs. "I said, go home," she repeated, then went to her car.

Boggs sat on the bleachers long after the last player had left the field. She couldn't stop thinking about what Vicky had said. But she also knew her own past, better than anyone else knew. She had never been able to stick with one woman longer than a few months. And when she did, she often thought of straying. If that happened with Toni, she'd never forgive herself. She couldn't let Toni go through that hurt. The best thing to do was to end it now, before it got too out of hand. Let Toni find someone who could settle down. That person couldn't be her. It never had been, so why would she think she could be that kind of person now?

She'd call her tonight and break it off. It'd be hard, but probably it'd be for the best. She'd just end up disappointing Toni or, worse, hurting her bad. She'd end it tonight. No big deal.

Boggs dragged herself to her car. She was convinced this was the right thing to do, but it was going to be incredibly hard. She felt sick to her stomach. She needed to get this over with fast. Before she could change her mind, she dialed Toni's number. She was both relieved and scared when the machine picked up.

"Hey, it's me, Boggs," she stammered. "Um, I forgot to let you know that I can't make it for Easter. You know, with your folks and all?"

She was beginning to panic. She hadn't thought out what she was going to say.

"I'm going to head up to see my mom. Yeah, and an old girlfriend will be in town, so I thought I'd spend some time with her. Sorry I forgot to mention it this morning." *Shit. That was cold. But I can't stop now.* "Um, so I'll see ya later. Um, 'bye."

Boggs disconnected and then stared at her phone. She sat in her car for fifteen minutes, desperately wanting to call back and say it was a mistake. But it would be a mistake to continue, she kept telling herself. This was for the best. She started the car and drove home. She had never felt worse in her entire life.

Toni walked in her front door after taking the trash out to the Dumpster. She had just finished the breakfast dishes when she noticed the flashing light on her answering machine.

"Hey, Mr. Rupert," she said as she crossed the room. "Why didn't you tell me someone called?" She was rumpling his fuzzy head as she pushed the play button.

When the message ended she sat in stunned silence. She tried to make words come out, but they wouldn't. Mr. Rupert crawled into her lap and she wrapped her arms around him. Still no words came. But the tears came, streaming down her cheeks. She sat with Mr. Rupert and rocked in silent agony. Her head was spinning, but no thoughts were forming. She was just feeling. After almost a half-hour, she took a deep breath and closed her eyes. Mr. Rupert licked the last tear from her cheek.

"I guess it's still just you and me, boy," she said quietly. "Now, at least, I know. She wasn't feeling what I was feeling. And that's okay, right? We had a few really good months."

The tears came again, but she was able to shut them down much more quickly. She got up and turned on some music.

"Come on, buddy," she said. "Let's finish the laundry, do some spring cleaning and then treat ourselves to some Chinese food!" She wished she felt as positive as she sounded. But at least it was a start.

It was nearly five o'clock and Toni's townhouse had never been cleaner. The laundry was done, the ironing completed and even the oven had been cleaned. Toni was scrubbing the floor in the downstairs closet when the phone rang. She froze. There was no way in hell she was going to answer the phone. She couldn't handle it right now.

"Hey, Toni," the voice said softly. "It's me, Vicky. Come on. I know you're there. Pick up, hon. Just pick up and talk to me for a sec, okay." There was a pause. "Listen," she said a little more sternly, "if you don't pick up, I'll be forced to come over there. I have a key, you know."

Toni tossed her rag into the bucket of soapy water and grabbed the phone. "Hey, Vicky," she said calmly. "What's up?"

"Are you okay?" Vicky asked softly. "I know what happened."

"Sure," Toni answered, trying to sound like it was no big deal. "I'm fine."

"I can come over if you want to talk or something," Vicky offered.

"No, no," Toni insisted. "I'm just fine." But then the tears started again.

"She's an ass," Vicky said.

"No, she's not an ass," Toni replied, choking on her words. "She just didn't . . . I mean, I guess I was feeling more than she was, that's all. It's not her fault. It's not like we said we were exclusive or anything."

"Is there anything I can do?" Vicky asked.

"No. I'll be fine. But thanks so much, Vicky. That means more to me than you know. Really."

"Well," Vicky said, "is that offer for Easter still open? I'm thinking I'd like to start a new tradition of eating a ton of food and candy with actual people instead of lying in bed feeling sorry for myself."

Toni laughed in spite of how she was feeling. "Absolutely. I'd love for you to come with me. We'll make it the most ridiculous candy hunt ever!"

"Perfect," Vicky replied. "I'll even bake a pie. Or at least I'll attempt to. This is going to be fun."

Toni found herself telling Vicky more stories about previous Easters and laughing more than once. By the time she hung up the phone, she was feeling a little better. Not great, but at least as though she'd be able to survive. And that was enough.

Chapter 21

Toni was somewhat surprised Monday morning when Cindy jumped at the offer to have lunch at Phil's Deli. They agreed to go at eleven thirty in hopes of beating the crowd. Toni called Patty and let her know the plan.

By eleven forty they were eating their sandwiches at a small table. Toni had seen Patty sitting at the counter when they entered and given her a quick wink.

"I've been hungry for a cheese steak all weekend," Toni said. "I'm glad you could join me."

"Thanks for asking me. This is wonderful." Cindy was grinning from ear to ear.

Time to gather some info here, Toni told herself. She still couldn't believe that lewd and lascivious charge. *Ugh. Gotta get rid of that visual.*

"I can't believe it's almost Easter," Toni said as an opening.

"Does your family do anything special?"

Cindy shook her head as she took another bite of her sandwich.

"My family is pretty ridiculous about the day." Toni explained the traditional candy hunt.

"That sounds so wonderful," Cindy said.

"Do you have much contact with your family?" Toni asked, trying again to get a feel for Cindy's past.

"No," Cindy admitted. "I've pretty much been on my own since I was a kid."

"Oh, I'm sorry," Toni said.

"Don't be, really. I like it that way. It was no big deal. Easier, in fact. I take care of myself."

"Well, I'd say you did a heck of a job," Toni offered. "Still, it must get lonely sometimes."

"Not really. I've got things all planned out." Cindy smiled up at her.

"That's great," Toni said, thinking she didn't have much to go on so far. Everything Cindy had said could be taken as a symptom of borderline personality disorder or just a messed up teenager, still trying to prove herself to society as an adult.

They finished their lunch and just chatted about mundane office things. Toni didn't feel comfortable going any further with her questioning. She still had to work with this woman every day, and if there weren't any more red flags, she'd leave it be. Toni insisted on paying, since she had asked her to lunch, and Cindy waited outside. Toni gave Patty a subtle nod as she left. Cindy was fumbling around in her purse as they walked back to Metro. She pulled out a pack of cigarettes.

"Nothing like a cigarette after a meal," Cindy said as she exhaled the smoke.

Toni was surprised but hid her reaction. "That's what they say."

The two walked in silence back to the office.

"Thanks for having lunch with me today," Toni said as they entered the building and went around the metal detector. The guards, seeing their badges, nodded as they walked by.

"No, thank *you*, Toni. That was really super of you to invite me. I hope we'll do it again real soon."

"Me, too," Toni said, but as she said it out loud, she realized that for some reason she didn't want to have lunch with Cindy again. At least not soon. She didn't know why, but she knew that's how she felt.

The rest of the afternoon went by quickly. Toni found she was able to concentrate on work for the most part. There were only a couple of times she found herself on the verge of tears when she thought of Boggs. Around four o'clock she received an e-mail from Anne telling everyone that the office would close at one o'clock the next day for Judge Smith's memorial service.

At the end of the day, Patty called. "Your sandwich looked better than my salad," she said.

"How could you order a salad at Phil's when all you can smell are those wonderful deli meats?"

"I was trying to watch my calories," Patty said. "And anyway, I'm supposed to go to The Cat's Meow tonight, where I plan to eat a giant burger. We're still on for tonight, right?"

"Yup," Toni answered. "I'm just going to sit at the bar and have a drink. No food or anything. I'm thinking I'll get out of here at five today. The bar shouldn't be crowded at that time."

"I'll get there before you and sit at one of the tables in front by the bar. I'll probably just be biting into my burger by the time you arrive. That way it won't look suspicious at all," Patty said. "God, I love this sleuthing stuff. I can't wait to take my detective's test next month."

"Oh, you'll be great as a detective, Patty," Toni said. "And look at all the practice you've been getting because of me."

"I'll thank you at the promotions ceremony, assuming I make the cut," Patty said, laughing.

172

"Perfect. I'll see you tonight. We'll talk about what we find out later, okay?"

"Sounds good to me," Patty said and then disconnected.

When Toni arrived at The Cat's Meow she saw Patty sitting at a nearby table. Just as she had predicted, Patty was taking what looked like her first bite of burger. She had a notepad and some reports on the table and it looked like she was doing paperwork. What a perfect cover, Toni thought. It looked like she was having a "working" dinner break. Toni couldn't help but grin. She sat at the bar. In less than a minute, Bert appeared from the back.

"Hiya, Bert," Toni called out.

"Well, hey, Toni," Bert said, smiling. "Can I buy you a drink?"

"I'd love a glass of white wine," Toni said as she set her keys and wallet on the bar. "I've had one heck of a day, so I thought I'd stop by for a drink. I'm glad you're here tonight."

Bert produced a glass filled to the top with white wine. Toni could barely get it to her mouth without spilling it.

"Bad day, huh?" Bert asked. "Someone give you shit?"

"Oh, no." Toni shook her head. "Just tons of paperwork. Sometimes that wears me out more than anything else. What's new with you?"

Bert leaned against the barback and opened a bottle of water for herself. She lit a cigarette with her Zippo. "Just working, mainly."

"Seems like you're here a lot," Toni said. "What do you do when you're off?" It was a little forward, but she took the chance.

"Oh, a little of this and a little of that. I'm doing some remodeling right now. That keeps me pretty busy."

"That sounds more like work than fun," Toni said, trying to be nonchalant.

"Not really. It's something I really enjoy. I think it'll turn out nice. Maybe I'll show you soon, huh?"

"Maybe." Toni decided to change the subject. The last thing she wanted was to get an actual invitation. "Hey, are you guys open on Easter?"

"Oh, sure. We won't open until about three, I think. But we're open. Why? Are you planning on coming by?"

"Maybe. My family has a big dinner early in the day, and then there's not much to do afterward," Toni explained. "How about you? Do you do anything special with your family?"

"Never," Bert answered. "They don't think too much of me. Pretty much disowned me when I was a teenager."

"Oh, I'm so sorry, Bert. That must be really tough."

"Not really," Bert said. "I'm used to it now. I do my own thing and I'm totally okay with that."

"That's great." Toni was trying to figure out how to handle the topic of whether or not Bert was seeing someone—without looking like she was interested herself. She didn't want to intentionally lead her on. "What else is going on around here?"

Bert filled her in on the upcoming events at The Cat's Meow, including several singles nights.

"Think you might go to those?" Bert asked.

"Maybe a bunch of us might check it out," Toni replied, realizing that she was in fact single. "Just to see what it's like." She was thankful that someone came up to the bar at that moment and ordered a drink. She had to blink back tears, thinking of Boggs. She downed the rest of her wine and waved good-bye to Bert. Even though she always felt comfortable talking to Bert, she couldn't handle it tonight. Anyway, Bert had a lot of red flags. There were the prior convictions for domestic assault and then her abandonment by her family. It was still hard for her to believe that it was anyone she knew, killing these men, but she had to keep an open mind. And, of course, be very careful. They love you one minute and hate you the next, she reminded herself. Never forget that. This person could turn on her at the drop of a hat.

Toni walked past Patty without so much as a glance. By the time she got to her car, tears were streaming down her face. She struggled to breathe. As she drove home her eyes continued to blur, but she made it home before she lost it. She dropped her briefcase and keys on the floor and fell onto her couch, sobbing uncontrollably. Mr. Rupert sat with her, gently pushing his giant head against her arm. It took almost a half-hour for her to stop.

"I'm sorry, buddy. You must be so hungry."

She fixed his dinner and went upstairs to change, then returned to the kitchen in search of food. The only thing that sounded good was wine, but at least she knew enough to nuke a frozen dinner. She poured herself a glass of wine while her food heated. She looked through her CD collection. *John Denver. Perfect. Just depressing enough.* She sang every song, and the tears reappeared on her cheeks. She brought her food into the living room. She ate most of it but tasted nothing. The sad songs filled her mind, body and soul. It was almost agonizing as she realized how much she loved Boggs.

"But you can't make someone feel what they don't feel," she said to Mr. Rupert.

He seemed to understand. He stayed close to her all evening. He'd been with her through her breakup with Sadie three years ago and he was with her tonight, through every John Denver CD and every Anne Murray CD. By the end of the night there were no more tears, and she was exhausted.

Chapter 22

Toni wore a black suit to work, assuming she would go to the memorial service straight from work. The rest of the gang would be there but not sit by her. They all wanted to see who, if anyone, would make contact with her.

Shortly before noon, Dorothy buzzed her. "Anne wondered if you'd stop by her office in a few minutes," Dorothy said.

"Absolutely. I'll be right there. Should I bring anything?"

"No, just you," Dorothy said. "See you then."

Toni pulled on her jacket and made her way to Anne's office. Dorothy motioned for her to go on in.

"You wanted to see me, Anne?"

"Please sit, Toni," Anne said. "Thanks. I've got a favor to ask you."

"Sure."

"Well," Anne said with a heavy sigh, "I've been asked by the chief judge to say a few words at the service."

"Oh, wow," Toni said without thinking.

"That's exactly how I feel," Anne said, smiling. "I've been racking my brain trying to think of something suitable. My husband, Bill, encouraged me to first write what I really thought. We both got a kick out of that one. Then we burned it in our fireplace!"

"I bet." Toni laughed.

"Anyway, I finally came up with a few short lines that are appropriate and dignified. At least I think so."

"What do you need me to do?" Toni asked.

"My little sister is coming to the service," Anne explained. "She was friends with Judge Smith's daughter. Anyway, she has trouble walking or standing for very long. She's got MS."

"Okay," Toni said, still puzzled at what she was supposed to do.

"I'm almost positive the press is going to be there, and I'll need to make a short statement after the service," Anne continued. "I usually let Rachel lean on my arm as we walk or stand, but I won't be able to do that if I'm talking to the media. I hate to impose, but would you mind just standing with her? If it goes on for more than a minute or two, you could walk with her down to my car. I know it's a lot to ask, but I'd really appreciate it. And I know Rachel would too. She didn't want to use her crutch."

"I'd love to help out," Toni said. "As long as it's okay with your sister, it's okay with me. I just want to make sure she's comfortable with me."

"I'm sure she will be," Anne said. "I've talked a lot about you, and in fact, she's anxious to meet you. She's working on her master's in counseling."

"Oh, that's great. We'll have a lot to chat about."

"Great," Anne said. "I'll see you at the service."

≪≫

177

Toni arrived at the memorial fifteen minutes early. It was a good thing she left the office when she had, because the parking was nearly impossible. This was definitely a "see and be seen" kind of event, judging from the crowd and the television cameras. She made her way inside and took a seat near the back. She spotted Anne in the front row. A much younger version of herself was seated next to her and Toni assumed it was Rachel. She scanned the room until she found Vicky and Patty. Boggs was nowhere in sight. Toni wasn't sure whether she was glad of that or not. She hadn't seen Boggs since the softball game. As she continued to look around the room, her gaze suddenly met Johnnie's. She smiled and Johnnie winked. Toni felt her face burn and she looked away.

Well, that was pretty brazen, but I'm sure no one else saw that. And anyway, I'm single now, right? At that thought she blinked back tears and focused on her surroundings.

The service was nice, but all the glowing descriptions of the judge hardly seemed to fit the man who Toni had come into contact with in the courtroom. She sat quietly and tried not to roll her eyes. After what seemed like hours, Anne finally had her turn at the podium. Just as she had said earlier, her comments were brief and very professional. *Ugh. The political side of being the prosecuting attorney. You couldn't pay me enough to have that job.*

There was one more speaker and then people began to file out of the building. Toni waited in the back for Anne and Rachel. Arm in arm, they made their way slowly down the aisle. Rachel was about five feet six and very slender. Not quite as athletic-looking as Anne, she shared many of her other features. Her eyes were a light brown and her hair was shoulder-length and slightly wavy. She wore a simple black suit with an ivory blouse. They both smiled at Toni in the same confident manner.

"Your comments were lovely," Toni said to Anne.

"And your sarcasm is duly noted," Anne replied. "Toni, this is my sister, Rachel Freemont. Rachel, this is Toni Barston."

Rachel reached out to shake her hand. "I'm very glad to meet you, Toni. Anne has said many nice things about you."

"Great to meet you, Rachel," Toni replied. "Anne tells me you're working on your master's in counseling."

"Yes, and I'd love to ask you some questions—if you don't mind, of course."

"I'd love to."

"Let's head outside," Anne suggested. Toni followed them. As Anne assumed, several members of the media rushed toward her. Rachel dropped her arm from Anne's and Anne moved several feet away to answer questions. When Toni extended her right arm, Rachel smiled gratefully and took her arm.

"Will you be okay standing here?" Toni asked. They had moved farther to the side.

"Oh, sure," Rachel replied. "Unless this goes on for thirty minutes, in which case I'll need to sit down somewhere. I sure appreciate this, Toni. I usually use a crutch, but I really didn't want to have it here at the service. I bet you think that's pretty narcissistic of me."

"No." Toni shook her head. "Actually I don't."

"Anne probably told you I have multiple sclerosis."

"Are you in a lot of pain?"

"Actually, I've been pretty lucky so far," Rachel said. "Some days are good and some not so good, but I feel very fortunate."

Toni raised her eyebrows slightly.

"At least I can walk," Rachel said. "I'm very grateful every day that I can get out of bed and walk. And I'm grateful for people like you that offer their help when I need it."

Toni squeezed her arm. "My pleasure. Just let me know if you want to head to the car, okay?"

"Deal," she answered. She shifted a bit and Toni noticed she wore a class ring suspended from a gold chain around her neck.

"Class ring?"

Rachel reached for the ring and held it up for Toni to see.

"This belonged to my grandmother." She had a wide grin on her face. "It's too small for me to wear on my hand. Granny gave it to me the day I was diagnosed. I was only nineteen. My prognosis wasn't very good and one doctor was really pessimistic. I've since dumped him, by the way."

Toni laughed. "Good move."

"Anyway, Granny said that no one thought she'd ever make it to college, let alone graduate. But she did and met my grandfather. He bought her this class ring. She wanted me to have it to remind me that I can do anything I set my mind to, and I have. It's been eight years and I've made it through undergrad and now I'm halfway through my master's degree. It's taken me a little longer than most, but I'm getting there."

"That's beautiful," Toni said. "Both the story and your determination. Now tell me about school."

Rachel talked about her classes and her desire to be a psychotherapist. She had just begun asking Toni questions about her previous career when Anne returned.

"Ready to go?"

"I didn't even have a chance to ask Toni all the things I wanted to ask," Rachel said, obviously disappointed.

"Let's have lunch this week," Toni suggested. "Or we can get together over the weekend if you've got classes."

"I'd love to have lunch," Rachel said. "I've got Thursday afternoons completely free."

"I'll check my calendar. Call me in the morning, okay?"

"I will. And thanks. I really do appreciate your help and advice."

Toni smiled. She really liked Rachel.

"I'll see you tomorrow, Toni," Anne said.

" 'Bye, Toni."

Toni waved and watched them walk away arm in arm.

Chapter 23

The woman grabbed a beer from her refrigerator and sat on the sofa. She put her feet on the coffee table and picked up the remote. The news would start any minute. She hit the record button on the VCR. She was sure there would be some coverage of the judge's memorial service. What a joke. He was such a piece of shit.

She thumbed through a magazine while she waited for the coverage. When it finally came on she turned up the volume. The newscaster was describing the service.

"That's crap," the woman said aloud to the television. "Why not mention his taste in little girls?" She laughed.

The next clip was that of Anne Mulhoney outside the building. She was talking about how her office would prosecute the killer to the fullest extent of the law. *Right. If you ever catch me.* The camera panned the people surrounding Anne. The woman froze. Standing to the side was Toni. Her Toni. And there was some woman holding on to her.

She got up off the sofa and sat on the edge of the coffee table, staring at the television. Toni and this "person" were arm-in-arm. This "person" was holding something in her hand and Toni was looking at it intently. The camera panned back the other way.

"Wait. Go back, you asshole. Show Toni. Show Toni."

The clip ended with the newscaster discussing more recent killings in Fairfield. A commercial came on next. The woman sat there stunned. She grabbed the remote, stopped the tape and rewound. She played the footage over. Then she played it again. And again. Each time she played it she felt her anger grow. Who the hell was that woman with her Toni? She had never seen her before.

She played the tape again, but this time in slow motion. She sat as close to the television as she could without distorting her view. On the third slow-motion replay she was sure the object the "person" was showing Toni was a class ring—she could tell by the onyx oval it had to be a class ring—that she wore around her neck on a chain. This "person" seemed to be so proud of that ring. She couldn't tell for sure, but it didn't look like Toni was wearing her class ring on her finger.

She got up and began pacing back and forth through her loft. She finished her beer and opened another, all the while pacing. She was trying to remember. Toni wore a class ring. She knew her Toni wore a class ring on her right ring finger. But was it there when she saw her last? Had Toni given this "person" her very own class ring? No. It couldn't be. Not her Toni. Toni would never give anyone her class ring. No. No. *No.*

She screamed out of sheer rage and threw her bottle of beer at the wall. It broke into about a hundred pieces and left beer dripping down the wall. With fists tightly clenched, she began pacing once again. Her jaw was taut and she kicked a dining room chair across the room.

How could my Toni do this to me? After all I've done for her? She'd worked night and day to make their home. To make it possible for them to spend their lives together and now this? *Fucking bitch. How could she be so ungrateful? How could she do this to me? To us?*

She took another beer from the refrigerator and downed half of it before taking a breath. She stared at the television and then drank the rest.

Goddamned fucking bitch. Who does she think she's messing with?

She screamed again, then slammed the beer bottle down on the floor, sending glass and beer residue across the kitchen floor. She paced again. She screamed again. Then she returned to the coffee table and pushed play for the tenth time.

As the footage rolled by again in slow motion, she studied Toni's face. She played it again. And again. And again. Her anger at Toni began to subside.

She realized Toni was puzzled. Or maybe concerned. No doubt she was wondering how this "person" got her class ring.

The woman watched the tape again.

Somehow this "person" had gotten Toni's ring. She was acting smug and showing it off as though it were a trophy. Toni was clearly confused, wondering why this woman took her ring and wouldn't give it back. Toni, of course, was too nice to demand its return. That bitch had taken her Toni's ring and wouldn't give it back. How could she do that to her Toni? *Bitch. I'm going to find you. I'm going to find you and end your miserable, fucking life. And take back what's mine.*

She went to her computer and began her search. She had resources. She was going to find this bitch if it was the last thing she did. Find her and shoot her in the head. *No. I'll shoot her first in the knee. That will bring her to the ground. Then I'll walk up to her and yank that stupid chain off her neck. I'll get Toni's ring back for her. I'll get it back. Then I'll shoot her in the head. No, I'll shoot her hand off first. The hand that took the ring. Then I'll shoot her in the head. Yeah. Then I'll shoot her in the head. Bitch. That will teach her a thing or two. No one messes with my Toni. No one.*

She watched the video one more time. That woman looked familiar, she thought. Had she seen her before or did she remind her of someone? After viewing it two more times, she realized that "the person" looked similar to Anne Mulhoney. On a hunch, she plugged in Anne's name on Google. After several minutes she found what she was looking for. There was a photo of Anne Mulhoney and "that person." The caption showed Anne, her husband and her sister, Rachel Freemont, at the mayor's swearing-in ceremony. There was no question that the person in the photo was the same woman that had been standing next to Toni.

With that information as a starting point, she worked at her computer far into the night. The Internet held a world of knowledge, if you knew where to look. She used a variety of search engines including Dogpile, Soople and Zabasearch. She made a few calls from her "safe," untraceable cell phone, the kind you buy with an allotted amount of time already programmed in. It was perfect for those times when you didn't want to be found. She went back to the computer. More phone calls. She cleaned up the glass and beer. She went back to her computer. By five a.m. she had her answer. Rachel was a graduate student at the University of Missouri, the Fairfield campus. She printed out a map of the campus that included all the buildings and the parking garages, along with a schedule of non-credit courses. She also found out that Rachel had an apartment a few miles from school and she had her phone number, but hopefully she wouldn't need that. According to the university's Web site, Rachel was the vice president of Psi Chi, a national psychological honor society. Their next meeting was tomorrow, Wednesday, at ten a.m. in Kaplan Hall. She wished she could kill the bitch right now; she didn't want to wait one more minute. She couldn't wait. The bitch had to die *now*. But she had to wait just a couple more hours. This would be her finest hour to date. She couldn't help but giggle.

She had enough time to shower, fix herself some coffee and a nice breakfast. By the time she left her loft that morning, she was feeling great. She drove to the university with her guitar case in the back of her SUV. She went to the registrar's office and enrolled in a weekend adult education class, Cooking on a Budget. It would be perfect. She paid the thirty-five dollar tuition plus ten dollars for a parking permit. She thanked the lady, went to her car and drove straight to the top floor of the parking garage. It was virtually empty. If all went as she'd hoped, Rachel would be dead and she'd be at work by noon. She felt proud and excited. It wouldn't be long now. Soon she would be sharing her loft with Toni. Her Toni.

Chapter 24

Toni grinned when Chloe buzzed her first thing Wednesday morning.

"Ms. Rachel Freemont is on line two for you," Chloe said.

"Thank you and good morning to you, Chloe," Toni responded.

"And good morning to you, Ms. Barston," she replied before clicking off.

"Hiya, Rachel. How are you this morning?"

"Great," she said. "Did I call too early? I wanted to catch you before I went to a meeting at school."

"Not at all. I already checked my calendar and I don't have court until two o'clock on Thursday. How about lunch Thursday at noon?"

"That would be perfect, as long as you're sure you have the time."

"Of course," Toni said. "I'm looking forward to talking to you again. It's fun to talk about psychotherapy and school. Where would you like to meet?"

"Whatever is convenient for you."

"Well, can you come downtown? We'll have longer to talk if I don't have to go too far."

"Absolutely," Rachel said. "What about Phil's Deli? It's just down the street from you."

"I love that place." Toni smiled. "That would be perfect. Noon on Thursday. Whoever gets there first should grab a table, okay?"

"Deal," Rachel said. "I really appreciate this, Toni. I'd love to get your advice before I enroll in summer school."

"I'm looking forward to it. I'll see you tomorrow. But let me get your number just in case something comes up, okay?"

Toni spent the rest of her morning in court dealing with a variety of misdemeanor cases. Most were taken care of in a matter of minutes. By the time she left the courtroom she had dealt with fifteen cases. She was ready for a break. As she passed by the secretaries' area she noticed another large brown envelope on Cindy's desk. It was addressed to her and was clearly another delivery from her anonymous writer. She looked around but didn't see Cindy anywhere.

"Hey, Phoebe," Toni said to one of the other secretaries. "Have you seen Cindy?"

"She had a doctor's appointment," Phoebe said without looking up from her computer. "I think she said she'd be back around one." She typed a few more lines and then looked up. "Is there something I can do for you?"

"Oh, no. But thanks anyway. I'll catch up with her later."

No sense in waiting for Cindy, she thought, then opening the damn thing and then taking it to Sam. She may as well just take it down now.

Toni retrieved a glove from the closet and carried the letter to

Sam's office. She was nervous about possibly catching a glimpse of Boggs at her desk, but it was empty. *Thank God.* She didn't want to cry at work. She took a deep breath and kept walking. She knocked lightly on Sam's open door. He grinned when he saw her.

"Hi, Toni." He motioned her inside his office as he took a sip from his Diet Coke. "To what do I owe this honor?"

"Can't a girl just come by and visit a handsome investigator without getting the third degree?" She flashed him a smile.

"Well, I can't argue with the truth," Sam said seriously. "But I must warn you. I am not going to leave my wife for you."

Both Toni and Sam laughed and she sat down in one of his chairs. She held up the envelope. "I have another gift for you."

"I'm truly touched," he said. "More candy?"

"I don't know. I didn't even open this one. Do you want the honors?"

Sam pulled gloves and a camera from his desk drawer, then took the envelope from her. He set it on his desk and took pictures before slitting open the end. He turned it upside down and several yellow Peeps and chocolate Easter eggs dropped out of the envelope. The Peeps were individually wrapped in plastic wrap.

"This is great." Sam took another slug of Diet Coke. He peered inside the can and drained the last few drops before tossing it in the trash.

"Great because you love marshmallow Peeps?" she asked.

"Well, that, too." He chuckled. "But actually we might have caught a break. These are wrapped in Saran Wrap or something. They're not in the original package. That means our guy, or girl, took them out and wrapped them. Maybe this doofus finally made a mistake and left fingerprints or something."

"Cool," Toni said. "So, Sam, how are things with you? And how's Betty?"

"Life is basically wonderful," he said. "Spring is here, I have a great job, and I get to go home to my Betty every night. What else could a person want? What about you? Are you settling into the felonies now?"

"I've got my second burglary trial coming up. I'm nervous, but I'm doing okay."

"Everything else okay?" he asked.

"Yes, Mr. Nosy. Everything else is fine. It's sweet of you to ask."

"I'm a caring kind of guy," he said, grinning. "And Betty would have read me the riot act if I didn't ask you. You should come over to dinner, you know. One of these days you won't be able to get out of coming over. Boggs, too."

"I will, Sam," she said, cringing inside at the mention of Boggs. "Honest. I'd love to have dinner with you and Betty."

"I'll have her call you, then. It's hard to say no when Betty asks you."

"Sounds good to me," Toni said as she got up to leave. "And thanks for looking into my anonymous guy. He's getting a little creepy."

"No problem. Do you want the Peeps back if they aren't tainted with arsenic or something?"

"Think I'll pass on that one. But thanks for asking."

Sam was still laughing as she left his office.

At two o'clock that afternoon Anne Mulhoney walked into Toni's office. It was the first time since she'd been hired by Anne that she had been in her domain. Toni was startled by her unannounced arrival.

"Hi, Anne. Is something going on?"

"I'm on my way to the hospital," Anne explained. "Rachel is at St. Mark's."

"What happened? Is she okay?" Toni asked quickly.

"She's fine. Just a sprained wrist. Thankfully not the one she uses with her crutch."

Toni was relieved. "How did it happen?"

"She told me she was coming down the stairs outside of a building on campus. Her crutch slipped off the stair and she went down."

"I'm glad it wasn't more serious."

"But there's more," Anne continued. "She said she heard a noise as she fell. It sounded like a firecracker. A woman several yards away from Rachel was hit by a bullet. The crime scene folks think the woman who was shot might have gotten hit from a ricochet. They found a mark on the concrete stairs near where Rachel was before she slipped. All this is just preliminary and frankly a few guesses, but I don't like the idea that someone is shooting at students. Captain Billings is looking into this. I just thought you'd want to know."

"Oh, my God," Toni said, shocked. "Is there any other evidence?"

"Frank is at the hospital. The woman is in surgery. The bullet is still in her leg. It's pretty bad."

"Will you let me know what you find out?"

"Absolutely." Anne nodded.

"And tell Rachel we'll reschedule our lunch tomorrow. She can call me when she's up for it. Will you tell her that for me?"

"Will do, Toni. I'll see you tomorrow, but I'll call and leave you a message if I find out more before then."

It was almost five o'clock when Chloe buzzed. "Detective Carter on line three for you, Ms. Barston."

"Hey, Vicky," Toni said after she punched line three. "What's up?"

"I'm down at the crime lab," Vicky said. "They haven't finished with ballistics, but they told me it's the same kind of bullet."

"I thought they already did that," Toni said. "I thought they matched the bullet from the parking garage to the one they found at the golf course."

"They did," Vicky said. "This is new. I was here when Frank brought in the bullet from today."

"What bullet? What do you mean, today?" Toni asked.

"At U.M. Fairfield," Vicky explained. "Didn't Anne tell you?"

"The woman who was hit? Well, yes, but we really only talked about her sister, Rachel."

"I know. I went to interview her. Frank was waiting at the hospital for that woman to come out of surgery, so I told him I'd talk to Rachel. That's when I found out she was supposed to meet you for lunch tomorrow."

"And?"

"And so I'm freaked out a bit, hon. The crime scene guys said it looked like the bullet ricocheted and hit the other woman in the leg. Nasty wound. But if it ricocheted, that means it probably didn't hit its main target, right?"

"Shit" was all Toni could say.

"Exactly," Vicky said. "Frank went back over to the hospital after he dropped the bullet off at the crime lab. He'll talk to her and see if there's any connection to the other murders. But I suspect there won't be."

"Are they sure it is the same kind of weapon or bullet or whatever?" Toni asked.

"The preliminary results are a match. It's a little hard to tell. The bullet ricocheted off the concrete steps and then went into the woman's leg. When the bullet hit the concrete, it flattened on one side, then smashed into her leg. The guys in the lab think it's the same type, though. Fired from a high-powered sniper rifle. Whoever's doing this is damn good. I can't believe he or she missed."

"No leads, I'm assuming," Toni murmured.

"Nope. None. Best guess is that they shot from one of the three-level parking garages next to campus. It was at least two hundred yards away. Several people heard the single shot, but no one saw a damned thing. At least no one they can find so far."

"My God, Vicky," Toni whispered. "What am I going to do? This person is really going off the deep end."

"I know," Vicky said with a sigh. "But at least you have an alibi for this one, which means you couldn't be a suspect for the others, right? Doesn't that make you feel a little better?"

"I guess so, but not really," Toni admitted.

"Okay, listen. I'm coming over to your place. I'll round up Patty and Boggs and we'll do some more brainstorming. Just go directly home and lock the door. We'll be there soon."

"No, that's okay," Toni said, stammering a little. She wasn't sure she wanted to see Boggs. "I'll be fine."

"No arguing. See you later." Vicky disconnected before Toni had a chance to protest again.

She sighed and began packing up her briefcase. She felt better knowing she wouldn't be alone, although she'd never admit that to anyone. She didn't feel like she was in danger herself, but she worried about her friends. Assuming the target actually was Rachel, a woman she had just met yesterday, they wouldn't think twice about killing someone Toni really cared about. She shuddered at the thought. She tried to push everything but the task at hand out of her mind. She finished putting her files in her briefcase and headed for the parking garage.

The woman was pacing back and forth, mumbling to herself. She had been doing that for almost thirty minutes now. She sat down on her sofa for a few minutes and then got up again and resumed pacing. She had been doing this most of the afternoon. Finally she sat back down on the sofa and removed her rifle from the guitar case. She pulled out her gun cleaning kit from underneath the sofa and began the task of cleaning. After a few minutes she could feel herself begin to calm down.

"I missed," she said aloud. "I goddamn missed the bitch." She could feel her anger growing again, so she concentrated on her weapon. The repetitive motion of cleaning her rifle did the trick. "I forgot to breathe, that's all. I pulled the trigger before I took my breath."

As if in response, she took a deep breath and let it out slowly.

"That's what I needed to do." She grinned. "It's all good. At least I scared the crap out of Rachel the Bitch. Hey, maybe that was better anyway. Then when I do kill her, she'll have been scared to death for a couple days. Yeah. That would be better."

She laughed, continuing to clean her rifle long after the job was done. She lovingly caressed the cold metal before finally putting it back in the guitar case. In fact, she was feeling quite good about the day. She decided that she would just stake out Rachel's apartment over the weekend. It would be perfect. She did feel like she'd forgotten something, but she couldn't put her finger on it. She brushed off the feeling.

Chapter 25

Vicky, Boggs and Patty arrived at Toni's within minutes of one another. After getting everyone a beer, Toni settled on the couch with the rest of them. She had smiled graciously at Boggs but kept her emotions in check. The pain she felt inside was killing her, but so far, so good.

"Okay," Vicky started. "I think things have really started to escalate here." She filled in Boggs and Patty. "Frank is looking into the connection this last victim might have had with the judge and Butch, but I think it's going to be a dead end. The woman is a math professor at the university and I don't think she was the target."

"I hate to admit it," Boggs said, "but I'm with you on this. I just don't understand how she could have missed. And I'm assuming for now it is a she."

"If she is escalating," Toni added, but not looking directly at

Boggs, "she might be getting more and more emotional. I think something must have set her off. My guess is she didn't take her time with her shot."

The three of them just stared at her.

"What?" She threw up her hands.

"Well," Vicky said, "that sounded, well . . . really cold and calculated."

Toni winced. "I'm trying to remain objective, okay? Anyway, when you shoot, you need to remain focused. If you get too excited, you shoot too soon."

"I totally get that," Patty said. "The first time I tried to qualify I nearly missed the target half the time, even though I did well in practice. I had to learn to relax."

"Exactly," Toni said. "So we need to figure out what set her off. And how the hell did she know I was taking Rachel to lunch? The only people who knew that were Rachel and Anne."

"Do you think Rachel told someone?" Patty asked.

"She didn't," Vicky answered. "I asked her that specifically."

"Then how the hell did she become a target?" Toni was exasperated.

"You were on the news," Boggs pointed out. "Last night. Anyone could have seen you."

"On the news? Why? When?" Toni frowned. She'd had no idea.

"It was just for a second," Boggs explained. "They were covering the memorial service and then Anne's statement afterward. They panned the crowd. You were standing there with some woman."

"And you think that our killer saw that?" Toni gulped.

"Absolutely," Boggs said. "Or maybe she saw you at the memorial service."

"But would that be enough to set her off?" Patty asked. "I mean, on the news, if it was just for a second, and you were standing there just talking to Anne's sister?"

"It would definitely be enough, I think," Boggs murmured.

"Well," Toni said to Patty, "if she thought I was interested in this woman, or that the woman was interested in me . . . I guess so." She thought for a moment and remembered Rachel showing her the class ring. "Oh, yup."

"What?" Vicky looked at her.

"Rachel was holding on to my arm," Toni demonstrated. "She didn't have her crutch with her, so I was her crutch, so to speak."

Boggs's eyes brightened. "She needed a crutch?"

"You don't know Rachel, do you?" Vicky grinned. "She's got multiple sclerosis, uses a crutch. But when she doesn't use her crutch, she usually leans on someone to walk."

Toni explained, "Anne asked me yesterday if I'd stand with Rachel during the press conference. She didn't want to use her crutch during the service. She knew the judge's daughter, by the way. That's why she was there. Anyway, she's working on her master's in counseling at U.M. Fairfield and was asking me some questions."

"I knew she was in grad school," Vicky said. "So you were talking about that when Anne was talking to the press?"

"Yes."

"Was there anyone else around you? Any of our suspects? Or someone who looked suspicious at least?"

Toni thought for a moment. "No. Not that I remember. In fact, the only 'suspect' I saw during the service was Johnnie. Did you guys see anyone?"

Patty and Vicky shook their heads. "I didn't see anyone looking at you, except Johnnie as she passed by," Patty added.

Boggs rolled her eyes. "Figures. Unfortunately, I can eliminate her as a 'suspect' for now. I was with her at the time of this shooting. In fact, she was sitting in my office when Vicky called me."

Patty beamed. "That's good news."

She was met by several raised eyebrows.

"I mean, well, at least that eliminates one person," she stammered.

"That's true," Vicky said.

"So I can at least relax where she's concerned?" Toni asked.

"Oh, I'm sure," Vicky said. Boggs shot her a look. "I mean, I don't think you have to worry that she's going to kill one of us or you, if that's what you're talking about."

"Okay," Toni said. "Let's try to figure this out. We still have the anonymous letter guy, Bert, Nancy and Cindy. Of course there's still the possibility that it's someone else, but let's stick to what we know." She filled them in on her lunch date with Cindy and the drink with Bert.

"I would say that they're both interested in Toni," Patty said. "They could hardly take their eyes off of her, but I didn't see anything else that would indicate they're crazy as shit."

"But I'm thinking she's now escalating," Toni said. "I'm going to assume she wasn't at the memorial service. And if she went a little nuts just seeing me on the news, that's not good. Especially if she did miss the shot because of added emotion. That means she's not thinking as clearly as she once did."

"Like, she was thinking clearly when she killed the judge or Butch?" Vicky seemed aghast. "You're kidding, right?"

"No. She was thinking a little more rationally then. At least rationally for her. She was able to think out her plan and then methodically carry it out. Now she's acting out in more of a rage. That's not good. Not good at all. It means that she's probably much more unstable." Toni slumped back against the couch. "If only I knew who she was. If I could just talk to her, maybe I could help her."

The room was silent, everyone apparently trying to figure out what to do. The quiet was finally broken by Toni's laugh. They looked at her with surprise.

"Sorry," Toni said. "In my opinion, this woman definitely has borderline personality disorder." She felt confident in her assessment. "If I had wondered in the past, I sure don't now. This happens. As a therapist, you think you can help, even if no one else has been able to. It's as though they suck you in. And they do. But she is a bit more violent than what I'm used to. I need to remember that. And we need to make sure that Rachel is safe. This woman won't let it go, believe me. She'll try again. And I'm pretty sure the next time she'll succeed."

"Already on that," Vicky said. "Rachel is staying with Anne and Bill. I know she'll be okay for tonight, but I think you should talk to Anne about this."

"I agree," Boggs said. "We need to bring Anne up to speed on what we're thinking here."

"And I think we need to bring Johnnie in on this," Vicky said, pointedly ignoring the stare from Boggs. "She has resources that we don't. And anyway, technically the feds are still on the case. If the bullets are a match, and we only just got the preliminary findings, then she'll be in this for sure. We might as well use her the best way we can."

"I'm all for that," Patty said, grinning.

"Okay," Toni said and Boggs gave a slight nod. "I want to see Rachel. I'm going to call Anne and see if I can go over there. That way I can talk to Anne and explain. And I just want to see for myself that Rachel is doing okay."

"Good idea," Vicky said. "But you can't go alone."

The sound of Boggs's cell phone interrupted the conversation. Boggs looked at the number and shrugged. "Boggs," she answered in a businesslike tone. "Slow down. Sharon, is that you? Slow down. Okay. Okay. Throw some clothes in a bag. I'll be there in ten minutes. Can you do it? Then get your stuff and run to the market on the corner. Go inside. I'm on my way." She closed her phone and was heading for the door. "It was Sharon. I could barely understand her. She's a witness for Elizabeth's drug trafficking trial tomorrow. The defendant is her boyfriend and he's threatened her. Poor girl is scared out of her mind. This guy is beyond cruel. I'm going to get her to a motel. I'll call you when I've got this straightened out." She made a move toward Toni, then stopped. "I'll call as soon as I can. Be extra careful."

Vicky must have sensed Toni's concern. "It won't take her too long," she explained. "We put up witnesses all the time."

Toni nodded. "Can I go ahead and call Anne?"

"Sure." While Toni made the call, Vicky took out her own phone. "I'm going to call Johnnie. I'll ask her over in, let's say an hour or so." She glanced at her watch and asked Patty, "Would you mind going to Anne's with Toni?"

Hearing that, Toni nodded her assent to Vicky.

"Not a problem," Patty said.

Toni got ahold of Anne, explained the situation and rang off. "Anne said to come right over," she said.

Patty stood and reached for her jacket. "Hello," she said, grinning. "My name is Patty and I'll be your escort tonight."

Toni laughed out loud, then sighed. "Thanks. I needed a laugh."

"So, if you don't mind, I'll stay here," Vicky said. "I'm going to make some calls. Can I use your laptop?"

"Sure," Toni said as she grabbed her favorite jacket from the closet. "It's upstairs. Help yourself."

"Try to be back by seven," Vicky said. "Johnnie will be here by then and I'll put in an order for pizza. Does that sound okay to you guys?"

"No onions for me and I'm good," Toni replied. "See you in about an hour." She grabbed her car keys and headed out the door with Patty.

Vicky had been sitting at Toni's desk in her bedroom for almost forty-five minutes when her cell rang. It was Boggs. "How's it going with Sharon?"

"She's still a mess, but I've got her calmed down," Boggs said. "We're in her hotel room. I got her some food and I'm waiting for a uniform to get here. It shouldn't be too long now. What's going on there? I was going to try Toni's cell, but—"

"But you're an ass," Vicky said. "Damn it, Boggs. I can't believe you broke up with her."

"Just drop it," Boggs said in a terse voice. "I don't want to talk about it, okay?"

"All right." Vicky softened. "But if you change your mind, I'm here, okay?"

"I know."

"Get back when you can, Boggs," she said, knowing that taking care of a witness in a trial was important to Boggs.

"Okay." There was an odd silence.

"Are you okay?" Vicky asked. "Is there something else going on? Say *pizza* if you're in trouble."

"No, I'm not in trouble. But thanks. It's just, oh, I don't know."

"What, hon?"

"I saw the news footage last night," Boggs said wearily.

"And?"

"Well, I went a little nuts myself," Boggs admitted.

"Because you saw Toni with Rachel?"

"Yeah," Boggs said. "I didn't know who she was. All I saw was some woman holding on to Toni's arm and I felt sick inside."

"Sick like you're going to toss your cookies?"

"Exactly," Boggs said. "And until I found out the real story, well, I felt sick all day."

"I think that's a symptom," Vicky said, wishing Boggs would just give in to the feeling.

"A symptom of what?"

"Love, you chickenshit." Vicky chuckled.

"Shit," Boggs mumbled. "Shit. Shit. Shit."

"Deal with it, sweetie." Vicky put on her tough-love voice. "I know it's scary, but I think you've got it bad."

"I've never felt like this, Vicky. But maybe I'm just coming down with something."

"You can tell yourself that if you want to, Boggs, but it won't go away. I know it's scaring the hell out of you, but it can be wonderful if you just let yourself accept how you feel. But you better figure this out quick, because you've already informed her she's single. Now it's going to take a hell of a lot to get her back. Think about it. Can you imagine your life without Toni in it? Have you tried?"

Boggs sighed. "Oh, I've tried. The harder I try to block her out of my mind, the more she's there. I can't even do my laundry without thinking about her."

"So you resolved the problem by breaking up with her?"

"No. Shit. I'm screwed. This is messing me up too much. I'm a player." Boggs was just trying to rationalize love as far as Vicky was concerned, but she let her go on. "It's who I am. I'm not the type to settle down and be an old married woman. That's not me." She paused. "Yeah. Thanks for straightening me out. I'm just gonna let this roll off me, like I always do. So I'll see you over there in a bit." She hung up before Vicky could say anything else.

Vicky just shook her head. She looked at her watch and dialed Patty. "Are you guys almost done?"

"Yeah. We were getting ready to leave when you called. Is there anything you need us to pick up?"

Vicky shut down Toni's computer and headed down to the kitchen. She looked in the refrigerator and sighed. "There's plenty of beer. How about some soda? It looks like she's running a little low here."

"Well, make yourself at home, why don't you?" Patty laughed. "Are you snooping in all her drawers as well?"

"No," Vicky said. "I did that the last time, smarty pants. See you in a few."

She called in an order for pizza, looked over her notes and had just sat down on the couch with Mr. Rupert when the doorbell rang. She peered out the peephole. It was Johnnie. She opened the door and waved her in.

"Just you and me," she said.

"This is becoming a habit," Johnnie said, scanning the room as she draped her coat over the dining room chair and placed her messenger bag on the floor. "Is this the local hangout now?"

"Pretty much, yeah." Vicky gestured for her to take a seat. "Besides, it's the only place that Mr. Rupert can join us."

Johnnie ruffled his head and sat down. "You were a little cryptic in your phone call. What's going on?"

Vicky got them a couple beers and joined her in the living room.

Johnnie was laughing by the time Vicky finished her explanation. "You mean I was on your suspect list?" she said, wiping her eyes.

"Absolutely," Vicky said, laughing herself. "Can't you see why? I mean, you literally came out of nowhere. And then you questioned Toni at her house, twice."

"Guilty," Johnnie admitted. "But not for that reason." She blushed just a little. "She's really attractive, don't you think?" She suddenly bolted upright. "Oh, shit. Are you a couple? I mean, I didn't think you were. Aren't you with Patty?"

Vicky chuckled. "No. The thing with Patty at the bar was a con, for you. And Toni and I are just friends."

Johnnie seemed to relax a bit.

"But I can't say the same for Toni and Boggs." Vicky knew it wasn't true at the moment, but she wanted to give them a chance to fix things without Johnnie complicating matters.

"Boggs? Oops. Shit." Johnnie was shaking her head. "No wonder Boggs is a little cold to me. I didn't have a clue. God, I'm such an idiot."

"We didn't want you to have a clue," Vicky explained.

"So," Johnnie asked tentatively, "are they serious? Boggs and Toni, I mean."

"I'm not sure." Vicky shrugged.

"Okay," Johnnie said. "I don't want to cause any problems. I'm not like that. Really. But if Toni were available, well . . . I'd be all over that."

"I'll let you all figure all that out," Vicky said. "But for now, let me fill you in on what we know about the shooter, or at least what we think we know."

Vicky had just about finished getting Johnnie up to speed when Toni and Patty arrived. The pizza man arrived at the same time. By the time they had gotten out the paper plates and drinks, Boggs had returned from the hotel. Vicky gave her a quick hug.

When they'd demolished the pizza and were working on another round of beer, Johnnie said, "I'd like to thank you all for taking me off the suspect list. And for inviting me over. I really like you guys." She smiled. "I mean, well, I do. I feel at ease with you guys, and that means a lot to me."

"We're glad," Toni said. "And I speak for all of us."

Johnnie blushed slightly. "Anyway, I think you're right on with the profile of this woman. Are you sure you don't want to join the Bureau?" She glanced at Toni.

"Yeah." Toni laughed. "I'm sure."

"Okay," Johnnie said. "Our loss. Back to business. There's no way the murders had anything to do with national security. That was just some political bullshit from the beginning. And I don't think it's connected to his penchant for pictures of young girls either. Especially since I know about the truck driver and now Rachel."

"Well," Toni said, "we're assuming she wasn't at the service and she must have seen me on the news last night, but it seems hard to believe that just a couple seconds of footage was enough to set her off. I wish I could have seen it."

"Hang on a sec." Johnnie hopped up and retrieved her messenger bag from the dining room floor. She pulled out her laptop and within a couple minutes she had a video of last night's news.

"Pretty slick," Vicky said as they gathered around the screen. The portion with Toni only lasted about ten seconds.

"Play it again," Vicky said, standing over Johnnie's shoulder. She watched the clip again. "Can you slow it down?" Toni moved in closer to see.

Johnnie pushed a few more buttons and the clip ran in slow motion. "What are you looking for?"

"She was showing me her grandmother's class ring," Toni said. "She wears it around her neck on a chain."

Johnnie ran the clip again. "Know anybody in the background?"

Everyone shook their heads. "No one that matters," Patty said.

"Wait!" Toni pointed to the screen.

"Did you see someone?" Johnnie asked, pausing the video.

"No. But I get it now," she said. "The ring."

"What are you talking about?" Vicky stared at the frozen image of Toni and Rachel.

"The ring," Toni explained. "The crazy woman sees Rachel with a class ring."

Vicky and the others just looked at her blankly. Toni held up her right hand. "And I'm not wearing mine."

"And if you gave it to Rachel," Johnnie continued along the same train of thought, "then you're in trouble. She'll kill you and Rachel, right?"

"Very possible," Toni said pensively. "Especially if she thinks I abandoned her, or dumped her or whatever. This could be the thing that sends her totally off the deep end."

"So what would she do next?" Boggs asked from the far end of the couch. It was the first time she had spoken more than two words. "You can't be alone, Toni. Or go out in public."

"We need to set a trap," Johnnie said. "We need to draw her out."

"What?" Boggs said quickly. "And use Toni as bait? I don't think so."

Toni was clearly surprised at Boggs's outburst. Boggs stood and started pacing back and forth across the living room. She went into the kitchen and retrieved another can of beer. She must have realized that everyone was staring at her.

"Anyone need another beer or soda?" she asked sheepishly, holding her can in the air.

Vicky followed her into the kitchen and grabbed a Coke from the refrigerator. "Try to keep it together, Boggs," she muttered. "You're not the only one who cares for her."

"The first thing we can do," Johnnie continued, "is to put a team on each of our suspects. At least then we'll know when one of them makes a move."

"Sounds good," Vicky said. "But we don't have enough evidence to warrant the extra people. At least not on our end."

"I can handle that," Johnnie said. "Off the record, though. My office is only officially involved in the judge's case and the lawyer's, but I can use a couple people to help out."

"We don't want to set her off in a rage," Toni said. "But maybe we can play on her desire to protect me, or take care of me."

"How?" Patty asked.

"Well, I'm not sure," Toni said. "What if we somehow let each one know that I'm in trouble. That someone hurt me. That would surely cause them to contact me, to find out who had hurt me."

Boggs was still in the kitchen, but Vicky could see the look of panic on her face.

"Let's save that for our last option," Vicky said. "Can we find enough to get a search warrant on any of these women?"

"We don't have squat for physical evidence," Johnnie said.

"What about the parking garage at the university?" Patty suggested. "Has anyone been over there yet?"

"Yeah." Vicky took a sip of her Coke. "Frank was going to follow up with the crime unit when they finished there."

There was a brief silence, then Boggs stopped pacing and rejoined them in the living room. "What about the ammunition?" she asked Johnnie. "Did you find anything there?"

"On Judge Smith's case, we checked all the gun stores in the surrounding area, fifty miles I think. We tried to match the names of any buyers of sniper ammo with anyone on our suspect list," Johnnie answered. "We went back six months."

"But that was the FBI 'terrorist' suspect list, right?"

Johnnie's eyes widened. "Shit. You're right. Let me pull up the list again and we'll see if we can get a match with our girls."

No one spoke as Johnnie punched several keys on her computer. After a few minutes the list appeared on her screen. Toni scooted closer to see. The movement, Vicky saw, did not go unnoticed by Boggs.

"Okay," Johnnie said as she scrolled through the names, "we're looking for Cindy, Nancy or Bert."

"I don't see them," Toni said, obviously disappointed.

"But maybe it's under their dad's name, or brother's or something," Vicky suggested. "Can we get addresses of the people who bought ammo and see if they match one of our girls?"

"Yeah," Johnnie said. "Hang on. Of course the shooter could have gotten the ammo a long time ago. I only went back six months, but at least it's a place to start." She continued typing.

"I think I've got a city map," Toni said. "Maybe that will help."

"I've got a big one in my car," Patty said. "It's laminated, so we can mark on it." She grabbed her keys and went out.

"I'll bring my laptop down," Toni offered. By the time she came back downstairs, Patty had returned and had the map opened up on the coffee table. Vicky had her notebook.

"Perfect," Vicky said. "Get on Mapquest and let's put in our girls' addresses." She'd gotten them from the database at Fairfield PD.

Toni sat on the couch. "Ready," she said.

"This is for Bert," Vicky said, and she read off her address. Toni nodded. When the information came up, she gave Patty the cross street so she could plot it on the map. "Wait a minute," she said. "That's an apartment complex."

"Yeah," Patty answered. "I know the one. It's three stories, six units per building. I think there are two buildings. Why?"

"Bert told me she's remodeling," Toni replied. "She even invited me to come over and see it when she's done."

"Okay, that's not good," Vicky said. "I highly doubt she's remodeling an apartment. Obviously either she's moved or she's not telling the truth. It could be something innocent like she's actually redecorating, or remodeling a friend's house. Or . . . I don't know."

"Can you find another address for her, Johnnie?" Toni asked.

"I'll try." Johnnie nodded. "Let me finish with this list first."

Vicky looked at Boggs. "Want to give it a shot?" she asked. She knew Boggs sometimes used questionable techniques to locate witnesses. She pointed to Toni's laptop. Boggs shrugged and sat next to Toni on the couch. Toni handed her the laptop.

It took Boggs about three minutes to hit paydirt. Vicky couldn't help but grin.

"I've got two addresses for Bert. The first one is the apartment complex. The other one is in the warehouse district." She read the address for Patty.

"That's not too far from The Cat's Meow," Patty said. "I didn't know there was any residential property around there."

"It's mixed," Boggs said. "On the west side most of the warehouses have been bought by big companies and are being rehabbed. When they finish those, they're going to cost a mint. But on the east side, closer to the gay bars, a lot of the warehouses are still up for sale. Not too bad—pricewise, that is."

"Going into real estate, are you?" Vicky asked.

Boggs grinned sheepishly. "Ah, no. I was just looking around last week."

"Cool," Patty said. "I think a loft would be really neat."

"Hey, wait," Toni said. "Cathy said something during her reading about a warehouse, but not really, right?"

"Shit," Vicky said, remembering the reading. "You're right. Okay. That moves Bert into the number one position in my book."

"She does have a lot of red flags." Toni ticked them off on her fingers. "Domestic abuse, abandonment by her family. Now we have a warehouse, and she smokes. Shit. I didn't want it to be her. I mean, I didn't want it to be anyone, but I like her."

"Let's go ahead and get the other addresses, okay?" Vicky said. She gave the names to Boggs.

"Are you kidding me?" Boggs said after she got the address for Nancy.

Toni leaned over to look at the screen and started laughing. "Are you ready for this? Nancy lives on Warehouse Street. No shit."

"Okay, that's just creepy," Vicky said. "Now she's on the top of my list also. If Cindy lives on Warehouse Lane I'm going to shit my pants."

"Hmm," Boggs said. "This is weird. I'll try another database." Vicky looked on as she plugged in a satellite view. "Okay, we've got another winner. Cindy lives in a vacant lot."

"What?" Toni leaned over again, then suddenly pulled away and sat up straight.

The tension between them was thick as molasses, and Vicky was about to suggest getting another soda when Boggs stammered, "Um, the address that Cindy gave for her driver's license and to work at Metro is a vacant lot."

"What the hell?" Vicky frowned at the screen. "How long has

she worked there?"

"About two years," Boggs said. "At least I think so. Hang on. Let me check the personnel records."

Vicky poked her. She didn't want Johnnie to think they were hacking into government databases.

Boggs cleared her throat. "I mean, hypothetically, if someone were to look at those records, they would probably be able to tell when she started working there."

"Understood." Vicky shot a questioning look at Johnnie and Patty. They both nodded.

"Okay," Boggs said. "Yes. Two years."

"What was there before?" Toni asked. "I mean at that address. Was there something there two years ago?"

Boggs tried a few more things before answering. "Yeah. There were a few old tract houses."

"Wait," Vicky said as an image came into her mind. "I remember. There was a fire. It took out at least two of the houses. I guess they just tore the others down. They were all in bad shape, as I recall."

"So maybe that's where she lived when she applied at Metro," Toni said. "Then she never changed her address."

"But we need to know where she is so we can watch her," Boggs said. "What about IRS records? Can you do that, Johnnie?"

"Technically, no." She keyed in a few numbers. "Post office box," she said after a couple minutes.

"Hell," Patty said. "I might as well just follow her home. It would be a lot more reliable than what we've gotten so far."

"And a lot more dangerous," Toni reminded her. "What about voters' registration, or credit cards or financial?"

"Oh, I can do that," Boggs said with a grin. A few keystrokes later, she read off the address and cross street to Patty.

"That's just a few blocks from the vacant lot," Patty said. "Zoom in on that satellite thing. See if it's a house or apartment or what."

"It's a little tract house," Boggs said.

"Okay," Johnnie said. "We've got the three locations. I'm going to have someone sit on these. Maybe we can at least get something suspicious enough for a warrant." She took out her phone and made a couple calls.

"Are you putting agents on this?" Toni asked.

"Kind of," Johnnie replied. "Just calling in some favors. Nothing official. At least not yet. Now let's look at the addresses and names I came up with for the ammo."

"It doesn't make me feel too safe knowing that this many people bought sniper ammo in the last six months," Toni said, looking at the list.

After about a half-hour the list was down to three people.

"The rest of these check out to real people with no apparent connection to our girls," Johnnie said. "But I'm still coming up with nothing on these three. How about you, Boggs? Anything?"

"Nothing." Boggs shook her head. "And they all bought at the same shop. I think we need to pay this guy a visit. Seems like he doesn't keep accurate records."

"Have you got anything going on in the morning?" Johnnie asked Boggs. "We could take a ride down there and scare the shit out of him."

"Sounds like fun," Boggs said with a grin. "Let's take pictures of our girls with us. I can stop by work in the morning, then meet you."

Vicky looked at her watch. It was late and she was tired. "Okay, ladies, it's getting late. Do we have our bases covered for tonight?"

"Rachel is staying at Anne's," Toni said. "And she's not going to leave the house tomorrow. I told Anne we'd keep her updated."

"And I've got people sitting on each address," Johnnie added. "Including here."

"Good," Vicky said. "But I don't think Toni should venture out on her own. And that means driving to work in the morning."

"I'll be fine," Toni said. "Especially if Johnnie has some of her people watching each of the houses. They can call me if Cindy, Nancy or Bert leaves before morning, okay?"

"I guess so," Vicky said. "Make sure your people have our phone numbers," she said to Johnnie. "And then you and Boggs can let us know if you find out anything at the ammo shop tomorrow. And maybe Frank will find something at the parking garage. I guess that covers everything for now. Do you all want to meet again tomorrow?"

They all agreed and began collecting their coats. Suddenly Toni pulled Vicky aside.

"You guys go ahead," she said to the rest. "I just want to chat with Vicky for a minute."

After they left, Vicky looked at her, curious as to why Toni kept her back. "Are you okay, hon?"

"Sure. Thanks. I just couldn't deal with either one of them tonight."

Vicky assumed she meant Boggs and Johnnie. "I know it's been really hard, but it'll turn out okay." She gave Toni a hug and headed toward the door. "Now, double-lock this thing, will you?"

"I will. See you tomorrow."

Chapter 26

The woman woke up very early Thursday morning. She fixed a pot of coffee and was waiting for it to brew. Things had gotten out of control. She missed an entire day of work because of that bitch, Rachel. She had lost her focus and that wasn't good. It wasn't good for her and it wasn't good for Toni. She needed to think. She still had a feeling that she'd forgotten something, or lost something, but she didn't know what. She paced back and forth across the kitchen floor until the coffee was ready. It smelled absolutely delicious. As she poured herself a cup, she took a deep, slow breath of the aroma. She closed her eyes and imagined her and Toni sitting in the kitchen on a lazy Sunday morning, enjoying a cup of coffee. They would be laughing and talking, looking deep into each other's eyes and planning their future. This was what it was all about.

She glanced around the loft. Their loft. It still needed a lot of work and she had been neglecting it. She looked at her calendar. It was a week and a half until Easter and Toni had been so excited about Easter. It would be perfect if she could finally bring Toni to their home on Easter. Yes, Easter.

She took out a pad of paper and refilled her coffee cup. Just for fun she got out her special mug that said *Toni*. She set it next to her on the table and began her list of things to do. She still had to put up crown molding, paint the living room, paint the kitchen, paint the bedroom, refinish the kitchen cabinets, lay the kitchen floor and hang pendant lights over the kitchen island. She needed to buy some new bed linens and towels and make sure the refrigerator was stocked. Oh, she still needed to take care of that bitch Rachel, but she would do that later, maybe over the weekend. She knew where she lived. It wouldn't be hard at all.

All this work on the loft was going to take more than one weekend to complete. Maybe if she took some time off work she could get it done. It probably wouldn't be a problem. She could call in sick today, then she'd work on Friday. She'd put in for next Thursday and Friday. That should give her plenty of time.

She poured herself another mug of coffee and smiled. This was going to work out just perfect. She looked at her watch. She still had to wait at least an hour before she could call in sick. That would give her enough time to get the walls prepped for painting. She already had the paint and supplies. This was going to be a great day.

Toni was ready to go to work. She peered out her blinds and thought she spotted an agent in a car across the street, but she couldn't be sure. She felt incredibly stupid, but she called Johnnie anyway. She answered on the second ring.

"Good morning," Johnnie said. "Is something wrong?"

"No." Toni took a sip of coffee. "I think I'm just being a little paranoid. I think I see one of your agents in a car across the street, but I'm not sure. Have any of our girls left their homes this morning?"

"Hang on. I'll check and call you back."

The phone rang less than five minutes later.

"No one has left," she said without preamble. "But the agent outside your place said he saw you peek out your blinds."

"Great." Toni looked out the blinds again, tempted to wave. "I bet he thinks I'm a crazy person, just like the one we're trying to find."

"No, I don't think so. You're just being careful, which is what's going to keep you safe." Johnnie paused. "How are you doing otherwise?"

"Okay, I guess."

"Well, I was wondering if, um, and it's okay if you say no . . ."

"Wondering what?"

"Um, if you'd want to go out for dinner or something, maybe Friday? Or if you're serious with Boggs, just say the word and I'll back off completely. Or if you just don't want to, that's okay, too." There was an awkward silence for a moment. "Shit, I'm sorry. I think this came out wrong."

"No, it's okay," Toni said. "Actually, Boggs and I aren't seeing each other anymore."

"Really? Great. Oh, I mean, shit. There I go again. I'm sorry."

"No apologies needed." Toni was actually flattered. "I'm just not sure I'm ready to really date or anything."

"Oh, I understand. Again, I'm sorry, Toni. I really stuck my foot in my mouth. Forget I said anything, okay?"

"No, Johnnie. I mean, heck. Why don't we have dinner? I mean, we've got to eat, right? I'd feel safer having you around, and I do enjoy your company, so let's do dinner Friday. Any place in particular you want to go?"

"Anywhere you want to go is fine with me," Johnnie said

quickly.

"How about Aunt Hattie's? I don't think we'll run into any of our suspects there."

"Perfect. Is seven o'clock okay with you?"

"That would be great," Toni said. "I guess I better go to work now. And I guess I'll see you tonight, right?"

"Oh, yeah. I think Vicky said we should meet at seven. I'll see you later."

Toni was shaking her head when she hung up the phone. What the hell was she thinking? Did she really want to get involved with Johnnie?

She thought about Boggs and how she had basically informed her she had been a casual fling. It still hurt like hell. She could feel the tears beginning to well up in her eyes.

How could she have been so stupid to think that Boggs felt about her the way she felt about Boggs? She realized she'd been falling in love. And she guessed she'd just assumed that Boggs was falling in love with her too. Why couldn't she just let things go on as they were instead of driving Boggs away? Now she was gone. *Idiot. I'm such an idiot.* Well, never again. She was just going to go out and have fun. Hadn't she told herself months before she even met Boggs that she'd probably always be alone? Why had she thought that had changed? *Idiot. Idiot.*

With this new resolve, Toni grabbed her keys and briefcase and headed out. She was determined to be one of those people who could lead a carefree and happy life and not worry about being tied down to any one person. As soon as this mess was over she was really going to live it up for once in her life. If she kept repeating this to herself, maybe even she would believe it.

By ten o'clock that morning, Toni had gotten the word that Cindy had called in sick and that none of their suspects had left their homes. This didn't help at all.

"We're still back to the same three," Toni said to Vicky on the phone.

"I know. I think it's weird that none of them went to work and none have left their homes," Vicky said. "Maybe Boggs and Johnnie will figure out something when they go to the ammo store."

"Oh, shit," Toni said. "I forgot they were going this morning."

"So?"

"Well, I guess it's nothing," Toni said.

"Puke it up, girl. What's going on?"

"I sorta told Johnnie this morning that I'd have dinner with her tomorrow night," Toni confided. "Do you think she'll say something to Boggs?"

"Ohh . . ." Vicky said. "That could be awkward, huh?"

"Just a bit. But, jeez, Boggs basically told me to go out and date the girls' football team, you know?"

"I know, hon. I know," Vicky said. "Boggs can be a shit, that's for sure. So, are you really interested in Johnnie?"

"Well, she is really attractive. And I enjoy talking with her," Toni admitted.

"But there's nothing else?"

"I don't know." Toni bit her lip. "It was stupid of me to agree to go out. When I met her the first time, in law school, I fantasized about her. I was with Sadie at the time, so obviously that went nowhere. When she asked me out this morning, well . . . I just thought about Boggs, and I guess maybe I was mad, or something. Oh, Vicky. I've made such a mess of everything, haven't I? I drove Boggs away, didn't I? I must have. Things seemed to be fine, then *boom*, she's off and running. I'm such an idiot."

"You've got it bad for Boggs, don't you?" Vicky asked.

"Yeah, I do. Or at least I did. There's not much I can do about it now, is there? I can't make someone feel something they don't feel, right? I might as well just get on with my life."

"Sometimes things work out for the best in the end," Vicky

said. "Don't ever give up on your hopes and dreams, okay? Now, let's get back to the big issue here. What are we going to do about this crazy woman of yours?"

"I think we should ask Cathy to come over again." Toni liked that idea. "She might have something new. But if not, at least it's another avenue we can look into, don't you think?"

"Sounds good to me," Vicky said. "Patty gave me her number. I'll call her right now and we'll meet at your house at seven unless you hear different, okay?"

"Okay," Toni said. "And thanks, Vicky. For listening, I mean."

"No problem, hon. I'm here for you anytime. Just quit worrying. We'll figure this all out."

Toni felt much better after talking to Vicky. She still didn't know what she was going to do, but it didn't seem as big as it had just minutes ago. She busied herself with work and the day passed quickly. There had been no word from Johnnie or Boggs all day. Well, she thought, at least she'd see them tonight and find out if Boggs knew about the date with Johnnie or not. She wasn't really looking forward to the evening, but Vicky would be there to help her.

Chapter 27

"Anyone want a beer?" Toni asked everyone. They all said yes. They ate and drank while chatting about nothing in particular.

After a bit, Cathy set her beer on the coffee table, took out a notebook and said, "Thanks for letting me take your things home with me. I was hoping to get something that related to this issue, but that only happened with Toni's ring." She handed Patty her necklace. "The strongest thing I got from this was odd. The only analogy I can come up with would be rewrapping a gift. It's the same thing underneath, just in a different wrapper."

Patty looked puzzled, but Toni grinned and said, "This is almost like a party game. No offense, Patty."

"None taken." Patty laughed. "Sometimes it's a real guessing game. What do you think it means?"

"Well, you'll be taking your detective's test in a few weeks.

That could mean you'd get a promotion. Same Patty, but not in a uniform. You'd be wearing the department blazer, right?"

"Hey," Patty said, "that sounds good to me."

"It doesn't mean you don't have to study," Vicky added. "Remember that."

Cathy handed Vicky her pinky ring. "This was interesting," she said. "You lost two things. One is a key, which is in a small blue box with a raised top. Like a cameo or something on top. The other thing lost is more like a passion, or a belief. Finding the key in the box will help you find the other. Does that make sense to you?"

Vicky was clearly stunned.

After a couple minutes, Toni reached out and touched her arm. "Are you okay?"

"Um, yeah," Vicky said. "That's amazing. I mean, wow." She looked at Cathy and smiled. "Thank you. Thank you very much. I know exactly what you're talking about."

Cathy nodded, then pulled the silver coin from her leather pouch and handed it to Boggs. "There is a lot of good energy in this coin."

Boggs nodded and put it back in her wallet. She said nothing else.

"And here's your class ring," Cathy said to Toni, who slipped it back on her finger. "It's moving you in a new direction," she added. "As to the current problem, I'm still feeling a warehouse of sorts. And I still hear that sound, like a tin bell. *Ting, ting, ting.* Three times. I don't know what that means. There also seems to be a slight lull, or a delay, as though nothing is going to happen for a bit. But I don't know how long that will be. Time is very difficult to interpret. It could mean two days, two weeks or much longer. Sorry. And last, there's also a sense of danger—but it's in regard to driving the wrong direction. The only way I know to explain it is if we said, 'Let's go to the bar,' but we turned south on Tucker instead of turning north. And we didn't realize we were going the wrong direction until it was too late. I know that's not much to go on, but it's the feeling I'm getting. I'm still no expert on this stuff, guys. I still have a day job, you know." She laughed.

"Oh, I think you've done a wonderful job," Toni said. "We have two of our suspects with a warehouse connection and all of them smoke cigarettes. We'll figure out more, you'll see."

"Well, I hope something will help," Cathy said. "I wish I could hang out, but I've got to hit the road. Thanks for the beer and pizza." She motioned for Boggs to follow her to the door.

Curious, Boggs got up and helped Cathy on with her coat.

"Your coin," Cathy murmured. "A lot of good energy."

"Yeah." Boggs shrugged. She wasn't quite sure what that meant, but she believed it.

"But I wanted you to know that just because things have always been one way doesn't mean they have to always be that way in the future. Like your coin, it represented one dollar in its inception. Then it was given to you by your father. Then it meant a dollar and the belief that you would always have money. Now it represents a dollar, sure . . . but more than that, it represents a strong bond you had with your father. It's changed because you've changed. To anyone else, this coin still represents one dollar, but not to you. Does that make sense? You've changed?"

Boggs just nodded. Cathy smiled and touched her arm. Then she waved good-bye to the rest and was out the door. Boggs slowly made her way back to the couch and the conversation.

"That's right," Vicky was saying. "We'll get a handle on this shit. But in the meantime, let's just have a drink and try to relax for once. Oh, what did you guys find out at the ammo store?"

"Nothing," Boggs replied as she sat down on the far end of the couch. The spot farthest from Toni. She pushed what Cathy had said from her mind and continued, "The owner wasn't there today and the asshole who was working said he was on vacation until next week. He could barely walk and talk at the same time. We looked at his records and they were a mess. Johnnie scared the shit out of him by flashing her shiny FBI badge. That was definitely worth the trip."

Johnnie was laughing. "Yeah, the guy was shaking so bad I thought he was going to have a seizure."

"Johnnie threatened to check into his credit and ownership of his piece-of-shit car. He would have given up his grandmother if it meant we'd leave him alone," Boggs said. "Johnnie 'borrowed' the records and told him to contact the owner. We'll try again later."

"Ah, the fun of being an FBI agent," Vicky said. "Scare the crap out of almost anyone."

"Well, we have to have some perks," Johnnie said. "Aside from the great salary and retirement package."

"Okay," Vicky interrupted. "Enough of the recruiting spiel. Is there anything else we can do?"

Before anyone could answer, Vicky's cell phone rang.

"Hey, Frank," she said. "What's up? Did they get a print? Shit. Okay, thanks for the update. Tootles."

"What did they find?" Toni asked.

"The crime scene guys found a shell casing at one of the parking garages at the university. It was apparently run over and in bad shape, but in my opinion there's no question it came from our girl."

"No print, huh?" Boggs asked, thinking they desperately needed to identify this shooter.

"Just a partial." Vicky took a swig of beer. "But at least we know the casing's from a sniper rifle."

"Well, the partial might be enough if we have something to match it to. Or maybe eliminate someone," Johnnie said. "Do all our girls have prints on record?"

"I know that Nancy and Bert do," Patty said. "But I think that Cindy's stuff was all juvie."

"Don't you all require prints to work at Metro?" Johnnie asked.

"We should," Boggs said, "but we don't. They shouldn't be too hard to get, though. I mean, she works in the same building. We could use a soda can or something."

"Why not just ask her straight out?" Toni suggested. "We could have Sam ask her. Tell her it's to eliminate her prints from some we found on the first letters from the anonymous letter guy. None of us used gloves on the first few letters. I could give my prints at the same time so there wouldn't be any suspicion on her part."

"Excellent," Johnnie said. "You should really get out of the lawyer business and start your own detective agency."

"Incredibly funny," Toni said. "It's just that most people will bend over backward if they think they're helping, but they'll put up roadblocks and become defensive if they don't trust you or think you've got some other agenda."

"I'll let Sam know tomorrow morning," Boggs said. "Hopefully she'll be in. Hey, did she say how she was sick? I mean, you know, a cold, flu, hangover?"

"Not that I know of," Toni replied. "I just heard from Phoebe that she called in sick. I didn't ask for details."

"I guess that's all we can do for now," Vicky said. "I'd love to be able to match the prints somehow, or at least get something solid on one of these people."

"Okay," Toni said. "I have an idea. Like Johnnie said, we need to draw this person out."

"We're not using you as bait," Boggs said sternly. "No way."

"No, not bait. At least not really." Toni smiled. "If the ring set her off, let's put her at ease a little. That should buy us a little time. And if what Cathy said is true, maybe there will be a lull, long enough for us to find something concrete to work with."

"What are you suggesting?" Boggs asked.

"What if I talk to each of them again? I can show them I've got my ring back. Maybe tell them I lent it to a friend for good luck. On an exam or something. If she's done her homework, as she obviously has, then she'll know that Rachel is in school. This might also keep Rachel out of harm's way."

"I can see how that might help us," Vicky said. "But I think you'll need protection. How can we go about this without her making a move, or becoming jealous if she thinks you're out with someone?"

"It would have to be someone she doesn't know, if we're talking about me having a bodyguard of sorts," Toni said. "And someone who she wouldn't feel threatened by."

"What about your friend Jake?" Vicky asked. "A gay guy shouldn't feel like a threat to her."

"No," Boggs answered immediately. Jake was the last person she'd recommend as a bodyguard. All eyes turned toward her. "I mean, he doesn't have any experience in protection, right?"

"She's right," Toni said. "Anyway, he's out of town for two weeks, so that won't work."

Boggs suddenly had an idea. "What about a relative? I don't mean a real relative, but someone you could introduce as a cousin or something. In town visiting for a week. That wouldn't be threatening at all. And one week should give us enough time to really concentrate on each of these women and hopefully come up with something solid."

"I like that idea," Toni said. "It would look perfectly normal for my 'cousin' to be with me, tagging along all the time."

"But there's one obstacle," Boggs said. "Our girl definitely has the ability to find information about someone. Take Rachel, for example. The news was on at six o'clock and by the next morning she had figured out who Rachel was and found out that she took classes at the university."

"Finding out that kind of information is not as hard as you'd think." Johnnie sighed. "I can make up an identity and I could do it pretty fast, but it won't be in-depth. Enough for the first couple layers of digging, but then it would end. What do you think?"

Boggs mulled it over. "You mean the 'cousin' could look like she's actually Toni's cousin, but if you dug any further then there would be no past?"

"Exactly." Johnnie snapped her fingers. "If we make her a little younger it would be easier. How about someone in graduate school?"

"Perfect," Toni said. "She could be visiting me on spring break."

"All I need is the name of an aunt and uncle, preferably ones that live out of town and are old enough to have a kid in graduate school."

"Aunt Doozie," Toni answered immediately. "She's my favorite aunt and she lives outside San Diego."

"Did you say 'Aunt Doozie,' or did I hear you wrong?" Vicky asked.

"Yes. Aunt Doozie. It's a nickname I gave her when I was a kid," Toni explained. "She has always been the 'cool' aunt. You know the type. The one who treats you like an adult when you're a kid? The one who actually seems to care what you think? Anyway, she lives out in California and has two grown kids. She could have a kid in graduate school."

Toni gave the specifics to Johnnie, who keyed in several bits of information into her laptop.

"Now all we need is someone to play the part," Vicky said. "Any ideas?"

"Ideally," Johnnie said, still clicking away on her laptop, "it's someone new in town. We don't want to run the risk of her being somehow known to one of our girls. And she needs to have some police or military background, know a little about protection and know how to handle herself in a crisis."

"Agreed," Boggs said gruffly. Experience, in her opinion was most important.

"What about someone just out of the police academy?" Patty suggested. "I know they don't have a lot of experience, but they'd be really eager. There were several in my class who came from other areas and had no connections to Fairfield. And the last class just graduated Saturday."

"That's an idea," Vicky said. "I'll call Captain Billings and see what he thinks. But that means we'd have to bring him in on this. I don't think that would be a problem, though. Anne is up-to-date on what's going on and would back us up. And anyway, if it meant we could stick it to the feds, Captain Billings would be all over that! Nothing personal, Johnnie, but you guys kind of squeezed him out of his own turf on this murder investigation."

"I know," Johnnie said. "And I don't blame him one bit. In fact, if I could apologize to him off the record, I would."

"Let's give it a try," Boggs said. "As long as we're sure Toni is protected." She couldn't bear the thought of anything happening to Toni.

Vicky grabbed her cell phone and dialed the captain as she walked out of the living room. She was on the phone for fifteen minutes before returning to the group. "I gave him the full account of everything we know so far. He seemed a little miffed that we kept him out of the loop for so long, but he agreed with our plan. He's going to make some calls and see if there's anyone from the graduating class that fits our needs. But he's only giving us one week, then he's pulling the plug."

"That sounds fair," Boggs said.

"More than fair," Vicky said. "I mean, we really don't have shit so far to even really point at these three. Most bosses would have called me on the carpet for what we've done so far, and maybe even fired me. But if we can figure out who killed the judge and Butch and make the feds look foolish, I think Captain Billings would be most grateful, off the record, of course."

225

Boggs grabbed another beer and everybody finished off the pizza.

Vicky's cell phone rang a while later and after about five minutes, she disconnected. "He's come up with two candidates. One male and one female."

"Female," Toni said immediately. "Aside from the obvious inclination I have"—she chuckled—"it would also make more sense that a female cousin would stay with me. And she could easily go with me into bathrooms or one of the bars."

"She's right," Johnnie agreed.

Boggs reluctantly agreed. She didn't like the thought of anyone being that close to Toni and the remark about the bathrooms hit a nerve with her.

"Well, that's good," Vicky said, "because I already told Captain Billings that we'd go with the female, so thanks for your input." She rolled her eyes. "Anyway, her name is Jessica Taylor. She's twenty-four and did a year stint in the army as an MP. Captain Billings said she graduated top in her class and he thinks she'll jump at this assignment."

"Perfect," Toni said. "What's the next step?"

"She'll be assigned to me for special duty. We do the same kind of thing when we need additional protection when a VIP comes to town or something. Anyway, Captain Billings is going to call her now and he'll call me back if everything is good."

"This is going to be strange," Toni said. "I mean, I know I had protection last fall, but at least I knew you guys. I felt comfortable. This will mean that I'm going to have a complete stranger in my house. What if we don't get along?"

"Well," Vicky said, "it's only for one week. And we get to meet her first. Captain Billings is just going to give her a vague idea of the assignment. Then we'll meet her and if we feel like it'll work, we'll clue her in on the details. Does that make it sound a little better?"

"Yeah," Toni said. "I guess so."

Vicky's cell phone rang again. "It's her," she said. "Detective Carter," she answered in her professional voice. She spoke for a few minutes and then gave directions to Toni's townhouse. "She'll be here in about fifteen minutes," she announced when she hung up. "She's got all the things we'll need, so it's just going to depend on our gut feeling about how she'll mesh with us. Let's just ask her some basic questions and get a feel for her personality, okay?"

"Okay." Boggs nodded. She hated the idea of Toni being in danger. She was going to make damn sure this rookie could handle herself in a dangerous situation. She remembered last fall when she'd been assigned to protect Toni, and she began to worry that the young police cadet would find Toni attractive and make a move.

The doorbell rang exactly fifteen minutes later and Toni let Vicky answer it.

"I'm Detective Vicky Carter," Vicky said as she shook the young woman's hand. "Let me take your coat and introduce you around."

The young officer handed over her coat and remained standing. She was about five feet eight inches tall with a lean build. Her dark brown hair was cut short with a style that looked like she just got out of bed.

Toni could feel the woman's nervousness from across the room. She approached her and smiled. "Officer Taylor, my name is Toni Barston, but please call me Toni." She shook her hand. She felt her relax just a bit. "This is my home. I'm glad you could come over tonight on such short notice. I know it's late. Can I get you a soda or something to drink?"

"No, thank you, ma'am," she said. "I'm fine."

"Do you mind if I call you Jessica?"

"I actually go by Jessie," she said quietly.

"Then Jessie it is," Toni said.

The rest of the women stood and introduced themselves. Toni gestured for everyone to sit down. Jessie even sat at attention.

"Can you tell us a little about yourself?" Vicky asked.

"Well," Jessie began, "I joined the army when I was seventeen and I was stationed at Fort Bragg. I was a military police officer. I've been working on my bachelor's degree in criminology and computer science. I'm fifteen hours short of my degree, which I plan on completing here in Fairfield. After my enlistment was up I went to the police academy."

"Where were you raised?" Toni asked.

"In Kansas City, the suburbs, on the Kansas side." She crossed her legs.

"Do you know anyone here in Fairfield, or have you ever been here before you started at the academy?" Boggs asked.

"I only know the guys in my class," Jessie said. "And I had never been to Fairfield before the academy."

"What brought you to Fairfield?" Toni asked.

"Well, the academy has a great reputation."

"And?" Toni prompted.

"I wanted to get away from my parents," Jessie said quietly.

"Problems?" Vicky asked.

"Not really. It just seems to work out better when I'm not living in the same general area. I stayed with them for a month when I got out of the army. That was enough."

"I can totally relate," Boggs said. "I find that four hundred miles is the best for me."

Mr. Rupert approached the new visitor. He sat on the coffee table and cocked his head to one side as he looked at her. Jessie smiled as she presented her hand for Mr. Rupert to sniff. He complied, then licked her hand.

"You've just been approved of by Mr. Rupert," Toni explained.

"He's beautiful," Jessie said. "And, well, he's a really big guy." She seemed to relax just a little bit more. Toni nodded to Vicky, who looked at Boggs, Johnnie and Patty with a slightly raised eyebrow. Each nodded almost imperceptibly.

"Captain Billings said you're up for a special assignment," Vicky said.

"Yes, ma'am." Jessie rubbed Mr. Rupert's head.

"Normally I'd be okay with a young police officer referring to me as ma'am," Vicky said. "But this assignment is a little different. We'll need to break you of that."

"Yes, ma'am," Jessie said. "I mean, yes."

"This assignment would require you to stay with Toni for a week," Vicky continued. "That means the only free time you'll have is a few hours during the day when she's at work. Will that be a problem for you?"

"No, ma'am. I mean, no."

"Great. Also, there's a good possibility that you'll have to go into a gay bar. Would you have a problem with that?" Vicky asked.

"Not a problem." Jessie shook her head.

"I'm gay," Toni said. "Will that be a problem for you?"

"Not at all." Jessie started to say more but Boggs stopped her.

"None of us care what your orientation is," Boggs said. "That's your business and it isn't important. We're not the army. We just want to make sure nothing interferes with your assignment. We need you to feel comfortable around Toni and not blow your cover, because that could put her in danger. That's our main focus here."

"I understand completely," Jessie said confidently. "And if you allow me, I won't let you down."

"You'll be fine," Vicky said. "Let me give you a rundown on what's going on." She took about twenty minutes to explain the situation, interrupted several times by Toni and Boggs, who added details.

229

"So what do you think?" Toni asked. "Can you do it? It means you and I are going to spend a lot of time together for a week."

"I'd be honored, ma'am. I mean, Toni."

"How long will it take you to set up her identity?" Vicky asked Johnnie.

"I can have it by tomorrow afternoon," Johnnie answered. "We'll keep your first name and change your last name to Phillips, same as Toni's Aunt Doozie. I'll have you enrolled in grad school at the University of Kansas. What would you like to study, Jessie?"

"Something close to my background, I suppose. It would be easier if someone asks me questions."

"What about a master's degree in sociology?" Toni asked. "That could incorporate criminology, and most people don't know what the hell it is. I think you could field most questions, especially if you're specializing in it."

"Done," Johnnie said when Jessie agreed. "Did you work anywhere in high school? Before you went in the army?"

"I worked at a pizza place," Jessie answered.

"Okay." Johnnie keyed in a few more things. "I've got you in here as working off and on through your college life at Big Cheese Pizza. I think that should just about do it. I'm going to use your current driver's license photo to make a new one for you. And a school ID. I'm pretty sure I can have these ready tomorrow. Oh, and I need your cell phone number. It shouldn't be a problem for you to keep the one you have. You won't be calling one of our suspects."

Jessie gave her the number and everyone put it in their own phones. They also gave Jessie their contact numbers.

"What about transportation?" Toni asked. "In case our girl has the ability to run her plates, that won't match."

"I can get her a car," Johnnie said. "We've got untraceable plates from every state. I'll put Kansas plates on it. Anything else you guys can think of?"

"That sounds like about it," Vicky said. "Now, when do we start?"

"The sooner the better," Toni said. "We want to get the message to our girl that the ring was not what she thought it was. That means tomorrow. How about having Jessie show up at work tomorrow? As long as Cindy doesn't call in sick, that is. Then we need to arrange to 'run into' Nancy. Maybe at city hall. She's always going to meetings there. Can we find out what's on the agenda there tomorrow?"

"I can do that." Boggs motioned for Johnnie to use her laptop.

"The only one left is Bert," Toni said. "We could go there after work. She seems to always be working."

"There's a meeting at city hall at three o'clock tomorrow. It's regarding that new city park resolution," Boggs said. "And Nancy is scheduled to speak. That would be perfect. If you guys could show up for some reason around two forty-five, I'm sure you'd run into her."

"I could just be showing my cousin around," Toni said. "No problem."

"Well, that's all set then," Johnnie said. "Jessie, if you could come by my office tomorrow around one o'clock, I'll give you your new identification and hopefully your car. Then you could head to Metro."

Jessie nodded. "I'm really excited about having this opportunity. I won't let you down."

"You'll do fine," Vicky said. "Just go home and pack for a week. You'll be paid your regular salary plus four hours of overtime a day. I'm sorry we can't do better. But at least your meals will be paid for."

"The experience alone is all I want," Jessie said.

"I guess that's all for tonight," Vicky said.

Everyone got up to go. Again both Boggs and Johnnie seemed to hesitate.

"You guys go on," Vicky said and Toni was grateful she'd stepped in. "I need to make sure Toni has all the numbers, for Captain Billings and the squad room."

That seemed to do the trick, although Toni guessed that neither Boggs nor Johnnie believed that was the reason Vicky was staying behind. Neither questioned her statement.

"Thanks, Vicky, once again," Toni said after they'd left. "I don't know if Boggs knows about my date with Johnnie tomorrow. Oh shit, what about that? If I'm supposed to be with my cousin the whole week, how can I go out with Johnnie tomorrow?"

"Well, it'll be a little awkward, that's for sure." Vicky laughed. "I guess you'll just have a chaperone, that's all."

"Maybe that's for the best," Toni said. "I'll think about that."

"Yeah, sleep on it," Vicky teased. "Before you sleep with her."

"Very funny," Toni said, but she couldn't help grinning. "I'll talk to you tomorrow."

Vicky was still chuckling when she headed out the door. "I crack myself up," she was saying. "Lock the damn door," she called over her shoulder.

Toni did as instructed, then went to bed. This was going to be one hell of an interesting week.

Chapter 28

Toni was at her desk for only about a half an hour when Sam ambled into her office with a Diet Coke in his hand. He grinned. "Hiya, counselor," he said as he plopped down in her only other chair.

"Well, hey, Sam," she said. "What brings you down to this end of Metro?"

He winked. "I'm working on an Academy Award," he whispered. "Can you get Cindy to come in?"

Toni buzzed Cindy and she answered on the first ring. Toni asked her to come over to her office and she appeared in the doorway almost before Toni could hang up on her end. She looked expectantly from Toni to Sam.

"Hi, Cindy," Sam said after he took another long swallow of Diet Coke. "We found a partial print on one of the first anonymous letters. We need to take prints from both of you.

Hopefully our guy made a mistake when he first sent the letters."

"I guess that makes sense," Toni said. "Neither of us wore gloves for the first couple of letters. What do you want us to do?"

"I'll take you over to the crime lab," Sam said. He drained his soda and tossed it in the trash. "They can do it digitally, which means you don't get that ink all over your fingers," he explained. "We can go now if you've got about fifteen minutes to spare."

"I've got the time," Toni said. "Can you get away, Cindy? That way we can walk over together?" She smiled broadly at Cindy, who beamed at her in return and nodded.

The procedure was painless, and Toni thought Cindy was rather nonchalant about the whole thing.

The three returned about twenty minutes later.

Sam stopped at the vending machine to get another Diet Coke. "Thanks, ladies." He took his first swallow. "I'll let you know if we come up with anything." He winked again at Toni and then disappeared down the hall.

Toni used this opportunity to make sure Cindy noticed she was wearing her class ring. "It feels good to have this back on." She looked at her hand and lightly touched the ring. "I loaned it to a friend for good luck. She was taking a really tough exam at school. This ring always brought me good luck at school, so I loaned it to her. I think it must have worked. She left me a message this morning that she got an A on the test."

Cindy looked a little puzzled and Toni wasn't sure whether it was because she was the 'one' or that Toni was telling her this information. Either way, there was no doubt that the message had been received. She felt pleased with her performance.

She waited about thirty minutes before she went to Sam's office. As she passed Boggs's office she both wished she would see Boggs and hoped she wouldn't. She realized she had been holding her breath until she made it to Sam's door.

This is so awkward. She chided herself. How many times had she given the wonderful advice to others, "Don't get involved with someone you work with?" Was she going to feel this way every time she passed by the investigators' offices? *This sucks.*

At Sam's office door, she said, "Hi, handsome. Am I interrupting?"

"Not at all," he said. "Come on in. How did I do?"

"I definitely think you deserve an Academy Award," she said. "You have a whole new career ahead of you."

"Thank you so much." He laughed. "And I'd like to thank all the little people that made this possible." He took a swig of his Diet Coke.

"Sam," she said, shaking her head. "Why don't you bring in your own Diet Coke and put it in the fridge? You must spend a fortune every day at the vending machine."

"I know," he said. "I tried that once, but it disappeared on me. People would help themselves and I ended up spending more money supplying Metro with Diet Coke than I did just buying it out of the machine. And anyway, it made me cranky."

"Cranky? Why?"

"Because every time I saw someone drinking a Diet Coke I would wonder if they bought it or if they just swiped it from me. Not good. Work crankiness led to home crankiness and that made Betty cranky. This is better for all, believe me."

"Point well taken," Toni said. "So, about the prints. Did you send Cindy's to Johnnie?"

"Yup. All taken care of. And I got some info this morning from the lab. They got some epithelia from the last package. The DNA didn't match anyone in the system, so the only info we have is that it came from a male. I guess that means these things aren't coming from one of your girls. Sorry."

"Thanks, Sam. I guess this crazy letter guy is a whole other story," Toni said as she was leaving. "And don't forget us little people when you're rich and famous," she said as she walked away. She could hear him laughing as she headed back to her office.

It was a little after two when Toni got a call from Johnnie, who let her know that Jessie was on her way over and that everything was in place. She also reminded Toni of their dinner date.

"But what about Jessie?" Toni asked, wondering how this was going to work out.

"Oh, yeah," Johnnie said. "I can't believe that didn't click in my head."

"Why don't we just ask her along?" Toni suggested. "It would look strange if she wasn't with me, and we need to feed her anyway. Would that be okay?"

"Sure," Johnnie said with a hint of disappointment in her voice. "I'll come by at seven and pick you both up, okay?"

"Perfect," Toni said. "Now I'm going to go out by the secretaries' desks so I can make my big scene when my 'cousin' arrives. I'll talk to you tonight."

She was surprised at how relieved she felt. It was probably too soon for her to go out on a date, anyway. That was especially evident when she went into the bathroom. The memory of Boggs hit her like a ton of bricks. She closed her eyes for just a moment and she could almost feel Boggs's arms around her, her lips brushing hers. Tears immediately slid down her cheeks. A paper towel with cool water barely helped. After almost five minutes she was able to pull herself together and leave the bathroom. She knew she wasn't able to get Boggs out of her mind and decided the night's arrangement would work out just fine. A chaperone would be perfect. She'd hate to have had one too many glasses of wine and then make a fool of herself. A little tipsy plus an attractive woman paying attention to her? What was she thinking? She might have easily fallen in bed with Johnnie before she even realized what she was doing. Vicky was right. She needed to sleep on this before she slept with Johnnie.

Toni wandered into the secretaries' area. In less than five

minutes she saw Jessie coming down the hall, peering all around. She looked convincingly lost.

"Jessie!" Toni called out as she went toward her. "I can't believe you're here." She grabbed her and hugged her tightly, then whispered in her ear, "You haven't seen me in almost a year."

Jessie responded by hugging her back. She was wearing a gray University of Kansas sweatshirt, compliments of Johnnie, and jeans. Her backpack was slung over her shoulder. She looked every bit the part of a college student.

"This is so great," Toni said so that anyone near could hear. "We're going to have a blast this week."

Toni then led her over to Cindy's and Phoebe's desks. "I'd like you both to meet my cousin, Jessie," she said. "She's spending her spring break with me." Both women smiled and nodded to Jessie.

"Where do you go to school?" Cindy asked.

"KU," Jessie replied easily, pointing to her sweatshirt.

"Are you studying law like Toni?" Phoebe seemed genuinely curious.

"Heck, no," Jessie said, then laughed. "No offense, Toni. I'm working on my master's in sociology," she said to the women.

"I hope you have a great time," Phoebe said.

"Oh, I'm sure you'll have fun with Toni," Cindy added.

Toni ushered Jessie into her office and closed the door. She motioned to her spare chair and Jessie sat down. "Are you doing okay so far?"

"It feels a little strange, but I'm feeling great," Jessie said, excitement flashing in her eyes. "Agent Layton gave me my new identification and the loaner car. Boy, you should see all the stuff they have in her building. It's amazing."

"A little starstruck?" Toni smiled, thinking that Johnnie must have really impressed her.

"I guess so," Jessie admitted. "I never dreamed I'd be working on a special assignment and be involved with the FBI."

"Well, you can pick her brain at dinner tonight. We're going out, the three of us. She's picking us up at seven. But now we need to go to city hall and see if we can catch Nancy."

By three thirty they were back in Toni's office. Toni had been able to introduce Jessie and work her class ring into her brief conversation with Nancy. All in all it went smoothly, Toni thought, but Nancy seemed unphased by the ring story. Jessie sat in Toni's office reading a novel while Toni finished up some paperwork. At a few minutes to five they headed out. Toni gave her directions to The Cat's Meow.

"Wait about five minutes before coming inside," Toni instructed before they left. "That way I'll be able to tell Bert that I'm meeting you, and hopefully get in my spiel about my ring. Are you ready for this?"

"Absolutely," Jessie said, grinning. "I think this will be the first time I've ever been told to order a drink while I'm on duty."

Toni smiled. "I'll see you there."

When Toni walked into the bar she didn't see Bert. There was another woman behind the bar. *Shit. I can't believe she isn't working tonight.* Before she could figure out what to do, Bert strolled through the front door.

She nodded to the other bartender and broke out in a huge grin upon seeing Toni sitting at the bar. "Hi, Toni."

"Hey, Bert. Are you working tonight?"

"Yeah. I'm running a little late. Hang on a sec." Bert disappeared behind swinging doors and reappeared behind the bar. The other bartender left. "Can I buy you a drink?"

"No, you don't need to buy one for me. But I would love a glass of white wine," Toni said. "I'm meeting my cousin here. She's spending her spring break with me."

Bert poured the wine. "Hey, that's cool."

"Yeah," Toni said. "It's been a good week. Jessie is here for a visit and I gave a friend some 'luck' this week."

"Huh?" Bert looked puzzled. "How'd you do that?"

"Well," Toni explained, "she was taking this big exam at school, so I loaned her my class ring." She held up her hand to show the ring to Bert. "She called me this morning and said her professor gave her an A on the test. Pretty neat, huh?"

Bert reached out and touched the ring. "Wow. That's pretty amazing." Her touch lingered and Toni fought the urge to pull away quickly. Fortunately Jessie walked through the front door at that moment.

"Jessie!" Toni said a little loudly. This time Jessie took the initiative and hugged her first. "Have a seat." She motioned to the barstool next to her. "Jessie, this is Bert."

The two exchanged nods and Jessie ordered a beer. While Bert busied herself behind the bar, Toni and Jessie talked about movies and books. Toni also brought Jessie "up-to-date" on things in her immediate family. Within an hour they'd finished their drinks and waved good-bye to Bert.

Once outside, Toni complimented Jessie on her performance. "You almost convinced me that we're related," she said as they stood by their cars. "Now, let's head to my place so I can get out of these clothes."

Jessie laughed. "I'll follow you," she called over her shoulder.

Chapter 29

Toni unlocked the door to her townhouse, Jessie right behind her. She locked the door behind them and noticed how Jessie scanned the room before she'd even set her duffle bag down. Toni decided she needed to tell Vicky that Jessie was doing a good job. She left her keys and briefcase on the dining room table and fed Mr. Rupert.

"Make yourself at home," she said. "I'm going to take a quick shower."

She glanced back before heading upstairs. Jessie was bending down to pet Mr. Rupert. Toni immediately recognized the bulge in the small of her back and saw the holster as her shirt crept up.

"Oh, I don't think this is good," she said.

"What's the matter?" Jessie stood, suddenly very alert. Her hand went to her gun.

"It's okay," Toni said, holding her hand in the air. "It's just that you're carrying. And if I noticed, then someone else might notice."

Jessie quickly pulled her sweatshirt down and stared at the floor as though she'd just been reprimanded.

"Hey, Jessie," Toni said softly as she went toward her. "You didn't do anything wrong." She put her hand on Jessie's shoulder. "Really."

"But that would have totally blown my cover. It wouldn't make sense for a grad student to be carrying a concealed weapon. And maybe that could've gotten you hurt."

"Now we know," Toni reassured her. "Do you have an ankle holster?"

Jessie shook her head. "I just got this holster last week for my off-duty weapon."

"I bet Vicky has one you can use. I'll call her right now. Don't worry." Toni quickly dialed Vicky and explained the situation. "She's got a spare in her trunk," she told Jessie after she hung up. "She'll drop it off on her way home. No worries, okay?"

Jessie nodded.

"I'm going to take a shower. Let her in when she gets here, okay? And help yourself to the fridge. There's beer, soda, wine or water. I'll be back down in a few." Toni trudged up the stairs. Seeing the pancake holster in Jessie's waistband brought back vivid memories. She remembered the first time she and Boggs had made love.

They had been in Toni's living room, very near where Jessie had been standing. Boggs had come slowly toward her, their gazes locked. Boggs had removed her holster and gun, placing it on the back of the couch. Toni had never felt so aroused in her life. The memory made her catch her breath.

As she took off her clothes in the bathroom, she relived that moment. She stepped into the shower and let the cascading water flow over her. Several minutes later she realized that she had lost Boggs, and once again the tears streamed down her face.

She tried to control her emotions but the pain was too great. She let herself sob until the water began to cool. She blinked away the final tears and hurried to finish her shower before all the hot water was gone. By the time she was drying her hair, sadness had turned to self-criticism.

"What's wrong with me?" she mumbled. "Am I that unattractive?" She looked at her body in the mirror and admitted it could use some work. Was she lousy in bed? Was she boring? She wondered if any woman would want to be in a relationship with her ever again.

Maybe she should just become a player like Boggs, she thought. She smiled and began to apply gel to her hair.

May as well have "date" hair if she was going to play the field, she told herself. What the hell, may as well go for broke. She pulled her white denim blouse from its hanger in her closet and grabbed a pair of jeans. She found her lacy bra and dug around in her underwear drawer for sexy panties. She only had one pair. *Well, that's going to change.* She finished the look with boots, gold hoop earrings and a spritz of perfume. When she looked in the mirror she was satisfied except for the puffy red eyes.

Nothing a glass of wine wouldn't cure, she thought as she headed downstairs. She heard Vicky's voice before she saw her. It reminded her of what Vicky had said about the buttons on her shirt. She looked down and unbuttoned one more before rounding the corner at the bottom of the stairs.

"Hey, Vicky," she called out. "Want a glass of wine or a beer?"

Vicky was sitting on the couch with her back to Toni. She raised her arm to show she was already drinking a beer. Jessie was on the couch facing Toni and also raised her beer. Toni went into the kitchen.

Vicky didn't look at Toni but noticed Jessie's eyes following her. She turned and saw Toni over in the kitchen, opening a bottle of wine. Well, she thought, it didn't take a detective to notice the red eyes and revealing blouse. Or to realize that Johnnie might get lucky tonight. And it didn't take a detective to notice Jessie's reaction. She shook her head. Rebound could be hell. She plotted and acted quickly.

"Hey, Toni," she said casually. "Do you have any books or journals about that borderline personality that I could borrow? I want to learn more."

"Sure," Toni said as she finished pouring herself a huge glass of wine. She brought her glass into the living room and set it on the coffee table. Vicky got a quick flash as Toni bent over. "I've got a couple upstairs."

As soon as Toni hit the stairs Vicky scooted over to Jessie. "I saw you look at her."

Jessie's eyes got big, as though she just got caught.

"I don't care, but Toni is my friend. And she's in a dangerous place right now. And I don't just mean the crazy woman."

Jessie looked both alarmed and puzzled.

"Normally I'd never tell you this, but I need your help tonight. From the looks of that huge glass of wine and the outfit you just drooled over, she's rebounding hard. You need to know that Boggs just broke it off with her, and Toni is in love with her. In fact, Boggs loves Toni too, but she's too stupid to realize that right now. Anyway, I want you to run interference between Johnnie and Toni tonight. Don't let Toni do something she'll regret later. In other words, I want you to be like a pesky little sister and don't leave them alone. Consider it a part of your job as bodyguard. If you feel out of your league, just call me and I'll be there as soon as I can."

Jessie nodded. "I understand," she said. "I can do that. I wish I had a friend like you."

Vicky winked at her. "You're halfway there, kid. And thanks." She moved back to her original spot just as she heard Toni's footsteps on the stairs.

"This is all I could find," Toni said as she put the books on the coffee table. "The DSM-IV-TR gives you the criteria for a borderline personality disorder, and this other book gives you case studies. These two journals have some excellent articles."

"This is great, Toni. Thanks."

"I completed my mission of showing off my ring today," Toni told her. "Maybe that will buy us some time and hopefully keep Rachel out of the line of fire. I wish I knew which one of these crazies was our girl."

"We'll figure it out." Vicky glanced at the books. "But do you have a gut feeling about any of them?"

Toni thought for a bit, consuming about one third of her glass of wine. "Well, Bert definitely has the most red flags."

"And she touched your hand tonight," Jessie added, "at the bar. She reached out and touched Toni's ring and kept her hand there," she explained. "I saw it when I walked in."

"That made me uncomfortable, I'll admit," Toni said. "And there's the domestic violence in her past . . . and she lives in a warehouse. But Nancy is still in the running. Her extreme anger at her ex was almost palpable. And she's got a stalking charge. Not good." She downed the rest of her glass of wine and she went to the kitchen to refill her glass. "Do either of you need another beer?"

"I'm good," Vicky said.

"Me, too." Jessie raised an eyebrow to Vicky and glanced toward the kitchen.

As long as Jessie held up her end of the plan, things would probably go off without a hitch. But Jessie would only be able to do so much, especially if Toni kept drinking. Vicky shrugged.

Toni returned with her glass filled again to the rim. "You know what keeps bugging me the most? The tin bell. *Ting, ting, ting.* What the hell is that all about?"

As if in answer, just then the doorbell rang. Toni jumped up and quickly ushered Johnnie into the room.

"Hey, Vicky. Hi, Cousin Jessie," Johnnie greeted them. If she wondered why Vicky was there, she didn't indicate it.

"Want a drink before we go to dinner?" Toni asked.

"Sure. Beer sounds good."

"Where are you all going for dinner?" Vicky took a sip of beer.

"Aunt Hattie's. Want to join us?" Toni called from the kitchen.

"Nah." She had considered it for only a moment. "I've got some things to finish up, but thanks. Hey, Johnnie, did you get any more info for us today? Prints perhaps?"

"Unfortunately, no. There wasn't enough of the partial to make any kind of match. We're still stuck with our three girls. How about you, Toni? Did you eliminate anyone?"

"Not completely," she answered, handing Johnnie a beer. "From a therapist's point of view, Bert and Nancy are at the top of the list. They have the most indicators. The only thing we have on Cindy is that she smokes and was a wild teen."

"In that case, you better put me back on the list." Johnnie chuckled. "Guilty. But seriously, I guess we should concentrate more on Bert and Nancy."

"I don't want to jump to any conclusions," Toni offered. "But at this point I guess you're right. I wish it were all over. The best answer would have been if Sam found out that the anonymous letter guy is the one. That way we could just go on with our lives. And believe me, I'm ready to just move forward. Speaking of which, are you guys ready to eat?"

"I'm hungry," Johnnie said as she finished her beer.

Toni took everyone's empty bottles and downed the rest of her wine. "I hope you're driving," she said to Johnnie.

As they headed out, Vicky gave a quick wink to Jessie before she went to her car.

❧

Toni thought the dinner went pretty well. She'd had two more glasses of wine along with her fettuccini. The conversation had been lively on the surface, but under the table was a different story. Toni had sat next to Johnnie, their legs only inches away. At one point Johnnie had reached down and rubbed her leg. The touch was brief but potent. Toni was loving the attention.

Afterward, they ended up returning to Toni's townhouse.

"Anyone up for an after-dinner drink?" Toni asked.

Johnnie opted for a beer and Jessie went for a soda, clearly aware she was on duty. Toni poured herself more wine from the bottle she'd started earlier. The sexual tension between her and Johnnie was still palpable. Nothing had been said, for which Toni was grateful, but it was clear both were feeling it. Of course, she was feeling a little tipsy. When she came back into the living room, she handed out the drinks and flipped on the stereo. Norah Jones, one of her favorites, was in the CD player. That would have been perfect for a romantic evening, she thought, if there hadn't been a chaperone.

She tried to remedy the situation. "If you're tired, Jessie, you can sleep upstairs tonight," she suggested. "I oftentimes sleep on the couch down here."

"Oh, I'm not tired at all," Jessie said, smiling. "I'm having a lot of fun. Can I look through your CDs?"

"Sure," Toni said, disappointed. "Or we can watch a movie." She went to the closet and brought out her box of movies and put it in front of Jessie, who was sitting on the floor in front of her CD rack. As she went back to the couch, she brushed Johnnie's arm with her hand. When their eyes met, Toni smiled slightly and winked. On an impulse she kissed her lightly on the cheek. "Thanks for dinner," she whispered.

Johnnie scooted closer to her on the couch. "Let's watch a movie."

Of course, Toni thought, anyone who had ever been on a first date recognized what watching a movie could lead to. Lights off with only the glow of the television. Yup. No question there. Jessie picked through the box and chose a stupid comedy.

Toni sighed. No sense in making it easy. She popped it in the VCR and grabbed the remote. "Would you hit the light in the kitchen?" She looked at Jessie, willing her to leave the room.

"Can we leave it on?" Jessie asked. "My eyes get a little funky when the only light is the TV. I'd really appreciate it."

"Oh, sure." Toni picked up her glass of wine and settled back on the couch, a little closer to Johnnie than she had been before. It wasn't perfect, but at least she was close to Johnnie. She took a big gulp of wine.

After about twenty minutes Jessie announced she was going to the bathroom. "I'll be back in a second. Can we pause the movie?"

Toni complied and the house was suddenly very quiet.

As soon as Jessie left the room, Johnnie leaned over and kissed Toni's ear. "You smell wonderful," she whispered. She kissed her neck. "And taste even better. Do you think we can lose our escort?"

Toni felt her stomach flutter. It felt so good. She had noticed Johnnie looking at her all night. She'd tried to remember the fantasy she had long ago about Johnnie, but it seemed to be hazy and jumbled in her mind. All she knew was that the kiss on her neck felt good.

Jessie returned in record time. "I just love watching movies," she announced, way too chipper. "The only thing that would make it better is if we had popcorn. Is there any?"

"Um, I think so." Toni reluctantly pulled herself up off the couch. "Let me go check." She touched Johnnie's hair as she passed by. "You're in luck," she called from the kitchen. "I'll pop us a couple bags."

Johnnie had followed her into the kitchen. At last they were alone, Toni thought, putting the first bag in the microwave.

Then Johnnie's arms were around her waist, and Johnnie was kissing her neck again. Toni leaned back, closed her eyes and sighed. Johnnie's touch felt so good. Johnnie kissed her ear again. Toni felt her body react and she moaned quietly. The sound of the beeping microwave interrupted them.

"Gotta put another bag in," she managed to say. She dumped the first bag in a large bowl and took a bite. She decided they probably wouldn't need salt.

"Smells great," Jessie called from the living room.

Toni turned to face Johnnie and was caught by surprise.

It's Johnnie, not Boggs. What am I doing? What am I thinking? She'd felt those arms around her and all she could think of was Boggs. *Shit. I can't do this. I don't want to do this. Shit.* She took a step back and put the second bag in the microwave. Jessie was now standing in the doorway. Great, Toni thought. How long had she been standing there? Had she seen anything? Would she say something to Boggs? *Jeez.* If nothing else, how awkward must this be for her?

Toni opened the fridge and grabbed a can of soda. She'd had enough wine. "Anyone for a refill?" she asked. Jessie nodded and she handed her a Coke. The second bag finished and Toni divided it into two smaller bowls. She handed the first big bowl to Jessie, giving a smaller bowl to Johnnie and taking the last small one for herself. "Now we're set."

Back in the living room, she parked herself in the corner of the sectional couch and called Mr. Rupert, who hopped up next to her. The rest of the movie was awful. Laughing at the appropriate times, she hardly paid attention.

The problem was, she wasn't interested in Johnnie that way. She was more excited by the *idea* of Johnnie, not Johnnie herself. Truth be told, she was still in love with Boggs. How did she let herself get into this mess? She must have been feeling sorry for herself, she decided, and trying to prove something. How pathetic was that? You need to get a grip, she told herself. Boggs had moved on. Time, that's what she needed if she was going to get over Boggs. At least wait until this crazy person was caught and she could feel safe again. And acting like a teenager in front of Jessie, how embarrassing. She should apologize to her. She couldn't believe Jessie had stayed in the living room with her and Johnnie. It was almost like . . . oh. *Vicky.* She smiled. Vicky must have told her to babysit. Well, thank God. No telling what she might have done if Jessie weren't here. *I'm such an idiot.*

She barely noticed when the movie ended. She knew she should tell Johnnie that they needed to be friends only. It wouldn't be easy, but it was the right thing to do.

"I think I'd like to call it a night," she said as the movie was rewinding. Both Jessie and Johnnie seemed surprised. It was, after all, still early, just past ten o'clock on a Friday night. "Jessie, could you give us a minute?" She saw the hesitation in Jessie's face. "It's okay, really. I'll only be a minute," she said, motioning for her to go upstairs.

Jessie complied.

"I think we moved a bit fast and too far," Toni said once she and Johnnie were alone. "I don't think I'm over Boggs, and that's not fair to either one of us. I'm sorry."

Johnnie sighed. "That's okay. I understand." She kissed her cheek. "But if you ever change your mind, let me know, okay?"

Toni grinned. "Absolutely. And thanks again for dinner. It was really nice."

"Anytime," Johnnie said as she put on her coat. "And if you just want to talk or something, feel free to call me anytime."

"I will, Johnnie. Good night." Toni closed the door and called for Jessie, who'd been sitting on the stairs. "Jessie," she said, shaking her head. "First of all, thank you. I believe Vicky roped you into protecting me on a whole new level, and I really appreciate that. I'm sure that's not what you signed up for." She sat back down on the couch. "If you're not too tired, do you want to chat for a while?"

Jessie seemed relieved and sat down too. "It was a bit awkward," she admitted.

"Well, I can't tell you how much I appreciate what you did. I almost made a big mistake. I'll thank Vicky in the morning, or are you supposed to report in to her?"

"Oh, no. She just said to call her if I got in over my head."

"I'll tell her you went above and beyond the call of duty. So, tell me, how are you doing so far? Is there anything that you need?"

"Nope. I mean, no, thank you."

"Relax, Jessie. You're fine. You're my cousin, right? Think of me that way, okay? Maybe that will help. I'm not your boss, just a woman who has a crazy person after her. No big deal."

Both of them laughed and they ended up talking for the next hour. Toni got Jessie to open up and learned more about her life and her dreams. By the time Toni went to bed that night, she felt closer to Jessie and better about her decision to shut down Johnnie. She was still missing Boggs, but she felt as though she would survive.

Chapter 30

A week had passed and the woman thought she'd been very productive. Every night she worked diligently on "their" loft. It was almost done. Just a couple of final touches and it would be ready for Toni. She had decided that she would bring Toni over on Saturday. She could hardly wait. Toni was going to be so surprised and so grateful. Now they could be together forever. She had waited so long and now everything was going to be perfect. No one was going to interfere. And if anyone did, she would take care of it.

She thought about the truck driver, the judge and that lawyer. They had hurt her Toni and no one would ever do that again. Her hands and jaw clenched, just thinking about how they had hurt her girl. But as she relived the moments when she pulled the trigger in each "incident," the rage subsided and she felt peaceful and hopeful. God, she loved Toni. She was the most wonderful person in the world. She had helped out that Rachel girl, too. She was the best. And she was all hers.

She hummed to herself as she mopped the kitchen floor. She put on her new silk sheets and made sure everything in the bedroom was perfect. She would sleep on the couch tonight, so as not to mess up the bed. Assuming everything went according to her plan, the next time she lay on this bed, Toni would be right next to her. Like it was supposed to be. *Me and Toni. Forever.*

Chapter 31

The next week was fairly uneventful for Toni. That was a good thing and a bad thing. She and Jessie had hung around the house with Mr. Rupert over the weekend, just reading and watching television. Toni had talked to Vicky several times, the first time thanking her for her interference. There had been no new information regarding any of their suspects. And thankfully, no new murders.

Work had also been uneventful. Jessie drove her every day and picked her up in the evenings. Toni had only seen Boggs once in the office and that was from a distance. Her stomach had flopped several times, but Boggs hadn't seen her, so there had been no conversation.

By Friday afternoon, Toni was beginning to wonder if this whole thing was just a bunch of crap and that the murders were not related to her. Jessie arrived at the office early and she told her what she was thinking.

"Well, maybe," Jessie said. "But there sure were a lot of things supporting our theory." She paused. "Have you heard anything from Johnnie?"

Before Toni could answer, her phone buzzed.

"Agent Layton on line two for you, Ms. Barston," Chloe announced.

"Thank you, Chloe." Toni punched the button on the phone. "Hi, Johnnie. Any news?"

"Maybe we got a break," Johnnie said. "Let's meet at your place, okay?"

"What is it?" Toni asked, a little worried.

"I'd rather talk to everyone at once," Johnnie said. "Maybe I'm just jumping the gun. Can you call Vicky?"

"Okay, I'll do that now. Jessie and I can head over there in a few minutes." She disconnected and immediately called Vicky, who answered on the first ring.

"That sounds a little cryptic," Vicky said. "But maybe at least we'll have something to go on now. I'm hitting dead ends everywhere I look. I'll let Patty know. Want me to call Boggs?"

Toni hesitated. She had thought about calling Boggs herself. "Yeah," she said. "I guess that would be good. I'll see you pretty soon." She told Jessie, "Johnnie thinks she may have something."

An hour later, Johnnie arrived with her laptop in tow along with a few folders. Patty came next, then Boggs and Vicky. Toni noticed her heart beating faster when she saw Boggs in the doorway, and she thought she saw a momentary sparkle in Boggs's eye when she opened the door. *Don't be ridiculous*, she told herself. Boggs was way over it. *Get a grip.*

Johnnie wasted no time getting started. "Okay," she began. "I was at The Cat's Meow and I happened to notice Bert's SUV in the parking lot. I wandered by and one of the windows was rolled partway down. On the front seat there was a folder."

Vicky grinned. "In plain view, I assume?"

Johnnie nodded. "Anyway, the wind must have made it move a bit." She shrugged slightly and Toni knew the wind had nothing to do with it. "Inside were pictures of Toni. Some from the newspaper. I think from that deal last fall. And then there were several taken at the bar. Probably with a camera phone."

"So it's her?" Toni asked in disbelief.

"It looks like it to me," Johnnie said. "And we've got nothing on the other two. I mean, this is nothing concrete, but it's enough to put someone on her tail all the time. I had to pull the other agents off after last weekend. Now I want to put someone on this, officially. What do you all think? Have you come up with anything?"

"Not a thing," Vicky said. "This is the only clear indicator we've gotten. And she had a crapload of red flags from a psychological standpoint. And she does live in a warehouse like Cathy said . . . and she smokes. I think this must be our girl."

"What do we do now?" Jessie glanced at Johnnie.

"I'm going to lean on her," Johnnie answered. "I'm going to question her, see if she has an alibi for any of the murders. And I'm going to have her watched. I don't know what else to do at this point. If that doesn't work, we'll have to think of something else."

"Get her a little nervous," Vicky said. "Then I've got a plan. Tell her that she doesn't have a chance with Toni. Tell her Toni has a girlfriend."

"What?" Toni's jaw dropped.

"Hear me out." Vicky held up her hand. "I've read up a bit on this personality disorder. Tell Bert that Toni is staying with her girlfriend at Oak Hill and Tenth Street. We have a safe house, of sorts, there. We'll have Toni's car parked out there. She'll go there. We'll have one of our cops stop her when she gets there. No one can drive more than a block without breaking some traffic law. Believe me. I don't care if she's stopped for 'weaving within the lines,' we're going to stop her. And you can arrest someone for a traffic violation. You don't have to give them a ticket, especially if she has an attitude. That should give us enough for an inventory search of her car. I'm betting there will be a gun in there."

"You're stretching the law to its very limits," Toni said. "Not that I wouldn't love to put an end to this, but I don't know."

"Okay," Vicky said. "Maybe I went a little far. How about just letting her get to the house and see what she does? She can't be up to any good. We'll have our people inside."

"That sounds a little better," Toni said. "I still can't believe it's Bert."

"Let me call Captain Billings and set this up." Vicky made the quick call then hung up.

Toni listened as Vicky, Patty and Johnnie began planning the details of their operation. Jessie was sitting close to them, apparently trying to soak up any information or expertise that she could.

Feeling out of the law enforcement loop, Toni went to the kitchen. "Beer anyone?" she called. She heard a chorus of yesses as she opened the fridge.

Just then Boggs appeared in the doorway. "Need some help?"

"Um, sure. Thanks." Toni set the beer on the counter as Boggs got the opener out of the drawer.

"How have you been?" Boggs asked.

"Okay, I guess. You?"

"Okay." Boggs looked at the floor. "I bet you'll be glad when this is all over. Then you won't feel like someone's watching you. That must be an awful feeling."

Toni was surprised that Boggs remembered that. She wanted to reach out and hold her, but she resisted. "Yeah," she said. "I'll be really glad when this is over, but . . ." She suddenly felt sad. She knew she would rarely get to see Boggs when this was over. Plus, something just didn't feel right.

"But what?"

"I guess I'm just in denial." Toni shrugged. "I can't believe it's Bert, that's all. Maybe it's just women's intuition, and God knows mine doesn't work too well."

Boggs didn't seem to notice the sarcasm. "It doesn't feel right to you?"

"No, but that doesn't mean anything." Toni needed to get out of the kitchen. It hurt too much to be that close to Boggs. She picked up three of the beers and went in the living room.

Boggs followed her, bringing in the other beers.

"So," Toni said, "when do we do this?"

"I think we should do it tomorrow, late morning," Vicky said. "Bert doesn't go to work until later, but we need you to be somewhere other than here, just in case."

"I'll go into the office," Toni said. "But I'll need a ride if you guys are hijacking my car."

"I'll take you," Jessie offered. "Then I can take your car over to the house." She was grinning.

"And yes, Jessie," Vicky said. "You can definitely be in on this. As soon as you drop off Toni's car, Johnnie will go into her act. That way we don't risk having you get there too close to when Bert does. How does this sound to everyone? Are we forgetting anything?"

"I think this is going to work," Johnnie said. "I'm betting that we're going to find that Bert has a sniper rifle and that the ammo matches the results from both the judge and the lawyer. We're close, I can feel it."

"I think we've got it figured out. I guess that's about it then," Vicky said. "But I'd feel better if Jessie stayed here tonight. Just in case. Is that okay, Jessie?"

"No problem." Jessie grinned. "I'm getting used to the couch and Mr. Rupert."

Johnnie was the first to put on her coat and leave. Patty went with her. Vicky and Boggs left minutes later.

"I guess this is our last night together," Toni said to Jessie.

"Another movie and popcorn?"

"Sounds great."

Vicky and Boggs walked to Vicky's car.

"Are you okay?" Vicky asked.

"Sure."

"Boy, you're a lousy liar," Vicky said.

"Go to hell."

"You look like crap, Boggs. I saw you talking to her in the kitchen. What happened?"

"Nothing," Boggs muttered. "I wanted to wrap my arms around her and beg her forgiveness, but all I could do was ask her how she was. I'm such an ass. I think she hates me."

"I doubt that," Vicky said. "So you've finally realized that you love her?"

"Does it even matter? I totally screwed everything up. Just drive me home, will ya?"

"All right." Vicky unlocked the car doors. "Do you want to be in on this tomorrow?"

"No," Boggs said. "I think I'll sit this one out."

"Are you still thinking about going to see your mom?"

"Oh, hell, no." Boggs laughed. "I don't think I could stomach that on a good day, let alone how I'm feeling now. I think I'll just stay home and drink. That sounds healthy and productive, don't you think?"

"Absolutely," Vicky said. "But I'm only a phone call away if you need anything."

Vicky drove in silence. Out of the corner of her eye, she saw Boggs wipe a tear from her cheek. When Vicky pulled up in front of her apartment, Boggs didn't even turn around to say good night. She just got out of the car and waved as she walked away.

Chapter 32

Toni awoke on Saturday morning with a feeling of resignation, having cried herself to sleep the night before. Seeing Boggs was almost too much for her to bear. She realized how deep her feelings were. And now that this whole situation with the crazy person would be over by tonight, she would probably only see Boggs at work. At least she hoped so. It would be incredibly hard to see Boggs with someone else at one of the bars. The thought of it made her feel sick to her stomach. She went downstairs to make coffee and feed Mr. Rupert, but when she got there he was already washing his face.

Jessie was sitting at the table sipping a cup of coffee. "I hope you don't mind," she said. "I've been up forever."

"No, not at all. Thank you." Toni poured herself a cup of coffee. "Too anxious to sleep?"

"I guess so," Jessie said. "This is the first real police work I've done. I couldn't stop thinking about it all night. Do you think it will go down the way Vicky said?"

"Nothing ever goes the way we plan it," Toni said. "But I'm hoping it's close enough. And I'm sure you'll be glad to get back to your own life after babysitting me for a week."

"Not really. I've enjoyed this. I've learned a lot from you guys. It'll feel strange to not be around you guys all the time."

"You can hang out with us anytime, Jessie. Really."

"Thanks, Toni. You've been really good to me. This week has been great, talking to you every night. You've given me some great advice. Especially the part about coming out to my parents. I'm feeling better about that."

"Are you going to drive to Kansas City tomorrow after this is over? For Easter?"

"No, I don't think so." Jessie refilled her cup and added some milk. "I don't want to do this when other family will be around. Anyway, I'm supposed to start with my training officer on Monday."

"Then I hope you'll come with me to my folks' for Easter," Toni said. "It'll be fun."

"How can I pass up free food and candy?" Jessie said. "I'll be there."

Just then the phone interrupted them. It was Cindy, calling from the office. Toni wondered why she was working on a Saturday.

"Sorry to bother you at home," Cindy said. "I came in to work today to catch up on some things. There's a box on my desk addressed to you along with a note from human resources. Apparently it was delivered to them by mistake. Anyway, it's from your anonymous letter writer, I'm sure. And it's big. Want to come and see what it is?"

"I was coming down there anyway. I'll probably be there in about an hour. Go ahead and leave it on my desk if you're not there, okay?"

"Oh, I'll still be here," Cindy said. "Lots to do. See you then."

Toni shook her head. "Another fun package from Mr. Anonymous," she said to Jessie. "Since he sent me Peeps last time, maybe this is a chocolate rabbit."

"Lucky you," Jessie said. "Hey, do you mind if I shower while you drink your coffee. I want to make sure I'm ready. It'll only take me a few minutes."

"Take your time."

Forty-five minutes later, Jessie dropped her off in front of Metro. Toni walked down the street to get a latté from the doughnut shop. At the last minute she decided to treat herself to a chocolate cake doughnut, so she sat at one of the tables with her prize and stared out the window. There weren't many people downtown. She glanced at her watch. Johnnie should be talking to Bert about now, she thought, and Vicky and her people should be staked out in the safe house. If things went as planned, this whole ordeal could be over in a couple hours. She finished her latté and headed to Metro.

Cindy was drinking a soda and sitting at her desk when Toni arrived. "Hiya, Toni." She pointed to the box on her desk. "This is it. Want to open it?"

"No, you go ahead," Toni said. Cindy had already gotten gloves from the closet. She carefully cut open the tape and gently lifted the flaps. Toni was standing near her and peered inside.

"Looks like a giant chocolate rabbit," Cindy said. "And it's packed in that green Easter grass. How cute is that? Creepy, but cute."

Toni nodded. It was making her uncomfortable. Again there was the signature card, "T.W.M.A." *Why is this guy doing this? Something is wrong.* She looked inside again. "Is there something else in there?"

Cindy fished around in the bottom. "I don't think so. I don't

261

feel anything else. Do you want me to dump it out on the desk?"

"Nah. It's probably nothing. I'll just take it down to Sam's office."

"I'll walk with you." Cindy was by her side before Toni could object. "I bet Sam will be able to get something from the box."

Toni agreed and they walked to the investigator's area in silence. She wondered why Cindy always came in on Saturdays. Maybe she got behind in her work. Or was she just lonely and bored? Toni knew how it felt, wanting to be anywhere but alone at home.

"Hey, Toni. Can I ask you a huge favor?"

"What is it?"

"Well, this is kind of embarrassing," Cindy said. "But I got something in the mail yesterday. It's from some lawyers and it has to do with a workers' comp claim from my last job. It sounded like they were threatening me or something. I can't understand what it means."

"I'd be happy to look at it for you," Toni said. "I don't know much about workers' comp, but I'll give it a shot. Do you have it with you?"

"No, I left it at home."

"Bring it in on Monday then," Toni said.

"Could you look at it today? Please? I know I won't be able to sleep until I know."

"Do you want to go home and get it? I'll wait here," Toni said.

"How about if we just buzz over to my house? I only live a couple minutes from here. It will only take a few minutes," Cindy begged. "Please? You'd be doing me a huge favor."

Poor kid. Toni guessed it wouldn't hurt. She was supposed to stay out of the way for at least an hour anyway.

"I guess that would be okay," she finally said. Cindy beamed in response. "But you'll have to drive us. My cousin dropped me off."

"That's perfect," Cindy said. "I'm parked at a meter just out front."

They dropped the box in Sam's office and Toni scribbled a note to him.

"Let's go, then," Toni said.

They walked outside and got in Cindy's SUV. She started the engine and had to immediately turn down the country music. "Sorry. I guess I had it up too loud on the way here." She pulled out and headed down Tucker.

Toni was expecting her to go the other way. She almost said something but then realized that she would have no reason to know where Cindy lived. If it hadn't been for the investigation, she would have never known. "Where do you live?"

"Over in the warehouse district," Cindy answered easily. "It's only a few minutes from here."

Toni's insides froze. *The warehouse district. Going in the wrong direction.* They'd turned down the wrong way on Tucker. If Cindy lived where they'd thought she lived, she should have turned left. *Shit.* This was exactly what Cathy said. Cindy lit a cigarette. *And she smokes. Shit.* Toni told herself to stay calm. She'd look at the papers and then just say she needed to go back to the office and do some research on workers' comp.

Cindy pulled down an alley and stopped in front of an old warehouse. She hopped out before Toni could say anything. Toni watched her unlock the padlock and open the huge metal door. She got back in the SUV and drove inside. Then she got out and shut the door, opened a small door leading to the outside and padlocked the garage door again. Toni sat in the vehicle and looked around the space. It was empty. She'd expected at least some boxes on shelves or perhaps a piece of furniture or two. There was nothing.

"Come on," Cindy said. "Let me show you." She was beaming even more than usual.

Watch what you do and say. You'll be back in your office in no time.

Toni got out and shut her door. There was a sound. It was unmistakable. *Ting, ting, ting.*

What the hell was that? she wondered. She looked down and saw a shell casing next to the front tire. It rolled just a bit. *Holy shit.* It must have just fallen from the vehicle. *No question, now. It's Cindy. Shit.*

Apparently Cindy hadn't heard anything. She was standing near the stairs. "Come on. I want to show you." She pointed to the red welcome mat. "Isn't this great? Come on up."

Toni hesitated only a minute. There wasn't much she could do. There was no doubt in her mind that Cindy was the one. She couldn't risk offending her or upsetting her. She needed to just remain calm. The idea that no one knew where she was didn't help. She patted her cell phone in her pocket, not completely reassured. She followed Cindy up the stairs, surprised to see the loft.

"Wow, Cindy. This place is amazing," she said, sincerely impressed.

"I knew you'd love it! Let me show you everything. I've been working on it for a long time."

"You did this by yourself?" Toni noticed beautiful khaki-colored walls and the crown molding. There were several framed movie posters hanging in the living area and a white shag rug under her feet.

"Sure," Cindy said. "I can do almost any kind of construction."

She spent the next thirty minutes showing Toni every corner of the loft. She pointed out clever storage spaces, the kitchen cabinets, the hardwood flooring and the crown molding she'd painted in a glossy white to contrast with the khaki walls. The last place she showed her was the bedroom. Painted the same as the rest of the loft, it was furnished with a queen-sized bed. The satin duvet cover was a deep red, accented with white pillows.

"This is my favorite part," she said, blushing just a little. "I got brand new silk sheets for us."

Toni heard the "us" loud and clear but did not show any reaction. On the inside she was screaming. She tried to transition the conversation to safer areas. "They are lovely," she said, admiring the bedding. "You've done a wonderful job here, Cindy." She left the bedroom area and went toward the kitchen. "Especially in here. You should be really proud of yourself. But I want to see those papers you talked about. I don't want you to have to worry about what they mean."

"Oh, I never got any papers." Cindy giggled. "I lied. But not to be mean or anything," she quickly added. "I just wanted you to be surprised at your new home. Do you really like what I've done?" She seemed almost jittery with emotion.

"I think you've done an amazing job. This must have taken you a long time." Toni smiled, hoping to keep her calm.

"I've been working on it for months and months, Toni. But it's been worth every minute. I just want to make sure you like your new home. Do you?"

Toni was careful how she responded. *Never lie. They will always see through you in the end and that will just come back to bite you in the ass. Take a deep breath. You can do this. You worked with borderline personality disorders for years. Never quite this disturbed, but still.*

"I like your home, Cindy. It is beautiful."

"But it's not just my home," Cindy protested. "It's our home. For you and me. We can finally be together, Toni."

"I know you've worked very hard on this," Toni began, careful not to patronize her. "And I think it's very kind of you to want to share it with me, really. But I don't think I'm ready for a relationship like that."

"What the hell do you mean, 'not ready' for a relationship? After all I've done?" Cindy was beginning to pace.

Toni tried another angle. "I'm just starting out in my new job, Cindy. I need to give that my full attention. That's only fair to

Anne Mulhoney, don't you think?" She knew that Cindy admired Anne.

"Well," she said. "I guess that is only fair to Anne. She's a good boss." Cindy frowned a little.

Maybe she'd hit it right, Toni thought. If Cindy believed the reasoning—not to let Anne down—maybe she'd back off a little.

Cindy suddenly grinned. "But that's okay. We won't let Anne down. I can help you. I mean, I work there, so I can help when you need to work late and I'll be here at home and cook for you. You won't have to worry about cooking, or cleaning or anything. That way you'll have more time to devote to work. See? This is going to work out perfectly."

"Let's sit down and talk this through," Toni said softly. She pointed to the stools around the granite-topped kitchen island.

"Why? Don't you believe me? If I say I'll do all that for you, I will." Cindy was getting a little agitated, but she sat as Toni asked.

"This is just a little new to me. You've got to understand that I'm a little surprised. That makes sense, doesn't it?"

"Well, I guess so." Cindy shrugged. "But you're used to the idea now, aren't you? I mean, what's there to think about? We have a great home and we'll be together forever."

"I'm not ready for something like this, Cindy. I'm sorry. I'm very flattered that you feel that way about me."

"So what? I'm not good enough for you? Is that what this is?" Cindy said, her voice rising.

"No, not at all," Toni said quietly. "It's that I'm not ready for a relationship like this. It's me, not you."

"Then it will be okay," Cindy said, apparently satisfied. "I'll take care of everything. You're ready for this. I know you are. I've planned this for a long time. It will work perfectly. You'll stay here with me in our home. I even have a coffee cup for you." She jumped up and retrieved a cup from the cabinet, proudly showing it off to Toni. "See? I made sure they spelled it right and everything. I wanted to make sure you had it for your first morning in your new home. Isn't it great? And see? I have one that has my name." She got out another mug and showed it to her. "We've got everything we need."

Toni set the mug down carefully on the counter. She knew she was in dangerous territory. Anything could set her off.

Cindy went to the refrigerator and opened the door. "See? I've got it completely stocked. And there's tons of food in the pantry. Plus there's a lot of places that deliver in case we decide not to cook. And I've got at least a hundred DVDs to pick from, so we can watch almost any movie. We could stay here for days without having to leave. Isn't that wonderful, Toni? Here, I'll make us some coffee right now so we can use our new mugs. I love you so much."

Cindy practically skipped over to the coffee machine and began making coffee.

This wasn't good. Cindy was clearly on the edge. Toni knew that love would flip to rage at the drop of a hat. She had to be careful. If Cindy thought she didn't love her, she'd turn on her. Toni didn't doubt that for even a minute. God, she wished someone knew where she was.

"Let me call my cousin and let her know where I am," she said as matter-of-factly as possible. She pulled her cell phone from her pocket and began to dial.

Cindy turned and snatched it away just as quickly. "I don't want anything to ruin our day." She put the phone in her own pocket and returned to the coffeepot.

"I just wanted to let her know she doesn't have to pick me up," Toni suggested. "That way she can do her own thing and not have to wait around for me."

"Are you trying to ruin the moment?" Cindy demanded.

Toni recognized that Cindy was now slipping into the world of psychosis. *Shit.* This was definitely not going the way she wanted it to go. Cindy was more unstable than she'd ever imagined. Toni sighed. Lying, she thought, might be in order now. *Lie and hope she doesn't realize I'm lying through my teeth.*

"I don't want to ruin anything, Cindy. I just didn't want my cousin to worry. I don't like to make people worry. That's just the way I am." *Maybe she'll buy into that.*

"You're a really nice person," Cindy said. "That's one of the many reasons I love you so much. I mean, heck, you gave your ring to Rachel for good luck, right? That was really sweet of you."

"So if I gave Jessie a quick call, she wouldn't worry." Toni held out her hand in hopes that Cindy would hand her back her phone.

Instead, Cindy grabbed her hand and pulled it to her lips. "You're such a sweetheart. But let's not worry about things like that, okay? The coffee is almost ready. I even bought your favorite, half and half, instead of milk."

Toni bided her time and drank the coffee, which was actually quite good. When she was almost finished with her cup she looked at her watch.

"I really need to get back to the office, Cindy," she said with a smile. "I want to work on my felony trial. I don't want to let Anne down."

Toni could tell that Cindy was considering this, but only for a moment. "No. I don't want to go back to the office. It's Saturday. Let's stay here and play all day. Do you want to watch a movie? Or are you hungry? I could fix us something to eat." She opened the large kitchen window. "A little stuffy in here."

"Even though that sounds like fun, I think I should go back to work. I feel like I messed up on my last trial and I want to do really well on this one. You could help me. It would go much quicker if you helped me."

Cindy's smile faded and her eyes got narrow. She slammed her coffee mug on the island. "You're trying to ditch me, aren't you? Do you think I'm stupid?"

"Of course I don't think you're stupid," Toni said with a puzzled expression. "Why would you say that? I would never think that." She tried to look hurt and wounded, playing on Cindy's need to take care of her and comfort her. It worked.

"Oh, I'm sorry," she said. "I didn't mean to hurt your feelings. I'm so stupid sometimes. Forgive me?"

"Well, okay," Toni said softly. "It's just that I would never think that about you."

Cindy beamed. She went to the pantry and got out some crackers, then gathered several types of cheeses from the refrigerator. "Let's have a snack and then we can watch a movie."

Toni assumed Cindy was trying to create a home-like experience by getting out the food and wanting to watch a movie. Her delusion was certainly complete, she thought. She needed to change Cindy's focus. "The food looks really good, Cindy. But I really need to get back to the office. Can you help me? It shouldn't take us too long if we work together."

Cindy stopped for a minute and Toni thought maybe she had gotten through, but she was wrong. Cindy threw the crackers across the kitchen. "Why can't we do what I want to do? Why is it always about you? I worked my ass off to get our home ready and you can't wait to get the hell out of here. What kind of thanks is that? Don't you understand what I've done for us? Can't you be grateful for once?" She was screaming, her face now bright red.

This was so not good. Cindy had blended this situation with one from her past and it was a good bet that the one before hadn't turned out too well. She didn't think it would matter what she said. *Shit. Stay calm.*

Toni took a deep breath. "Of course I'm grateful. I know how hard you must have worked. I mean, look at this place."

"You don't know shit," Cindy screamed again. Now she was pacing back and forth in the kitchen. "You always do this to me. I work my ass off and you complain. It's never good enough, is it?

There's always something that could be a little better. And you're always pointing that out to me. You're such a bitch."

"I think this loft is absolutely perfect and I wouldn't change a thing," Toni countered.

That stopped Cindy for a minute. She shook her head and blinked a couple times. Toni knew she had gotten her off that path, if only for a moment. At this point the only hope was to keep Cindy's anger from escalating. That wasn't going to be easy. And the longer Toni remained in the loft, the more danger she could be in. Cindy picked up the box of crackers from the floor. She started the task of setting out the plates with the cheese.

What the hell should she do now? Toni asked herself. She had to get the hell out of there, but it would have to be Cindy's idea. She dutifully ate some of the offered crackers and cheese, all the while desperately trying to think of something that would make sense to Cindy but still get them out of the loft. One more dose of psychosis and Toni was afraid Cindy might stay there.

Think, Toni. Think. Then it dawned on her. *Easter! Tomorrow was Easter.*

She looked at her watch. "Oh, my gosh," she said. "It's getting late. I need to pick up the ham I ordered for Easter. Will you take me?" Cindy began to scowl, but Toni continued. "What would happen if you and I showed up tomorrow at my parents' house and we didn't have the ham?"

"Your parents' house?"

"Of course. Tomorrow is Easter. We have to be there by eleven at the very latest. But if we don't get the ham before the store closes today, we're screwed. What will everyone eat?"

"I didn't know you ordered a ham," Cindy said, almost apologetically, the scowl gone. "Let me clean up here real quick and we'll go." She was humming as she cleaned.

"Here, I'll help," Toni offered, bringing her mug to the sink. She saw a McDonald's bag on an end table in the living room and started to walk toward it. "Is this bag trash?"

Cindy suddenly rushed past her and grabbed the bag. She turned toward Toni, her face red with rage. "You bitch," she screamed. "Do you think you can fool me that easy?"

Toni was dumbfounded. She had no idea what had just happened. Cindy ripped open the bag and out came a handgun, which she threw to the floor. It had just registered in Toni's brain that the gun was real and not a toy when the back of Cindy's hand slammed into the side of her head, sending her toppling over the coffee table. Her head hit the wooden arm of the couch. She saw Cindy's face begin to blur, then everything went black.

Chapter 33

Boggs got up Saturday morning with one hell of a hangover, having left Vicky the night before feeling worse than ever. She realized how much she missed Toni and how much she had hurt her by ending it the way she did. She thought about what Cathy had told her, how she was different now. While she cleaned her fifty-five-gallon fishtank, she kept thinking about what that meant.

"Does that mean I'm not a player anymore?" she asked her albino frog, who was swimming around in the tank. He paused for just a moment, but that was all. "I didn't really expect you to answer."

She poured herself another cup of coffee, glancing at the clock above her computer desk. She bet they were already talking to Bert. This whole thing would be over in a couple hours. She wondered if Toni was still down at Metro, if she should go down there too. She could at least apologize for being such an ass, although she knew she'd never forgive her completely. Still, showing up at Metro might help.

This decision made, Boggs showered and got dressed in record time. She was at the Metro building within thirty minutes. She tentatively headed toward the attorneys' offices. It was very quiet. She poked her head into Toni's office. No one was there. Funny, she thought. Toni was supposed to be here this morning. Maybe she was in the lunchroom.

Boggs checked out the lunchroom. Empty. Then she checked the file room and the copy room. No one. She headed over to Anne's office and found Anne was sitting at her desk working on a file.

"Hi, Anne," Boggs said.

"Well, hello, Boggs. What brings you down here?"

"Um, I was just looking for Toni. Have you seen her?"

"No." Anne shook her head. "But I've only been here about an hour. Has anything happened yet? Captain Billings filled me in last night."

"Not yet. At least not that I know of. Toni was supposed to hang out here this morning."

"She's probably around, then. Did you check the AV room? She had some tapes to look at for her trial."

"No, thanks. I'll try there. See ya, Anne."

Boggs looked in the AV room, but no one was there. *Where the hell is she?* Thinking she'd head over to her own office and make some calls, she passed Sam's office and noticed the box on his desk. Curious, she went in to look at it and found Toni's note to Sam. Well, she thought, at least she knew Toni had been in this morning. Boggs went to her own office, unsure what to do. There was no real reason she needed to talk to Toni. At least not officially. But she sure would like to apologize to her. She called Vicky.

"Hey, what's going on?" she asked.

"We're still sitting here on our butts," Vicky said. "Johnnie

273

leaned hard on Bert, but so far Bert hasn't left her house. We're still waiting and watching. This is crazy. I thought this would work for sure."

"Is Jessie still there or did she already pick up Toni?" Boggs asked.

"No, she's still here. Are you kidding? That kid is drooling over the chance to get in on this."

"Oh," Boggs said, thinking that something just wasn't right.

"Why? Is something wrong?"

"No. I just wanted to talk to Toni for a second. I'm down here at Metro and I can't find her."

"She's probably in the lunchroom or something," Vicky suggested.

"I looked there," Boggs said. "But I probably just missed her. Hey, give me a call on my cell when Bert shows up, okay?"

"Will do. Are you okay?"

"Sure," Boggs said. "I'm just an ass, but I'm okay."

"Tell me something I don't know." Vicky laughed. "I'll call you later."

Boggs made another circuit around Metro. No sign of Toni. Her office light wasn't even on. If she had just gone to another part of the building, she would have left her light on. Boggs started to get worried.

This is stupid. Just because she couldn't find her didn't mean anything. Maybe she went out to get lunch. She could just call her. She was probably right around here and they just keep missing each other.

Boggs dialed Toni's cell number. It went to voice mail. She hung up without leaving a message. *She probably saw it was me and decided not to pick up.* She didn't blame her. On the other hand, she'd just hung up on her. That was stupid. She could at least leave a message.

She dialed again and got the voice mail again. "Hey, Toni. It's me. Um, Boggs. I just wanted to talk to you for a second. I'm down here at Metro. Give me a call if you've got a minute. Thanks."

Boggs stared at her phone, hoping it would ring as soon as Toni played back the message. Several minutes passed. Nothing.

Something was wrong. She could feel it. Just like Toni had said last night, something didn't feel right. *Go with your gut, Boggs.*

She went to the main entrance of Metro and saw Wilbur, the weekend guard. "Hey, Wilbur," she said. "How's it going?"

"Not bad, Boggs. Kinda slow day."

"You haven't by any chance seen Toni Barston have you? You know who she is, right?"

"Sure I know her. That new attorney. She's really sweet. Gave me a box of candy for Christmas. Yeah, I saw her earlier."

"Did she leave?"

"About an hour or so ago, I think. She and that really cute secretary left together."

"You mean Cindy Brown?"

"Yeah, that's the one. They got in an SUV and left."

"Thanks a lot, Wilbur. You've been a great help." Boggs was on her way out the door with her phone to her ear. "Vicky, we've got a problem," she said as she got in her car. "I think we're on the wrong track. Toni left Metro with Cindy about an hour ago. She's not answering her cell. I want you to call her in case the reason she's not picking up is because it's me. Then call me right back."

"Got it," Vicky said and then hung up. She called back a minute later. "I got voice mail, too. Are you on your way to Cindy's?"

"Yes. I'm going there now. Can you meet me there?"

"I'm on my way out the door. This is a bust here, but I'm leaving Patty here with a couple guys. I'll bring Jessie with me. See you in a few. Wait for me, okay? Don't do anything stupid."

Boggs disconnected without answering. She was flying down

the streets to get to Toni, but as soon as she pulled up in front of the house, she knew it wasn't right. She sat in her car and waited for Vicky. She hopped out before Vicky's car came to a complete stop.

"This isn't the place," Boggs said. "I know it isn't. It doesn't feel right."

"Slow down, Boggs. Have you looked around or anything?"

"No, and I don't need to. Toni isn't here. I would know if she were here, believe me." Boggs was pacing in the street. "We've got to find her. She knew something wasn't right last night. It's Cindy. I know it's Cindy. We've got to find her."

"Okay, we will. We just need to figure out where to look," Vicky said quietly.

"Her phone," Boggs said. "Her phone."

"But she isn't answering," Jessie said.

"It has a GPS, right? Can't we find her that way?"

"It would probably take some time," Vicky said.

Boggs had an idea. She pulled out her phone and dialed. "Johnnie? I need you to find out where Toni is. With that GPS shit on her phone. You can do it quick, can't you? What? No. I'm positive. Please, do it now. Okay. Call me back. I'm with Vicky and Jessie."

Jittery, Boggs couldn't stop pacing. She needed to know where Toni was.

"She said she'd do it now," she told Vicky. "What's taking so long?"

"It hasn't even been two minutes," Vicky said. "Calm down. We'll find her."

It took ten long minutes for Johnnie to call back. "I've got a location and one very pissed-off boss. Something about protocol. Anyway, it's in the warehouse district." She gave Boggs the address.

"Follow me," Boggs yelled to Vicky as she ran to her car.

When they arrived, there was no sign of life. No vehicles, no people. Boggs ran back to Vicky's car.

"I'm just going to break down the damn door," she said to Vicky.

"No. Wait a minute." Vicky grabbed Boggs's arm. "This woman is crazy, remember? If Toni isn't answering her phone, it's because she can't, not because she doesn't want to. That means this woman is probably holding Toni against her will. If you break in there, no telling what she'll do."

"Can we call SWAT or something?" Jessie asked.

"I don't think that will help," Vicky said. "Remember what Toni told us? This woman might think, 'If I can't have her, no one can,' and that isn't good."

"Then I'll get Cindy to go after me," Boggs said. "That will give you an opportunity to get to Toni."

"Boggs, you're not thinking straight," Vicky argued. "Cindy is an expert shot. She could take you out right here."

Boggs couldn't listen to her anymore. She turned to go. She needed to take action. She needed to get to Toni.

"Wait a sec." Vicky rummaged through her glove compartment and grabbed a wireless microphone for the police radio and switched it to channel four. "Put this on so at least we can hear what's going on. I'm calling Johnnie and Captain Billings."

Boggs took the piece.

Vicky grabbed her vest from the backseat. "And put this on, for God's sake."

Boggs peeled off her jacket and put on the vest, which was a little snug. She was pulling her jacket back on as she ran to the small door. "Just back me up," she called over her shoulder.

Boggs pounded on the small door next to the larger garage door. She wasn't positive this was the right place, but the padlock on the garage door looked fairly new. She pounded anyway.

"Hey, Cindy," she yelled. "It's me, Boggs. Can I come in? I need to talk to you. It's important."

There was no response. She waited about thirty seconds,

knowing Toni was inside. She could feel her.

She pounded again. "Come on, Cindy. Let me in. I really need to talk to you."

Inside the loft Cindy was pacing back and forth, mumbling to herself. Her Toni was still lying on the floor next to the couch, a pool of blood under her head from a gash just above her left ear. She was unconscious.

Cindy looked over at her lifeless body. "See what you made me do?" She kept pacing. "See what you made me do?"

Toni slowly began to regain consciousness. She could hear someone talking. *What happened? Who is that?* She tried to make her eyes open, but they wouldn't obey. *Cindy? Shit.* Toni tried to take inventory of her body. Her head was pounding. She tried to open her eyes just a little bit. It worked. She concentrated on the movement across the room. Cindy was still agitated. *Great.* Cindy no doubt thought Toni caused all this. *She'll turn on me again. I need a plan.*

Toni tried not to move. She didn't want Cindy to know she was conscious. At least not yet. Her eyes were still open only a little bit and she tried to see what was around her. She spotted the McDonald's bag on the floor. It looked empty. But next to it was the gun. It was at least three feet away. If she could just get to that gun. She took a deep breath. *Here goes.* She made her move, but her body wouldn't react as quickly as she wanted. She had barely reached out two feet when Cindy noticed her movement and ran over. She stepped on Toni's outstretched hand.

"You bitch," she screamed. "I can't believe you did this to me. After all I did for you, for us. And now what? You're trying to kill me? You ungrateful bitch."

She stepped down harder and Toni heard the sound of her

own bones breaking. She tried to pull herself up in hopes of pushing Cindy back, but that only succeeded in angering Cindy even more. The room began to blur again and Toni felt the impact of another blow to her head. As her world faded back to black, she thought she heard the sound of Boggs's voice. Or maybe she was just dreaming.

Cindy was pacing again and stopped in midstride when she heard someone pounding on her door. She checked the outside monitor and saw Boggs, her fist clenched and starting to pound on the door again.

She looked over at Toni's body on the floor. "See what you did? You are such a bitch. You messed up everything. We had a perfect life here and you made Boggs show up."

Furious, she picked up Toni's coffee mug and threw it across the room. It crashed on the floor just inches from Toni's face.

"You cheated on me, didn't you?" The realization made her livid and she wanted to scream. "With Boggs. You're such a whore. I can't believe you would cheat on me. While I was slaving over our home, working day and night. And you were out with her? Bitch. I should just kill you now. Or kill her now and torture you."

Floating back into consciousness, Toni could hear Cindy yelling at her. She knew if something didn't happen to change Cindy's frame of mind, she would end up dead on this floor. And more than likely Boggs would be dead too. *Think, Toni. Throw a wrench in her thought process.*

Toni tried to speak, but only a mumble came out of her mouth.

Cindy ran to her and spat on her face. "What did you say, bitch? You have no right to speak to me. Do you hear me?" She spit again.

Toni swallowed and tried again. "She loves you."

"You piece of—what? What did you say?" Cindy leaned down closer to her.

"Boggs," Toni repeated. "She loves you. She wants to be with you."

Cindy was pushing some broken bits of something—the coffee cup?—out of the way to sit on the floor next to her. She could hear pounding on the door again. Boggs? Toni strained to hear. It was Boggs.

"Come on, Cindy," Boggs was yelling. "Let me in. I really need to talk to you."

"See," Toni said. "She loves you and wants to tell you."

"How do you know that?" Cindy frowned.

"She told me," Toni said slowly. She tried to pull herself up again. Cindy didn't interfere. She just sat there on the floor with her legs crossed and stared off into space. Toni mustered all the strength she had and was able to sit up and lean back against the couch. The room was spinning and everything was blurry, but she didn't black out. *I can do this. Just give her a reason to let Boggs in.*

Boggs pounded again.

"Let her in," Toni said quietly. "Let her tell you that she loves you."

Cindy got up. She ran over to the monitor and stared at the screen. Then she ran back to Toni. "Does she really love me?" Her eyes were sparkling. "She told you that?"

"Yes, she told me."

Again Cindy ran to the monitor, then back to Toni. She was smiling. "Do I look okay? Is my hair okay?"

"You look great, Cindy. Boggs loves you. Let her in. Don't make her wait."

Cindy ran toward the stairs, then stopped. She turned to Toni, the smile replaced by that now-familiar scowl. "Are you lying to me? Are you trying to make me look stupid?"

"Of course not. She's right outside, isn't she?"

Cindy had to think about that for a minute. She started toward the stairs again but stopped. Instead she went into the bedroom and returned with what looked like a guitar case. What the hell was she doing with a guitar? Toni wondered. Cindy opened it and gently pulled out not a guitar but rather a rifle. Toni gulped in fear. Cindy chambered one shell and worked the bolt action like a professional.

Holy shit. It was a sniper rifle. Toni suddenly felt sick. Well, she thought, Cindy only had one shot. She hoped if Cindy hit one of them it'd be her and not Boggs. She saw that the handgun was still only about two feet away from her. She would have one chance when the time came.

Cindy went to the top of the stairs, her rifle cradled in her arms. She was smiling and, for all intents and purposes, she looked quite happy. "Okay," she said. "I'm going to buzz Boggs inside. If she tells me she loves me, then we'll all celebrate, okay? But if you're lying to me, well . . . I guess I'll just kill you both."

"Let her come upstairs first," Toni said. "Then she can tell you in front of me. I'm sure she wants everyone to know how she feels about you."

"Okay," Cindy answered in a singsong way. She pushed the button and Toni heard the buzzer. Then it sounded like the downstairs door opened.

"Cindy?" Boggs called. "Where are you?"

"I'm up here, Boggs," Cindy called. "Shut the door first. This is a bad neighborhood. Then come up here. You can tell me your news when you're up here."

Boggs slowly made her way up the stairs. She held her gun down by her leg. She saw Toni first, sitting on the floor next to the couch. One side of her body was covered in blood. She resisted running to her and instead scanned the room. Cindy was against the far wall, pointing a rifle in her direction.

"Hiya, Boggs." Cindy blinked several times and even seemed to blush. She kept the rifle leveled at Boggs. "You wanted to tell me something? Something important?"

"Um, yeah," Boggs stammered, not sure what the hell was going on. "I sure did."

"Well, put your gun down and come in," Cindy said in a chipper voice. "Put the gun down or I'll go ahead and kill Toni." She was smiling.

Boggs quickly assessed the situation. There was a rifle pointed at her and she had no doubt Cindy could—and would—shoot her. She placed her gun on the top stair and entered the room.

"Now tell me," Cindy said in a singsong fashion.

"She's a little shy," Toni said to Cindy.

"Shut up!" Cindy screamed. "Boggs is trying to talk to me. Go ahead, Boggs. It's okay, sweetie. You can tell me."

Boggs hesitated.

"I was just saying," Toni said, "give her a minute. It's hard to tell someone you love them for the first time."

Boggs looked over at Toni. She saw her eyes move slightly toward Cindy.

Boggs grinned. She got it. "Yeah, Cindy," she said. "This is kind of hard for me. I've never told anyone that I love them."

Toni said a silent prayer of thanks. Boggs understood. Now, hopefully, she could diffuse the situation and get them out of there alive. But Cindy could change in a second and she was still holding the rifle, pointing it straight at Boggs.

"How long have you loved me?" Cindy asked.

"A long time," Boggs said. "Why don't we celebrate? Let's go out to The Cat's Meow." She took a step toward Cindy. Cindy was beaming and she lowered her rifle just a bit. But then Boggs glanced at Toni.

Cindy pulled the rifle level again. "Why are you looking at her if you love me?" Cindy yelled. "You're lying to me. You're both lying to me. Do you think I'm stupid?"

"She's just shy," Toni said quickly. "She probably is shy about kissing you in front of me. But it's okay, Boggs. I don't mind. I'm fine, really."

Cindy wasn't buying it. "Boggs isn't shy," she said in a loud voice. "She's a player. She's probably done a hundred women. Some in public, I bet. She doesn't love me." She put her eye to the scope.

"I used to be a player," Boggs murmured. "But when I met you, all that changed." She took another step toward Cindy and kept her eyes forward.

Toni could see that Cindy's eye was on the scope. Her other eye was closed, which meant she could see only Boggs. Toni inched to her right. The gun was within inches of her hand. She moved again. Cindy hadn't noticed. She felt for the gun, but her fingers wouldn't work. She blinked away the tears. There was no doubt that at least two bones were badly broken, possibly shattered. She hooked her thumb under the trigger guard and slowly pulled the gun to her lap. She was staring at Cindy. Still no movement. But her vision was beginning to blur, so she blinked again. Now there were two Cindys. *This isn't good.*

"I really love you," Boggs was saying.

Toni tried to focus and kept staring at Cindy. The gun was in her lap, but she'd have to use her left hand if it was to be of any use to her. Slowly she willed her left hand toward the gun. Still two Cindys. Only inches to go. She felt the cold metal as she gripped the gun. She blinked several times, but it didn't help. She was still seeing double.

Boggs had moved one step closer. "I know I used to be a player, Cindy. But I've changed. I've really changed," she said softly. "I met you and my whole world changed. I'm in love with you and I want to be with you. Only you."

Cindy lowered her rifle about an inch and took her eye from the scope. She was grinning. "I think you're telling the truth. You do love me, don't you?"

"Of course I love you," Boggs said in a tender voice. "I want to spend my life with you, if you'll let me. And I want to meet your parents."

The room went still. Everything stopped. Toni suddenly realized that Boggs had been talking to her, telling her how she really felt. But Toni knew that Cindy's parents were not in the picture. It would only take a second for that to register in Cindy's mind. Boggs looked at Toni with a world of emotion in her eyes. *She knows she messed up. She's telling me she loves me and she's saying good-bye. Everything I wanted and now it's about to come to a horrible end.*

Cindy looked at Boggs and then looked at Toni. *Shit*, Toni thought. Cindy knew Boggs was lying to her. Cindy's smile disappeared and her eyes narrowed. She began to raise the rifle. It was happening in slow motion. Toni gripped the gun in her lap, raised her left arm and squeezed the trigger. As the shot went off she prayed. Cindy had squeezed her trigger just a fraction of a second later than Toni. Both Cindy and Boggs fell backward to the floor. Toni slumped down and slipped into her own world of darkness.

Seconds after the shots were fired, Vicky kicked in the door downstairs and she and Jessie ran up the stairs. Vicky ran to Cindy and kicked the rifle across the floor from where it had dropped.

Jessie went to Toni. "She's alive," she yelled. She ran to the bathroom and came back with a towel which she placed under Toni's head. Vicky breathed a sigh of relief. It looked like Toni was starting to come around.

Vicky went to Boggs. There was blood spreading across her upper arm. She grabbed a kitchen towel and applied pressure. "Hold this," she said to her. "Officer down," she said into her radio.

Already she could hear sirens. Captain Billings had been en route and, like everyone else she'd radioed, would be tuned into channel four.

She went back to Cindy, who was still on the floor and holding her shoulder. Blood was oozing between her fingers. Vicky got another towel and pressed it to the wound. Cindy was crying.

"Hold this on there tight," she said to Cindy. "The ambulance is coming."

She hurried across the room to Toni, who was holding the towel to her head and at the same time trying to sit up. Vicky motioned for Jessie to go over to Cindy.

"Guard her," she instructed. "Don't let her move an inch."

Grinning, Jessie ran over with her weapon drawn.

Vicky looked at Toni and smiled. She was still holding the gun. Vicky gently took it from her. "Where are you hurt?" she asked softly.

"Is Boggs okay?" Toni asked.

"She'll be fine. It's just her arm. Now, where are you hurt?"

"What about Cindy? Is she okay?"

"She'll be fine. You hit her in the shoulder. Nice shot." Vicky could see that there was quite a bit of blood on the floor near Toni. She saw the gash on the side of her head when Toni pulled the towel away. It was still bleeding, but only slightly. Toni looked very pale.

"I'm bleeding," Toni said, looking at the towel. "I didn't know I was bleeding. I just thought my hand hurt."

Vicky smiled. "Yeah, I'd think your hand hurt. I think you broke a couple fingers."

Toni nodded.

"Well, shit," Vicky said. "I guess you weren't kidding."

"What?"

"You can shoot pretty good." She laughed. "You shot with your left hand?"

Toni looked down at her left hand. "Yeah. I couldn't get a grip with my right one, so I had to use my left. I was seeing double so I just aimed between them, hoping I could hit the real Cindy."

Vicky put her hand on Toni's shoulder. "You did good, Toni."

The ambulances arrived and a medic took over. Jessie was to ride in the ambulance with Cindy, still keeping guard. Once Cindy was on the gurney and handcuffed to the rail, Vicky had to tell Jessie to holster her gun.

"I don't think she's going anywhere now," Vicky said. "You did good, Jessie. I'll see you at the hospital."

Boggs watched the medic load Toni on another gurney. Toni was clearly having a hard time staying focused. Finally she managed to keep her eyes opened.

"Are you okay?" she asked Boggs.

"I'm fine," Boggs replied. She held Toni's good hand. Her own arm was bandaged where she'd been hit, but the bullet had only grazed her and she barely felt any pain. "Just relax. I'm right here." She looked at the medic.

"She's lost a lot of blood," he said. "And I'm sure she's got a concussion, but she'll be fine."

Boggs followed them down the stairs and watched them load her into the back of the ambulance. Exhausted, she walked toward her car.

"You're going in the ambulance," Vicky said, suddenly appearing at her side.

"I'll drive myself," Boggs said. She pointed to the bandage on her arm. "I'm fine."

Vicky grabbed the keys from her. "No," she said sternly. "I'll have one of my officers drive your damn car. Get in the ambulance."

Vicky strode away, leaving Boggs standing alone. Resigned to the inevitable, she went to the ambulance and got in the back. The medic rechecked her arm.

"This will be okay until we get to the hospital. Just sit here and don't move around much, okay?"

Boggs nodded, then sat on one side of Toni and watched as the medic started an IV. Toni raised her left hand. Her eyes remained closed.

"Is that you, Boggs?" she whispered.

Boggs took Toni's uninjured hand in hers and squeezed. "I'm right here. You're going to be fine. I'm right here."

"You were talking to me, weren't you?" Toni asked.

"Yes," Boggs said softly. "I was talking to you. I'm so sorry, Toni."

"Is that how you really feel?"

Boggs squeezed her hand again. "Yes. I love you, Toni."

Toni opened her eyes and a single tear ran down her cheek. "I love you, too." Her eyes closed.

Alarmed, Boggs looked at the medic.

"She's going to be fine," he said. "She just needs to rest."

Boggs let out a long sigh and wiped her own tears from her face.

Chapter 34

Vicky was standing in the hall of the emergency room, waiting for the doctors to finish with Boggs. The doctor was shaking his head when he came out of the room.

"She's a pain in the butt," he said to her. "But she's fine. It's basically a bad flesh wound. She's stitched up and ready to go. Make sure she fills the prescription, okay? Pain meds and antibiotics."

Vicky laughed. "I'll make sure she fills it, but that doesn't mean she'll take them."

The doctor shrugged and walked away.

Vicky went inside. "You look like crap."

"Hangovers are hell," Boggs replied, but she was grinning. She was pulling on a blue scrub shirt that the nurse had given her. "Where's Toni?"

"Down the hall." Vicky helped Boggs up and led her to the

room. Toni was lying on a bed with an IV dripping. There was a doctor looking at her chart.

"How is she?" Boggs asked.

The doctor looked at Boggs. "Are you family?" he asked.

"Yes," Boggs said.

When he hesitated, Vicky showed her badge. "And Toni is an officer," she said sternly.

"Oh, well," the doctor said. "She's doing fine. We're giving her fluids. She lost a lot of blood, but she'll be okay. We stitched up the laceration above her ear and set the bones in two fingers of her right hand. She has a concussion and will need to be monitored for at least twenty-four hours. If her MRI comes out okay, I'll write a script for pain medication."

"Can she go home today?" Boggs asked.

"Sure. As long as the scan is fine, she should be ready to go in about two hours. But someone has to stay with her. The nurse will give you instructions."

Boggs nodded and he left the room.

"Well, he was charming," Vicky said.

"An officer?" Boggs said.

"Well, she's an officer of the court." Vicky snickered. "Close enough."

"Damn right," Toni said.

Boggs rushed over to her side. "How are you feeling?"

"I've felt better," Toni said. "My head is killing me."

"Doc says you have a concussion, but you can go home. You have to have someone watch you." Boggs hesitated. "Do you want me to call your parents?"

"Can you stay with me?" Toni asked.

Boggs held her hand and brought it to her lips. "I'll stay as long as you want, Toni. As long as you want."

Vicky smiled from the doorway. "This is really disgusting," she said, putting on her tough-guy attitude and coming over to Toni. "But it's about time."

Both Toni and Boggs blushed.

"But seriously," Vicky said, "I know you guys would love to be alone, but I don't think that's a good idea for tonight."

"What the hell are you talking about?" Boggs protested.

"You've got pain meds," Vicky explained. "There's no way you're going to be able to stay awake or function well enough to watch out for her."

"I just won't take my pain meds tonight," Boggs said, as if that were perfectly reasonable.

"Too late," Vicky said. "I knew you'd do that, so I told the doc to give you a shot. It should be taking effect pretty soon."

"You're an ass," Boggs said. "But you're probably right. I was just being selfish. We need to be sure that Toni is okay. I've got the rest of my life to be alone with her."

Toni squeezed Boggs's hand. "That's right. We've got all the time in the world."

"Disgusting," Vicky said, grinning. "So here's the plan. Jessie and I will hang out with you guys tonight. We'll make sure you're still breathing or whatever. You can watch us drink. Then tomorrow we can all go over to Toni's parents' house for Easter. How does that sound?"

"Perfect," Toni said. "Now, when can I get out of here?"

It was nearly six o'clock when the four women arrived at Toni's townhouse. The pain meds had already kicked in for Boggs, or so she'd said, and the doctor had approved pain medication for Toni once he determined her concussion was not serious. They had filled the prescriptions at the hospital and Toni had taken some immediately.

"The meds should kick in any time now," Vicky said. "Do you want to go upstairs and get in bed?"

"No," Toni answered, petting Mr. Rupert. "I just want to change clothes, then come back down here with you guys."

She headed for the stairs but still felt a bit wobbly.

"How about some help?" Vicky asked. Boggs started to walk over, but Vicky stopped her. "Sit down," she snapped. "You're not supposed to move that arm much. And anyway, I think you'd be more of a hindrance right now. Wait for us on the couch."

Vicky helped Toni up the stairs and into the bathroom. She took off Toni's shirt and gently washed the dried blood from her neck and shoulder. She found an old flannel shirt in the closet and helped Toni put it on. Toni's hand was in a cast and she was unable to navigate the buttons.

"I guess it will take me some time to get used to this," she said. "Thank you for helping me."

"I'm just glad to be able to help you at all. I thought you were a goner for a minute," Vicky said quietly. "And I'm so glad you and Boggs finally figured things out."

"How did you know?"

"She was wearing a wire. We heard everything."

Toni blushed. "Everything?"

"Yeah." Vicky laughed. "She forgot to take it off when she got in the ambulance, so we pretty much heard it all."

"Oh, jeez."

"Well, look on the bright side," Vicky said. "Maybe it's a good thing you were kind of out of it at the time. If you'd been in better shape, we probably would have heard a hell of a lot more, if you know what I mean."

Embarrassed, Toni laughed. "You're probably right."

Vicky grabbed a couple pillows from Toni's bed and helped her back down to the living room. She propped her up in the corner of the couch. Boggs sat on one side and Mr. Rupert crawled in her lap. Jessie was in the kitchen taking drink orders.

"I don't think you're supposed to have alcohol," she said to Boggs, who rolled her eyes.

"Fine. I'll have a Coke then."

"Could I have a Sierra Mist, Jessie?" Toni asked.

"Sure," she said.

"And beers for us, Jessie," Vicky yelled. "After a day like today, I think we deserve a beer." Vicky's cell phone rang. "It's Johnnie," she said before answering. After a couple minutes of conversation she disconnected. "Johnnie is coming over. I told her she was welcome to visit the patients here as long as she brought food."

While they waited, Toni filled them in on what had happened on the way to Cindy's loft.

"And Cathy was right," she continued. "We turned the wrong way on Tucker. I had a bad feeling then, but when I heard the sound of that casing hit the floor, I knew it was her. And it sounded just like Cathy described. *Ting, ting, ting*. But here's what I don't understand. How did you guys know it was her? And how did you know where I was?"

"That was all Boggs," Vicky said. "She said she 'knew' that something wasn't right. That you were in trouble. She went looking for you at Metro."

Toni grinned. "You came looking for me?"

"I wanted to apologize," Boggs said. "I wanted to see you. But when I couldn't find you, I knew something was wrong. And it was because you told me last night that something didn't feel right about it being Bert."

Toni just looked at her, saying nothing. Just smiling and holding hands.

"Um, hello?" Vicky said. "Other people in the room here."

"Sorry," Toni said, snapping to. "But how did you know where we were? It wasn't the address we had for Cindy."

"We went there first," Jessie said. "But then Boggs went nuts and demanded that Johnnie get your location from the GPS on your cell phone."

"Smart." Toni squeezed Boggs's hand and kissed her cheek. "Thank you."

Boggs blushed.

The women discussed what clues they missed with Cindy until Johnnie arrived. She was carrying four pizza boxes and a six-pack of Coke.

"I hope this is okay," she said as Vicky took the pizzas from her. "I didn't know what everybody wanted."

Jessie got paper plates from the kitchen and refilled drinks.

"So fill us in on what you know," Vicky said, taking a bite of her slice.

"Well, first of all, Cindy is out of surgery and, physically, she'll be fine," Johnnie said.

"I'm so glad," Toni said, meaning it. "I didn't want to hurt her, you know."

"You saved both our lives," Boggs said. "You did good." She caressed her shoulder.

"Yeah, Toni," Johnnie said. "You did an excellent job. I still think you should join the Bureau."

That comment was met by groans. There was no way, Toni thought.

"Anyway," Johnnie continued, "I talked to Captain Billings for quite a while. And I apologized to him off the record, just so you know. He said there wasn't any question that Cindy killed the judge and Butch. And he was pretty sure the ballistics would match on the nine-millimeter with the truck driver."

"I guess this is all over, then," Toni said, relieved at last. "Thank God."

"And I went back and talked to Bert," Johnnie said. "I told her a little bit about what was going on and apologized for leaning on her. But then I told her she was no longer a suspect. We chatted for a while. She's pretty cool, actually."

"What did she say?" Toni was curious. "Was she upset?"

"Just a little, when I told her you really did have a girlfriend. She has one hell of a crush on you. That's why she had your pictures and stuff. She was working up the courage to ask you on a date. I guess I sort of burst her balloon on that one."

293

"But she's okay with the rest?"

"Absolutely. In fact, she said if we ever needed her help, she'd be glad to do whatever she could. As long as she wasn't a suspect."

"Good," Toni said. "I feel better about that. I like Bert."

Johnnie finished her piece of pizza. "I guess I should be going and leave you guys alone. I really enjoyed hanging out and I appreciated you letting me in on this."

"Do you have to go?" Boggs asked.

"Yeah, can't you stay and hang out?" Toni said.

"Really?" Johnnie said.

"Sure," Vicky said. "You're one of the gang now. You can't abandon us now. We might need some FBI shit one day." She laughed. "And you can help Jessie and me watch these two and make sure they continue breathing or whatever."

"That would be great," Johnnie said, sitting back down on the couch.

Toni smiled. "And I'd love for you to come with all of us over to my parents' house tomorrow for Easter. I'll finally be able to introduce all my friends to my folks."

"Sounds great to me," Johnnie said.

Vicky got up to get more drinks.

"Hey, Jessie," Johnnie said. "I think I've got a shoulder holster you could use in my trunk. Want to take a look?"

"Sure." The two of them went outside.

Toni pulled Boggs closer to her. "Are you sure you're up to meeting my parents?"

"I'm a little nervous," Boggs admitted. "But, yes. I'm ready."

"Do you want me to introduce you as my girlfriend, or just my friend?"

Boggs thought for a minute. "Well, neither, actually."

Toni frowned. "What should I say? I could just say your name. Is that what you were thinking?"

Boggs held Toni's hand and looked in her eyes. "I don't want to be just your girlfriend," she said softly. "If you'll have me, I'd like to be your partner. For life. I love you."

A tear welled up in Toni's eye. "Oh, Boggs. I would love to be your partner." She put her arms around her as best she could and kissed her. "I love you, too."

They were still snuggled together when Vicky returned to the living room. "Ugh. You guys are so disgusting," she said. "And I'm so glad."

Johnnie and Jessie returned and Vicky put in a movie. While the three of them watched the film, Boggs just held Toni in her arms.

"I can't wait to consummate this," Toni whispered.

"We've got a lifetime for that," Boggs answered. "A lifetime."

Toni drifted off to sleep, happier than she'd ever been in her life.

Publications from
BELLA BOOKS, INC.
The best in contemporary lesbian fiction

P.O. Box 10543, Tallahassee, FL 32302
Phone: 800-729-4992
www.bellabooks.com